# THE FORGOTTEN BOOK

## MECHTHILD GLÄSER

FEIWEL AND FRIENDS

NEW YORK

A FEIWEL AND FRIENDS BOOK
An imprint of Macmillan Publishing Group, LLC
175 Fifth Avenue, New York, NY 10010

Library of Congress Control Number: 2017944811

ISBN 978-1-250-14679-3 (hardcover)/978-1-250-14678-6 (ebook)

Our books may be purchased in bulk for promotional, educational, or business use.
Please contact your local bookseller or the Macmillan Corporate and Premium Sales Department
at (800) 221-7945 ext. 5442 or by e-mail at MacmillanSpecialMarkets@macmillan.com.

First American edition, 2018
Originally published in 2017 in German by Loerve Verlag GMbH under the title *Emma, der Faun und
das vergessene Buch.*

fiercereads.com

*In the beginning was the Word*

John 1:1

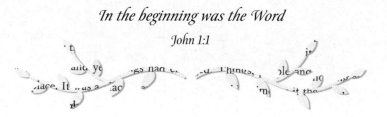

# ONE NIGHT

S HE WAS CRYING AS SHE TURNED THE HANDLE AND TUGGED AT it. The window was stuck—it was old, antique, like everything else in this place. It was a place seemingly untouched by time, as if the decades simply blew past like leaves in the wind. A place where nothing ever changed, where seconds and years had no meaning. Even the night felt centuries old, as if this was the same night that had fallen for hundreds of years. Somber, blacker than black, it loomed over the treetops and cloaked the high walls the way it always had—and yet, things had changed. Things, people, and words.

And not necessarily in that order.

Her legs trembled as she climbed onto the window ledge, blinking back the tears and breathing in the ancient darkness. Not even the moon, it seemed, wanted any part in this—it was very high in the sky, very far away. But she'd known she was alone in this from the start. She hesitated a moment longer, then closed her eyes, and everything happened in a flash. The night air flooded her lungs. The blood roared in her ears as she leaned forward, loosened her grip on the window frame, and slid her feet over the edge. Words flashed through her mind, trying to tempt her. But they couldn't reach her anymore—she was leaving them behind, just like everything else.

She jumped off the ledge and the voices in her head fell silent.

For the space of a heartbeat she was part of the never-ending night, and then the ground came up to meet her, fast. She was surprised in spite of herself.

The landing wasn't as hard as she'd feared. But it was hard enough to sprain her ankle. She gritted her teeth and ran. Her feet felt as though they were moving of their own accord.

Pain shot through her with every step, hot and sharp. But she kept running. She couldn't go back now, even if she'd wanted to. And it was too late, anyway—there was nothing she could do. No way of changing things. Not far to the Rhine.

He was waiting for her.

# 1

IT IS A TRUTH UNIVERSALLY ACKNOWLEDGED THAT RETURNING home after a long absence is one of the best feelings in the world. That's how I felt, anyway, when I arrived back at Stolzenburg one rainy Friday afternoon to find the keep swathed in fog and the castle courtyard gray in the hazy afternoon light. It was unusually cold for August.

Nevertheless I stood for a long moment outside the double entrance doors, closed my eyes, and breathed the smell of wet, age-old masonry deep into my lungs. Raindrops splashed down onto my face like a blustery welcoming committee, while the wind tugged at my ponytail as if trying to get it to dance.

At last! I was home at last!

This was the place I'd called home for the past four years, at any rate: the first place I'd ever known that felt like a real home.

I spread my arms wide and was about to spin on the spot for joy when I heard the noise of an approaching car and decided against it.

Through the gate came a gleaming black limousine, and out of it stepped Helena von Stein (the best student in my class, and currently head girl). She wafted toward me, opening an elegant umbrella.

I let my arms fall back to my sides.

"Emma." Helena eyed my sodden suitcase and the mud stains on my red summer coat as the chauffeur lifted her luggage (suitcases, hatbox, and vanity case) out of the car. "Oh, dear. Did you *walk* here?" She raised one eyebrow.

"Hi, Helena." I beamed at her. Not even Princess von Stein, as I liked to call her, could put me in a bad mood today. True, I'd had to walk some of the way to the castle because my dad had forgotten to pick me up at the airport again. In fact, I'd taken one train and two buses from Cologne Bonn Airport and then walked almost two miles from the village to the castle; all in all I'd been traveling for over eight hours. But I certainly wasn't going to tell Helena that. "I like walking," I said. "Anyway, how was your holiday? You didn't get stalked by that boy at the pool again, did you?"

Helena's lips twitched. "Of course not," she said, pointing to her tanned face. "I've just got back from Mauritius, and it was amazing. And you? I'm guessing you went to see your mom in England again, right?" She made the word *England* sound not unlike a yawn. But Helena, whose parents were diplomats, had been to so many different countries that anything less than a trip to the moon probably wouldn't have impressed her.

"This time we went on a road trip," I offered nonetheless. "A, um, a cultural study tour, to be exact. It was fascinating."

4

"Er, sure . . . how exciting. Anyway . . ." She flicked back her dark hair and followed her suitcases up the steps and into the castle before I could reply. Which was probably for the best, because I would honestly rather have dragged my suitcase another couple of miles uphill than give Helena any more details about my supposed "study tour." And to think it had sounded like such a good idea when my mom had first suggested it. . . .

Initially, the fact that the summer holidays coincided with my mom's new boyfriend's lecture tour had seemed like a golden opportunity. "We've got invitations from all over the country," Mom had gushed. "It means you'll get to see a bit more of England this time, not just Cambridge." Even though my mom had a habit of putting on a husky voice and obsessively touching up her makeup whenever John was around, I'd still been looking forward to spending the seven-week summer holiday with her. We'd made plans to explore London, Manchester, Brighton, and Newcastle together.

It soon transpired, however, that John (a distinguished professor of literature) didn't approve of our proposed mother-daughter excursions. Instead he insisted we accompany him wherever he went, carrying his papers, pouring him glasses of water, and handing him pens with which to sign his books. By the end of the holiday, having sat through forty-two lectures in forty-two stuffy town halls the length and breadth of England, I felt that if I ever had to listen to John's four-hour lecture on eighteenth-century women writers again, I would literally die of boredom. Some holiday this had been! But in spite of everything I'd decided to come out of it feeling positive—*re-energized*, even. True, I hadn't spent weeks being "pestered" by a good-looking pool boy or the wealthy heir to a Cornish country estate. But my holidays had been so dull that they might almost have been described as . . . *meditative*. Yes, that was definitely the right word. There were people who would have spent seven weeks on a bed of nails in a Tibetan mountain monastery to achieve the kind of inner enlightenment I'd achieved (in a less monastic fashion, admittedly) over the course of forty-two lectures in a series of British town halls.

Because, in between John's pompous speeches and my mom's breathless giggles at all his lame jokes, I'd gradually formulated a plan. I was sixteen years old now, and I felt it was time to take a few things in hand. Things that were long overdue. It was about time I challenged Princess von Stein for the role of head girl, for example. And tidied up the library. And started being more elegant and intelligent and independent in general. And then, of course, there was Frederick . . .

Once Helena had disappeared I thought about having another go at dancing in the rain, but I was afraid the chauffeur might come back at any moment and that the other pupils might start arriving— and besides, I was starting to get cold—so I decided against it.

Instead, I made do with turning my face to the sky and taking one more deep breath. Pure, cool Stolzenburg air, fresh with rain. It really did feel good to be back: back in Germany and back at the castle. The gardeners had even planted out some of the pots around the entrance with pink fuchsias, which I loved. I smiled to myself.

The new school year was starting on Monday and I, Emma Magdalena Morgenroth, felt readier than I had ever been. Ready for Year 11. Ready to grow up. I heaved my suitcase up the flight of steps, squared my shoulders, and stepped inside the imposing entrance hall of Stolzenburg School.

That was the day I found the book.

Later on, I sometimes wondered what would have happened if I hadn't stumbled across it. If we'd never gone into the library in the first place. Or if I had found it, but I'd cast it aside, just shoved it away on a bookshelf somewhere. What would have happened then?

The west wing library was located, unsurprisingly, in the west wing of the castle, which was hardly ever used for day-to-day school life anymore. The classrooms were all in the northern wing of the castle and the common rooms and bedrooms where the school's elite boarders lived and slept were situated in the east wing. Most of the west wing, however, had stood empty since the last time the castle had been renovated some eighty years earlier.

At that time, one of the school's former headmasters had decided that the teaching staff should no longer be housed in the castle itself but in apartments in the neighboring farm buildings. Ever since then the west wing, which was also the oldest part of Stolzenburg Castle, had been used mainly for storing tattered old maps, discarded furniture, and boxes full of yellowing exercise books. With its meter-thick walls and stone staircases, it was difficult to heat, and the water pipes often froze in winter. Only the ballroom on the first floor was in regular use. The rooms on the floors above remained for the most part in a state of cold, dusty hibernation.

I'd always thought it was a bit of a waste, especially considering how beautiful the west wing library was. I'd had an inkling that the room was going to be perfect for our purposes, and now that I saw it with my own eyes I was delighted: Bookshelves covered the walls from floor to wood-paneled ceiling. Even around the windows, shelves had been put in, and all of them were full of old, expensively bound books. (These had long ago been superseded by the school's media center, of course, which gave every student access to library books online.)

There was also an open fireplace and a huge oak desk, several armchairs and sofas with carved wooden feet, a small intarsia table, and an impressive chandelier, which must have dated right back to the early days of electric lighting. There were a few things that were surplus to requirements—broken bits of furniture, antique lamps, piles of tattered papers, boxes full of old atlases bedecked with a thick layer of dirt and cobwebs—but it wouldn't take long to get them out of the way. I rolled up the sleeves of my sweater.

"Nice," said Charlotte, taking a photo on her phone of the clutter around us; no doubt she would post it online later. "But are you sure your dad's okay with it?"

Charlotte was English, a little shorter and slimmer than me, and had the look of a porcelain doll with honey-colored curls. She had a thing about cats (the top she was wearing today had two black cats on it, with their tails entwined to form a heart) and she was also my best friend in the world. For four years now, ever since my first day at Stolzenburg, we'd sat next to each other in classes and shared all our secrets.

"'Course he is," I said. "The room never gets used, anyway."

During the most boring holiday in the history of holidays, I'd pictured exactly how it was going to be: We would commandeer the library and turn it into our own private retreat, somewhere to get away from the stress of lessons and the hustle and bustle of the dormitories. I was sure my dad would agree—he let me do whatever I wanted most of the time, so asking his permission was really just a formality. I'd run it by him when I got the chance.

We clambered over cardboard boxes and other assorted clutter. "Just look at all these books. Isn't this amazing?" I said as we stood in the center of the room. "And the fireplace! In winter we'll have a fire, drink tea, and read the classics while the grandfather clock strikes the hour and ice crystals form on the windows. It'll be lovely and cozy."

Charlotte eyed me skeptically. "The classics? You mean like *Nathan the Wise?* And other such thrilling reads?"

She had a point. Charlotte clearly remembered my scathing comments about Lessing's eighteenth-century play, which we'd read the year before.

I pushed a rickety floor lamp out of the way. "It's not necessarily all about the books. I was thinking more of a kind of secret society." I'd read an article recently about famous student fraternities in the USA, and ever since then I'd been toying with the idea of starting my own elite little club at Stolzenburg. This was one of the oldest and best schools in Europe, after all, and secretly I was imagining a society like Skull and Bones at Yale University. But without any embarrassing rituals like lying around naked in coffins and stuff. "We could just meet here and chat, watch films, do our homework, whatever. It'll be awesome."

"The idea of not having to fight for space on the common room sofas does have a certain appeal," Charlotte conceded. She looked around the room for a moment, then sighed. "But we're going to have to do some dusting."

"Thank you!" I brushed my bangs out of my face and launched into a detailed explanation of my idea: "So, I've got it all planned out. The first thing we need to do is get rid of all this junk. I thought we could shove it in the bedroom opposite; there's plenty of room in there. Though I don't know if we'll be able to carry everything ourselves. But we'll give it a try. Then we'll sweep the floor and get rid of the spiderwebs and their delightful inhabitants. And this chest of drawers here—oh!" Charlotte had suddenly enveloped me in a bear hug.

"I missed you. I didn't even realize how much till now," said Charlotte, still with her arms around me. She smelled a little of sea and sunscreen; she'd only just got back from holiday, too. Her family had been to Lanzarote. "I'm guessing it didn't go the way you wanted with your mom?" she asked.

"Nah, it was fine," I mumbled. Charlotte knew me too well. She knew that the more enthusiastically I threw myself into school life, the worse it meant things were going with my family. Although Mom and I hadn't actually argued the whole holiday. "It was bearable. It was just . . ." I thought for a moment, wondering why the disappointment of the holiday was bothering me so much. Being bored wasn't the end of the world, after all, but . . . "I think the whole thing just made me realize that I can't expect my parents to sort anything out for me anymore. That's all," I explained at last.

It wasn't exactly a groundbreaking realization, to be fair. I'd had to learn to rely on myself since my parents split up four years ago. My dad had been wrapped up in himself and his job as a headmaster, and my mom was preoccupied with her own chaotic life in England. Since the age of twelve I'd been washing my own clothes, checking my own homework, and deciding what to have for breakfast, lunch, and dinner.

No, my realization was really more of an admission to myself that what I'd always thought of as a sort of temporary state of affairs was never going to change. My dad was always going to be a workaholic, and my mom was always going to be busy "finding herself." And I was sixteen now, and officially not a kid anymore. Only *I* could decide what to do with my life, and from now on that was exactly what I was going to do. It was that simple. From now on, I was going to be in charge of my own destiny.

Charlotte pulled at my ponytail. "All right then," she said. "Let's make this year our best one yet. And let's make this library our headquarters."

We grinned at each other and set to work. Together we lugged boxes and stacks of paper, three-legged chairs and crinkled lampshades into one of the rooms across the corridor. On top of those we piled globes with out-of-date borders, moth-eaten cushions, and moldy tennis rackets. It took nearly two hours to empty the library of all the things we didn't need. Eventually, however, all that remained was an old chest of drawers in the middle of the room, which absolutely refused to budge. The thing weighed a ton! We leaned our whole weight against it, dug in our heels, and pushed and pulled with all our strength. But the beast didn't move an inch.

After a while Hannah (my new roommate—today was her first day at Stolzenburg) came to give us a hand. But not even our combined strength was enough to shift the chest of drawers. "Do you reckon it's screwed to the floor?" Hannah panted as she and Charlotte pushed and I pulled as hard as I could.

"It feels like it's put down roots," I grunted through gritted teeth. "Anchored itself in the bowels of the earth. They probably built the whole castle around this chest of drawers."

Hannah giggled.

The two of us had immediately clicked. I'd taken to Hannah the moment I'd seen her empty the contents of her suitcase unceremoniously into her closet, saying it didn't matter because she was going to be rummaging through her clothes like a raccoon every morning, anyway.

Of course, I would have loved to share a room with Charlotte now that Francesca, my old roommate, had left Stolzenburg. But Charlotte had been sharing with Princess von Stein for years, and Mrs. Bröder-Strauchhaus—who taught biology and math, and was also in charge of bedroom allocations—was less than accommodating when it came to changing people's sleeping arrangements. (She had some inane reason for this—something to do with us developing good social skills.)

Luckily, Charlotte was the most tolerant and good-natured person I knew and had managed to put up with Helena von Stein's moods without complaint since Year 6. We were also lucky in that Hannah (unlike Charlotte and me) was not afraid of spiders, and she released several of them in quick succession into the ivy outside the library window.

Meanwhile, Charlotte swept the wooden floor and I confronted the chest of drawers again. I'd decided to empty it out. That would make it lighter—hopefully light enough to lift. I started rifling through the drawers. First I unearthed a collection of hideous dried flower arrangements, then a stack of even uglier painted porcelain plates. These were followed by an assortment of candlesticks, broken bits of soap, and yellowed handkerchiefs.

And then I found the book.

It was inside a sort of secret compartment, hidden under a wooden slat in the bottom drawer that I'd almost overlooked. The grooves in the wood around the edges of the slat were practically invisible, and it was only when I happened to graze my left wrist on one of them and thought I'd gotten a splinter that I noticed them at all. But then I ran my fingertips over the bottom of the drawer again, and sure enough I felt the furrows in the wood around the edges of the slat. I dug my fingernails in underneath it, jiggled it about a bit, and finally managed to lift it out. In a compartment below, one that looked specially designed for the purpose, lay the book.

It was old. You could see that from the worn, dark cloth binding. The corners were frayed, and the fabric was so stained that I couldn't even tell what color it must once have been. Gray? Brown? Blue? I lifted the book carefully out of its hiding place. It was heavier than I'd expected, and warmer. *Alive*, I thought, and the thought startled me.

I rubbed the cover with my sleeve, raising a little cloud of dust. As I wiped the dust away, delicate lines became visible on the cloth binding: not letters, not a title, but the vague outline of a figure imprinted on the fabric. I could only guess what it was supposed to be. Was it a man? Or . . . no, the figure didn't really look human. It had what looked like curling horns on its head, and its legs were strangely crooked.

I ran my fingers over the rough fabric. What was inside this book? Why had someone hidden it? And from whom?

Suddenly there was a whispering in the air, a sigh, so quiet that I felt rather than heard it. A rustling murmur, a hum that made the hairs on the backs of my arms stand on end. It sounded almost like a name.

My name.

Er—okay . . .

*Emma*, whispered the book. *Emmaaa*.

I shivered, then shook my head firmly. This was ridiculous! My ears were obviously playing tricks on me.

It had been a long day, after all. Too long. The flight back from England, the journey from the airport to the castle, and the hours spent clearing out the library. I'd been on my feet for so long, it was no wonder I was in a bit of a daze. I was completely worn out: Obviously the book was *not* calling my name, or anything else for that matter. It certainly wasn't alive. I needed to get a grip. Or some sleep. I yawned.

"Let's sort out the rest another time. I reckon that's enough for today," I announced after a moment. But I found it hard to tear my gaze away from the shadowy figure on the front of the book.

When I did, I saw that Charlotte and Hannah had already called a halt to the cleanup operation. The broom stood propped against the wall in one corner, and my friends were leaning out of the window, peering down into the courtyard below.

"Are they students here?" Hannah was asking. She stood up on tiptoe, leaning out of the open window as far as she could go without falling.

"I don't think so," Charlotte replied. "They look a bit too old—though it's hard to tell from up here."

"Well, they're not bad-looking—I can tell *that* from here!"

"Hmm," said Charlotte, looking over her shoulder at me. "Do you know these guys?"

I joined them at the window in time to see two tall young men climbing the steps to the entrance. They disappeared into the castle before I could catch a glimpse of their faces. "I don't think so," I said, looking at the Mini Cooper with the British license plate that was parked on the gravel right at the foot of the steps. "But whoever they are, they clearly think they're too important to use a parking space like the rest of us mere mortals."

I'd promised my dad I'd eat dinner with him that evening. So when Charlotte and Hannah eventually set off for the dining hall, I made my way across the courtyard to my dad's apartment.

My dad lived in the old coach house, in an apartment with light parquet floors and windows that looked out over the gardens. On the walls hung a collection of African masks and drums. Dad himself had never left Europe (partly due to his fear of flying) but he often got presents from parents or ex-pupils or people who were both at the same time. It was well known that he had a penchant for the exotic.

So, when we sat down to dinner I was relieved to see that none of his students had brought him back honey-roasted locusts or other such insectile delicacies from their travels this year. The last time we'd eaten together before I left for England there'd been insects on the menu, and it had put a bit of a damper on things. However nutritious Dad claimed they were, I was never—I repeat, *never*—going to let an exoskeleton pass my lips. And any creature with more than four legs was also out of the question.

Luckily, however, he'd ordered tonight's dinner from my favorite Chinese restaurant, and the polished mahogany table was littered with boxes, chopsticks, and paper napkins.

"My poor little Emma," Dad said now for the third time, picking at his sweet and sour chicken (and probably inwardly lamenting the fact that it wasn't as crisp and crunchy as a giant grasshopper). "I'm so sorry I wasn't there to pick you up. I hope you didn't catch cold. And in the pouring rain, too! Why didn't you call me?"

"I did. Your phone was off." As usual. My dad and modern technology really did not mix. The fact that he'd finally started communicating by email at work was nothing short of a miracle. If he'd had his way, he would still have been writing letters on a typewriter and only ever using the Internet to observe other countries from a safe distance on Google Earth. If at all. The Internet, according to my dad, was a force for evil, and a source of "uncontrolled overstimulation." (At least that was how he'd described it eighteen years ago in his famous parenting guide *The Modern Child*, a seminal reference work that appeared on many a parental bookshelf to this day, and which was essentially responsible for landing Dad this job and for the fact that I—perhaps the ultimate "modern child"—had been permitted to have a smartphone last year only after a series of tense negotiations.)

"What about the landline in my office?" my dad continued. "You could have reached me there."

"It was busy."

"Really? All that time?"

I raised my eyebrows. "I tried seven times. At one, at quarter past, and half past, at quarter to two, at . . ."

My dad put his head in his hands and sighed. "Ah, yes—that blasted sheikh. Exasperating! He seems to want to know the shoe size of every member of staff at the school before he will even consider sending his son here," he muttered. "I was on the phone with him for three hours. I feel a migraine coming on just thinking about it."

If you'd had to hazard a guess at my dad's age—given his aversion to technology and the myriad ailments and illnesses he suffered from (or thought he suffered from) on a daily basis—you could have been forgiven for thinking he was about 120 years old. In actual fact he would be celebrating his fifty-sixth birthday in two months' time. But his eccentric manner belied his age (and as an eminent authority on pedagogical matters and a holder of two PhDs, he got away with it without anybody questioning his ability to manage an elite institution like Stolzenburg).

"How did it go with your mother?" he inquired between two mouthfuls of rice.

"Fine. She says hi," I said, taking a bite out of a spring roll. I usually tried to avoid talking to Dad about Mom whenever possible. This was because of the look that came into his eyes at the slightest mention of her—a look that gave him the air of a mournful old dog that has just been kicked. Now, as ever, he looked as if he were simply awaiting the next blow.

"Thanks. Is she . . . is everything all right?" he went on gamely.

"Oh, yes—she's still living in Cambridge. She only cooks ayurvedic meals now. *When* she cooks, that is. We mostly ended up having pizza. . . . Well, you know what she's like." I cleared my throat. "But how was your summer, anyway?"

"Hmm . . ." He swallowed a mouthful of rice and then, visibly relieved at the change of topic, launched into a detailed account of his recurring sore throats; problems with the caretaker, Mr. Schade; bouts of fever; applications from new students and meetings with prospective parents; and, of course, the attack of flu that had left him a shadow of his former self. Not to mention the migraines he'd been having the past few days. "And now these two young men turn up here unannounced, demanding to be housed here for several weeks. As if we had anywhere to put them, with three hundred students on the waiting list! But what am I supposed to do—I can't exactly have them camping out in the courtyard, can I?" he concluded, and he began massaging the bridge of his nose with his thumb and forefinger, presumably to fend off another migraine.

"Why not?"

He sniffed. "Well, I'd have no qualms about sending one of them packing—a certain Toby Bell—I don't know him from Adam. But the other one, you see, is Darcy de Winter, which means, of course . . . But all I could offer them at such short notice was a couple of rooms in the west wing."

"I see," I mumbled with my mouth full, though I didn't see at all. No, hang on . . . the name de Winter *did* ring a bell. It was the name of the English lord whose family had once lived at Stolzenburg and had set up the school. It was well documented that a son of the

Stolzenburg family had married into a branch of the British de Winter family several hundred years ago, and that when the Stolzenburg line had died out the castle had passed to the de Winters. I'd never heard of a boy called Darcy de Winter, though. "Did they say what they're doing here?"

"Not exactly. Apparently they're on a road trip around Europe and thought they'd make a stop here."

"For several weeks? It's not like there's a lot to see round here." Dad sighed.

"Strange," I murmured, but my mind had already started to wander, from the boys who were to stay in the west wing to my beautiful library and from the library to the book I'd found. Especially the book.

Somehow I just hadn't been able to bring myself to put it back in its secret compartment, so I'd taken it away with me for a closer look. I wasn't quite sure why. There was just something about that book—something that made me curious. Intrigued, even.

"Anyway, I've said they could have two of the old guest rooms on the second floor. I was planning to make them available for the sheikh's entourage, in case he should decide to grace us with his presence, but it'll be all right for a few nights, I suppose, and after that we'll see," Dad went on. I was still thinking about the book, lying in my shoulder bag a few inches from my chair, waiting to be read. It looked like a perfectly ordinary book, the same as hundreds or possibly thousands of others in this castle. It was probably just an old textbook. Or a deathly dull treatise on garden herbs, or a corny old-fashioned love story. Nothing that could possibly be of any interest to me. And yet . . .

Wanting, if nothing else, to silence the nagging voice in my head that kept telling me there was something special about the book, I took it out again later that evening when I got back to my room.

As Hannah slept soundly in the bed opposite mine, dressed in a mismatched pair of pajamas (the top was pink and the bottoms were red with little Santa Clauses on them), I leafed carefully through the book by the light of my bedside lamp. I was struggling to stay awake, but I wanted to do this before settling down for the night. A sneaking suspicion that you might not be of sound mind is not exactly conducive to a good night's sleep.

As it turned out, of course, the book was just a book—just as I'd expected—though not a novel or a gardener's handbook. It seemed to be some kind of chronicle. I thought at first that it was a diary, because it was full of dates followed by separate paragraphs. All the entries were written by hand, and by lots of different people. The paragraphs at the beginning of the book were in an archaic script full of flourishes—more painted than written—but there were passages in the middle written with fountain pen in an old-fashioned hand, and sections toward the end with more recent dates that someone had written in ballpoint, and in some places even in felt tip.

Most of the entries, as far as I could make out, talked about Stolzenburg. Chroniclers from different eras had recorded all sorts of events, both major and minor, throughout the castle's history. I found accounts of a kitchen fire in the summer of 1734, the founding of the school in 1825, and an unusually large snowfall in 1918. One diarist had written about the night-time bombing raids during the Second World War, and someone else had described the opening of the new chemistry lab five years ago. And the paper was so gossamer-thin that the book must have a lot more pages than I'd thought at first glance.

Okay, so the book was a bit special after all. Just not in a freaky, name-whispering way.

I flicked back and forth through the pages for a while. Right at the beginning was a very old text that seemed to date back to the time when the castle had first been built. It even mentioned the former monastery (which now lay in ruins in the woods near the castle) and the monks who had once lived there and produced a special type of paper from which to make their books.

A few chapters on, I found an ink drawing of the figure on the cover. Somebody had captured the creature on paper in sharp pen strokes, and it was much clearer here than in the embossed image on the cloth binding. Its upper body was human, but it had the legs of a goat and cloven hooves. From its misshapen head sprouted two huge, curling horns encircled by a crown of leaves and insects. It reminded me of those creatures you find in ancient myths and legends—a faun, perhaps. Yes, a faun, with a mournful look in its eyes.

I flicked through to the entries written after Stolzenburg had become a school. This was the most interesting part of the book. There were descriptions of balls, new headmasters and headmistresses, and visits from peers and politicians and famous actors. Information that might be worth its weight in gold next spring, when the school would vote to pick the next head girl.

Information that meant—I felt sure of it—I had been destined to find this book.

Yawning, I put it down on my bedside table. I'd have a proper read through it tomorrow, when I felt a bit more awake.

I soon drifted into an uneasy sleep, full of disorienting dreams. In one of them, the west wing library had turned into a classroom. John was the teacher, and he was giving one of his interminable literary lectures. To my surprise, my classmates were hanging on his every word as if they found the whole thing incredibly exciting. Charlotte in particular was absolutely spellbound. Helena, meanwhile, who was sitting in the row in front of me, turned round and asked me why I'd walked all that way in the rain—my hair was a mess. Frederick, in the seat next to mine, said it didn't matter: Even with wet hair I was gorgeous. And behind the screen where John's Power-Point presentation was displayed, oblivious to everything around them, my parents were dancing the tango.

Then, all of a sudden, something landed on my hand.

An animal.

For a moment I was afraid it was one of the spiders Hannah had released into the ivy. I often had nightmares about spiders. But even as I wondered how it was that I was able to think so clearly in a dream, I realized the creature was not a spider at all but a kind of dragonfly. It was a strange color for a dragonfly, though: Instead of a shimmering bluish-green body, it had a snow-white back and pearly round eyes. There were gray flecks on its body that, upon closer inspection, turned out to be tiny little letters. This was probably because the thing on my hand was not a real live dragonfly but an elaborately folded piece of paper made to look like an insect. A piece of origami fashioned from the page of a book, perhaps.

But then, just as I was thinking this, the paper dragonfly started to flutter its shimmering wings and rose into the air. It buzzed away over the heads of my classmates and flew in a circle around John and then my parents. Then it came back to me, flew away again, came back again.

Nobody in the dream seemed to be aware of the creature. But it looked as if it wanted me to follow it. I got up from my seat and clambered over the legs and schoolbags of my fellow students.

The paper dragonfly was flying more quickly now. It led me through the school corridors and out of the castle, through the castle gardens and deep into the woods. The moonlight gleamed on its blanched paper body and its wings rustled quietly like pages turning.

Not until we reached the bank of the river did the creature come to a halt. It landed on a rock (or was it the remnants of an old stone wall?) and stretched out its antennae toward me. I crouched down in front of it in the grass and watched it crawl on its delicate little paper legs until it was only inches away from my face. It blinked its pearly eyes as I tried to decipher the letters and words on its body.

*Emma*, whispered the dragonfly suddenly, making me jump. *Emmaaa!*

"This is ridiculous," I scoffed. My breath sent the dragonfly tumbling backward, almost into the water. But it managed to cling on to the rock and immediately came crawling back toward me. *Emma*, it whispered again. *Emmaaa!*

"Stop it," I said. "You're made of paper. You can't fly and you can't talk."

But the dragonfly said my name again, and this time I'd had enough. I took a deep breath and blew the dragonfly off the rock.

It rustled angrily as it whirled away from me, far, far away across the moonlit Rhine.

A moment later I woke up in my own bed, bewildered. A talking dragonfly? I'd had some bizarre dreams in my time, but this one was definitely the weirdest!

13th August, in the year of our Lord
sixteen hundred and three

On this day the brothers from the Abbey of Saint George did deliver to my master, His Grace the Earl of Stolzenburg, the three reams of paper that they had promised him from their new paper mill, whereupon His Grace requested that they make and bind six books and decorate them with beautiful illustrations, like to this volume that His Grace hath kindly given me for my records. The Earl doth wish to give the six illuminated books as a gift to his most excellent lady wife upon the birth of his second child.

Unhappily one of the brothers was crushed between the mill wheels as he worked, and the monks have asked that they might be given a week's grace to bury their

brother and mourn his death. The Earl hath most graciously granted their request.

Yet since the unfortunate event took place, some of
the holy brothers do seem to fear the mill and the paper
that doth issue from it. 'Tis likely owing to the shock they
suffered, for many of the men did witness the accident
with their own eyes.

# 2

Darcy de Winter and Toby Bell—good-looking and expensively dressed—entered the castle vaults around quarter past nine the next evening. Since arriving at Stolzenburg they had been *the* primary topic of conversation among the students, particularly the girls. But until now only a few people had been able to catch a glimpse of them—they'd been holed up somewhere in the west wing. I still hadn't met them, either, and I observed them with curiosity as they entered the main vault where the dance floor was.

Hannah's long-distance assessment had been accurate: They were an attractive pair. One was tall and blond and covered in freckles, and looked as though he'd spent the summer surfing on the west coast of America. He grinned at the partying students as he squeezed through the crowd to the bar.

His friend, on the other hand, was of a much less sunny disposition; his mouth was set in a sullen scowl. He, too, was tall, half a head taller than his friend, with neatly parted dark hair that was exactly the same color as his eyes. Unlike the surfer, he hovered by the door as if wondering whether he should stay or go.

His doubts were not unfounded, as far as I was concerned. No one had invited him, after all. The "First Lesson" (the name of the party that had been held on the last Saturday before the start of term for as long as anybody could remember) was organized entirely by Stolzenburg students. Once upon a time, when education had been more of a luxury than it was now, the students really had attended their first lessons on the Saturday before term started. Pipe-smoking professors with whiskers and stern faces had taken it in turns to give inaugural lectures, and the assembled students had sat through these lectures on hard, uncomfortable chairs until late into the night (preoccupied mainly, I imagined, with trying not to fall asleep).

But the First Lesson had long since been declared a teacher-free zone. Not even Frederick had come, which I was a bit annoyed about. I'd taken extra care with my appearance and Charlotte had put my hair up in an elaborate bun. But Frederick was no longer a student here—he just worked on the estate during the summer holidays. Of course I understood why he hadn't come, but I'd been hoping until the last moment that he would.

So what were the two unexpected visitors doing at the party? Nobody but me seemed to mind very much that they'd showed up: On the contrary, the uninvited guests had soon found themselves surrounded by a large gaggle of female students.

I sighed and turned my mind back to more important matters. The decorations, for example. This year it had been my class's turn to organize the party, and before the holidays Charlotte and I had spent several weeks' worth of art lessons making decorations out of papier-mâché and tinfoil. This was another school tradition: The outgoing students picked a theme for the next academic year, and the students in the years below had to organize the First Lesson around that theme. This year it was *2001: A Space Odyssey*, and relatively speaking I felt we'd got off pretty lightly.

I still shuddered to think of the spider-themed party we'd had the year before last. There'd been hairy legs and fake cobwebs strung up everywhere, and unfortunately it had been impossible to tell them apart from the real thing (of which there are a fair few in the castle vaults). I was much happier with our papier-mâché planets. At least they didn't have legs.

It had taken Charlotte, Hannah, and me almost all day to arrange the decorations the way we wanted them. The lower years in particular seemed impressed with our efforts (and I hoped they would remember that fact when the head girl elections came around next spring). The pièce de résistance was a huge satellite made from shoe boxes and mirror shards, with a built-in motor that made it rotate like a disco ball. In theory, anyway.

I was just wondering whether it would be a really bad idea to go and stand on a chair in the middle of the dance floor and try to fix the stationary satellite while everyone around me danced to an *NSYNC song (the playlist was also from 2001), when I spotted Hannah standing by the wall gazing at Sinan, a boy in our class, as he sipped on a lemonade. She was absentmindedly tugging at the bow on her dress, which already looked pretty rumpled. Uh-oh.

"Everything okay?" I asked once I'd worked my way over to her.

Hannah nodded. She was still gazing at Sinan, who was leaning against the wall a few feet away from us.

"You're . . . um . . . you're being a little obvious," I ventured cautiously. "Shall we go over there?"

"Over where?"

I nodded in Sinan's direction.

Hannah blushed. "What d'you mean? What makes you say . . . ?" She looked down at the crumpled bow.

"Come on. I'll introduce you."

"What? No! I don't know. No, let's not." Hannah's face had gone as red as a cooked crab. A Madonna song was playing now, and the surfer dude was dancing—to the great annoyance of all the Year 7s—with . . . Charlotte! The two of them seemed to be getting on swimmingly. The surfer's friend, however, was still leaning against the door with his arms folded, surveying the room with a bad-tempered expression. Why was he even still here, since he so clearly thought the party was rubbish?

No, Charlotte had the right idea—we were here to have fun. Determinedly linking arms with Hannah, I pulled her onto the dance floor. "Come on then. Let's dance," I said, and we lost ourselves in the music, spinning each other round and round as we celebrated the beginning of the new school year.

We were in Year 11! My fifth year, and Hannah's first, at the best school in the country—maybe even the world! "You're going to be so glad you came here," I told her. "Stolzenburg is amazing."

"I know!" Hannah called happily, as Megan Stevens danced past us with Karl Alexander von Stittlich-Rüppin (he came from an old aristocratic Swedish family, hence the ridiculous name) yelling, "Damn right, baby!"

Charlotte danced to a few more songs with the surfer, and after a while the two of them came over to join us.

"This is Toby," said Charlotte. She was slightly out of breath, and her eyes were shining.

"Hi. I'm Emma, and this is Hannah."

"Nice to meet you. Do you girls want a drink?"

We nodded.

"I'll be right back." He disappeared into the crowd.

"He seems nice," I said as soon as he'd gone, studying Charlotte attentively.

She grinned. "He is. Super *super* nice, actually." Her cheeks were a bit flushed, too. "Isn't his accent the cutest thing ever?"

I couldn't help laughing. "It's exactly the same as yours, Charlotte. Probably something to do with the fact that you're both English." Stolzenburg had always taken lots of British students; it was a very international school. Foreign accents were nothing unusual here.

"But *still*," sighed Charlotte.

"Did he tell you what's wrong with his friend?" I gestured toward the party pooper in the corner. "He seems to be hating every minute of this."

"I didn't ask," said Charlotte. "But I remembered something— the de Winters used to be students here. Till about four years ago. Darcy and his twin sister, they must have been about sixteen then—I was twelve. I only saw them a couple of times. And then after—you know—what happened to Gina, Darcy left and went to Eton."

"Was that *her*?" I asked.

Charlotte nodded, and Hannah asked, "Who?"

"Gina de Winter," I murmured. Yes, now that Charlotte mentioned it . . .

Just then, Toby returned holding four Cokes.

"Thanks." Charlotte beamed at him as if he'd just saved the world, and sipped at her Coke.

I took a sip of mine, too. "So," I began, looking the surfer dude square in his blue eyes. "Who are you guys, and what are you doing in our castle?"

He smiled. "Darcy and I are at Oxford together," he explained. "But we don't have any lectures till next month so we decided to take a road trip around Europe. We've just come through France and we thought we'd stop off here. Darcy reckons he owns the place." He grinned and made a sweeping gesture that I took to indicate not only the vault where we were standing but all the floors above our heads.

I sniffed. "Well, I very much doubt that he *personally* owns this whole castle." Unbelievable! Toby must have misunderstood. The school was a charitable foundation, and . . . I definitely shouldn't have drunk so much Coke. I was on my third glass of the evening. "Back in a minute," I said.

When I returned from the toilet a few minutes later, Darcy had at least stopped glowering silently in the corner. Unfortunately he was now talking to Princess von Stein, of all people.

". . . kids' disco with all these stupid decorations . . . looks like a primary school, doesn't it? And that shoe-box satellite! It's hilarious!" Helena was exclaiming as I walked past. She pointed at the papier-mâché planets above our heads.

I came to an abrupt halt.

Darcy nodded. "Ridiculous. But what do you expect—Stolzenburg is basically the whole world to these kids, and this party is the highlight of their year."

"Not mine," said Helena.

"I know." He heaved a sigh. Why? I wondered. Because he'd turned up here uninvited? Because the decorations were not to his taste? Seriously?

"Hello," I said loudly, before I could change my mind.

Darcy de Winter turned and fixed me with the same look that had already caused so many of the younger girls to beat a hasty retreat. It was a cold, haughty look, and there was an inscrutable expression in his dark eyes.

Nevertheless, I smiled my most endearing smile and pretended not to have heard what he'd said about our lack of sophistication. "I'm Emma. I heard you used to be a student here. Welcome back! Are you not enjoying the party?" I asked with studied friendliness.

"No, not particularly," he replied. He was about to turn away again, but quick as a flash I inserted myself between him and Helena, who was forced to take a step backward. "It's, um . . . it's a shame you've found it boring," I went on. What was I even doing here? I should have just left him to it—if he wanted to stand here sulking all night, that was up to him. It was no skin off my nose. I decided to go straight back to my friends.

But my feet felt rooted to the spot.

He frowned, suddenly seeming to properly see me for the first time. "Er—excuse me, do we know each other?"

"No. I'm Emma."

"Yes, you said."

"Yes."

"Mhm."

We stared at each other. His nose really was very aristocratic. As if it was accustomed to being wrinkled in disdain at every opportunity. And indeed, it was starting to wrinkle a bit now. In amusement, or in contempt? Or a mixture of the two? And why on earth was I still standing here talking to this thoroughly unpleasant person? Oh God! The giant bun on the top of my head must have been interfering with the proper working of my brain. I took a deep breath. The moment dragged on.

"What do you want, Emma?" Helena asked eventually.

"Can we help you?" added Darcy.

"Er—no. It's just that I . . . *we* happen to like our 'kids' disco,' " I informed him without looking at Helena. My thoughts were gradually becoming clearer. "Perhaps you've forgotten, but the First Lesson is supposed to be for everyone—including the younger students. It's about doing something together, something that everyone at Stolzenburg can get involved in. *We* happen to think that's important."

Darcy's lips twitched. "So I see. I didn't mean to offend you— I'm just not really in the party mood."

"No worries." I made a sound that vaguely resembled a laugh. "It takes more than that to offend me."

"Really?" He raised one eyebrow. "You look a little annoyed, if I'm honest."

"No, no. I just noticed you've been standing here for about twelve songs looking as if you were being subjected to a particularly cruel form of torture. And since I'm the school council representative, I thought I'd come and ask why?"

"Well, Emma the school council representative: If you really want to know, Toby persuaded me to come. But forgive me if I'm not fantastically excited about hanging out with a load of thirteen-year-olds in a cellar decorated with balloons and tinfoil, dancing to the songs that were in the charts twenty years ago. Community spirit or no community spirit," he replied, as I finally started to regain control of my feet.

"That's a shame," I said. "You know, sometimes you can have a much better night if you just forget about the big wide world and all its hipster clubs for a while. Even if that involves cardboard satellites." I turned to go.

"Oh, Emma," sighed Helena. "Ignore her, Darcy. She's been gluing mirror shards to shoe boxes for weeks: She's probably still high from the fumes. Shall we go and get a drink?"

I turned away and headed off across the dance floor.

"Thanks, I was actually just leaving, anyway," I heard Darcy say before a new song came on and the DJ turned the volume up full blast.

It took me a long time to get to sleep that night. The First Lesson had finished, as always, at midnight on the dot, and on the way back to our room Hannah and I had been treated to a detailed account of Toby Bell's freckles, his sense of humor, the dimples in his cheeks, and, of course, his accent, which was apparently the cutest thing in the world *ever.* Charlotte was walking on air—but I was still fuming about Darcy de Winter.

"The party wasn't stupid," I muttered at last, when Hannah and I were both tucked up in bed. "That's just how we do things at Stolzenburg."

Hannah sighed. "I thought it was awesome and you did a brilliant job of organizing everything. Why are you letting that guy get to you so much? I hardly even noticed him. And the two of them will probably be off on their travels again soon, anyway."

"Don't let Charlotte hear you say that."

"Well, it's true. What's he doing here, anyway? Has he just come back to reminisce?"

"Hmm."

As far as I knew, Darcy had left the school not long before I'd started, because of the girl who'd gone missing—Gina de Winter, his twin sister. I'd heard about what had happened, of course. Gina had disappeared a few months before my dad had taken the job as headmaster. In fact, it was rumored that her disappearance was the real reason the previous headmaster, Mr. Bäuerle, had finally decided to retire. Gina had been a quiet student, people said, unassuming but friendly. She'd joined the drama club to help her get over her shyness.

And then, one night, she'd suddenly vanished without a trace. Nobody knew where she'd gone. She hadn't taken any of her belongings with her and she hadn't triggered the castle's alarm system. The police had mounted a search for her but had found nothing, and eventually closed their investigation. Gina had never been seen again. Naturally, rumors abounded at Stolzenburg as to why she had disappeared, from abduction to a romantic elopement with a mysterious stranger. Some people even said Gina had gone to America to pursue a singing career and was earning a living by appearing in TV commercials.

Either way, her disappearance had attracted a lot of attention, and her brother had returned to England shortly afterward. And he probably wasn't going to stay long at Stolzenburg this time, either. Hannah was right: I shouldn't let him get to me. With any luck he would leave as quickly as he'd arrived. Although I hoped his friend might stick around a little while longer, for Charlotte's sake. I'd hardly ever seen her look so happy.

The last time Charlotte had been this excited was in the run-up to her visit with the Queen last autumn. Her family had been invited to tea at Buckingham Palace along with a select handful of other guests, and Charlotte had spent weeks planning what she was going to wear. Unfortunately, however, the visit had ended in disaster, and Charlotte and her younger sister, June, had been splashed across the front page of the British tabloid the *Sun*. Charlotte was still so embarrassed by the "incident" that we'd never spoken of it since. She even feared she might never be able to show her face again in her native England. I was sure people would forget about the story in time (and anyway, it wasn't Charlotte's fault that she and June had eaten some bacon of questionable quality that morning and that they'd both started to feel queasy right in the middle of their audience with the Queen). Toby hadn't mentioned the incident at all yet. Perhaps he hadn't heard about it—after all, not everybody in England read the *Sun*, thank goodness.

The *Sun*, I thought . . . what a strange name for a newspaper. Had they called it that because it came out in the morning? Or did it have something to do with the day of the week?

At some point during these ruminations I must have fallen asleep, because I suddenly became aware that the illuminated numbers on my alarm clock read 03:47 and that I was freezing cold.

And no wonder, because the bedroom window was wide open. I switched on my bedside lamp and glanced over at Hannah. But she was fast asleep with the duvet pulled up over her head, a muffled snoring noise issuing from beneath it. Why had she opened the window? Did she want us to freeze to death? Or had the window not been properly closed in the first place, and blown open in the wind?

The curtains were billowing in a rather ghostly way, and it took a certain amount of willpower to leave my warm bed. I scurried quickly over to the window and closed it, turned up the dial on the little radiator, and finally fished a pair of thick socks and a woolen blanket out of the wardrobe before crawling back into bed. It was a very cold night for the end of August. It was odd how the temperature had plummeted over the last few days.

I carried on shivering for a little while, but eventually I started to warm up under my multiple blankets. My eyelids began to droop. I felt around for the switch to turn off my bedside lamp. My fingertips brushed paper and frayed cloth and . . . hang on. Had the wind really been that strong? I turned my head and blinked.

Suddenly I was wide awake again.

The book was open.

It was still lying where I'd left it, on top of the little bedside table by my pillow. But now it was open, to a page fairly near the end. I picked the book up and looked at it more closely.

The diary entry that filled these pages was one of the more recent ones, written in modern handwriting in what looked like felt-tip pen. It was dated to an evening in August four years earlier. In fact, it seemed to be talking about that year's First Lesson. I skimmed a few lines and sighed. The text gave a detailed description of people, dresses, drinks, and music, none of which I had a burning desire to read about at four o'clock in the morning. I let the pages slip through my fingers, and as I did so I caught a glimpse of something about smoked salmon canapés, mmm . . .

Now I came to think of it, I realized I was quite peckish. There hadn't been any snacks at the party this year, and it was several hours since we'd had dinner. And I really liked smoked salmon. And canapés. And my stomach had now started to rumble. Damn it!

With a great deal of effort I managed to haul myself out of bed once more, this time with the intention of creeping downstairs to the kitchens and making myself a cheese sandwich. I pulled on a sweatshirt over my pajamas, picked up the book and my flashlight, and set off down the dark hallway. The thick carpets swallowed up my footsteps and made me feel as if I was gliding soundlessly along the castle corridors. The building itself, however, was far from silent—it was never that. There was always a creaking from some-where in the woodwork, a rustling in some dark corner. Shadows danced across the paintings and suits of armor. I was used to it by now, after four years at the school, and it didn't scare me at all. Stolzenburg wasn't reputed to be a haunted castle, and even if it had been, it wouldn't have bothered me: I didn't believe in all that crap. Stolzenburg was my home.

I carried on flicking through the diary as I walked, the beam of my flashlight revealing entry after entry penned in felt-tip. Whoever had last written in this book had certainly been prolific.

Downstairs, in the main kitchen, there was a fridge that had been the target of nighttime raids by Stolzenburg students for generations. It was not my first foray to the fridge, and I soon found what I was looking for and more. Ten minutes later, armed with a cheese sandwich, a carton of chocolate milk, and a banana, I headed back to my bedroom. But when I got there and pushed open the door, a chill ran down my spine.

Hannah was lying in the same position as when I'd left. She was still snoring lightly, wrapped up in her duvet, sound asleep. And everything else in the room looked exactly the same as before.

Except the window.

The window was open again.

~~In the year of our Lord, blah blah~~
August 2013

The venerable students of Stolzenburg celebrated the beginning of the school year again as usual this summer. The smoked salmon canapés donated by Mr. Bäuerle were delicious, but unfortunately they ran out very quickly. I should have grabbed myself a handful right at the start.

Frederick Larbach was the hero of the hour: He managed

to repair the speakers after they got knocked off their stand by Darcy de Winter and Helena von Stein, who were getting a little too energetic on the dance floor.

Yes, it was great fun.

For most people.

# 3

STRAIGHT AFTER BREAKFAST WE ASKED MR. SCHADE, THE caretaker, to have a look at the lock on our bedroom window. Then I gave Hannah a long-overdue tour of the school. Yesterday I'd been too busy with the First Lesson to show her around. But today I intended to devote myself completely to helping Hannah settle in.

First I showed her the classrooms, the chemistry lab, the biology department, the music room (which was on the top floor of the north wing of the castle, right under the roof), the art studio, and, of course, the computer room, which had been renovated over the holidays, complete with brand-new computers. Then we paid a visit to the staff room, empty and silent on this Sunday morning.

Next on the agenda were the kitchens, where I introduced Hannah to the Berkenbecks (mother and daughter, both getting on in years and sporting identical poodle-style perms), who may have looked as though they were on a permanent diet but were in fact very talented chefs. They were busy peeling and chopping a huge heap of carrots as we walked in, and broke into enthusiastic chatter the moment they saw me.

"Emma, love, good to see you back again! How've you been? Did you have a nice time with your mom?" clucked Berkenbeck the younger, but before I'd even opened my mouth to reply she had embarked on a lengthy account of the three emails she'd received over the holidays from her niece Marie. "She's teaching herself to knit, and last week she cooked a meatloaf, all by herself, using the recipe we sent her. Do you remember, Mom? Must have been two or three months ago. She followed all our instructions to the letter, bless her. . . ."

I listened politely, as I always did, although I had never met this Marie and I was not particularly interested (to say the least) in what she cooked or knitted, or in the fact that she was, as we now learned, suffering from another bout of athlete's foot.

Despite their foibles (treating every email from their long-distance niece as a small miracle, reading every celebrity gossip magazine from cover to cover the minute it came out, and always taking rather a long time to get to the point) the two chefs were kind-hearted women, and were always ready with a bowl of chicken soup when I was ill. On my last birthday they'd even baked me an impressive cake with marzipan decorations in the shape of roses. I liked them both very much—but they did get on my nerves sometimes.

"Oh, and we still haven't told you our biggest news," piped up

44

Berkenbeck the elder, leaning closer to us with a solemn expression. "It's about Cheyenne. We read a blog recently that gave us an idea we'd never even thought of. And then we had another look at the photos in this week's *In Touch*." Her voice had dropped to a whisper. "Two words: Lady Gaga."

"Um . . . ," I said, "isn't she a bit young to have a daughter that age?"

The Berkenbecks exchanged a triumphant glance. "True. But what about a younger sister? Well? Are we close?"

"Um . . . ," I said again, shrugging my shoulders. Cheyenne, a twelve-year-old girl with short brown hair, had started at Stolzenburg last year and the Berkenbecks had been pleading with me ever since to tell them which celebrity she was related to. It was common knowledge that Cheyenne was here incognito—my dad was the only person who knew who her parents were. The Berkenbecks, however, were convinced that he must have let me in on the secret. (He hadn't, but the Berkenbecks staunchly refused to believe that.)

"So we're wrong again?" asked Mrs. Berkenbeck with disappointment.

"No idea," I said. "But can I introduce you to Hannah Neuler? She's a new student. She's also lactose intolerant."

"Oh, I do beg your pardon—how rude of us!" exclaimed Miss Berkenbeck, beaming at Hannah. "Can you have soy milk? Tofu? Marie had a terrible reaction to dairy, too, a couple of years ago—do you remember, Mom? She ordered that omelet in a café and—"

"Soy is fine," said Hannah, and I decided she'd heard enough Berkenbeck anecdotes for one day.

"Oh, yes!" cried Mrs. Berkenbeck. "That was at Easter-time, when she'd just got the new magazine subscription from that sales rep who came to the door the day after the cycling trip. . . ."

"We have to go now," I muttered, dragging Hannah with me by the sleeve. We slipped discreetly out of the kitchen, leaving the Berkenbecks to their gossip and their mountain of carrots.

The student common room, where tea, hot chocolate, and cookies were served in the afternoons and where the students met to chat or do their homework, was situated in a long conservatory that opened onto the castle grounds. Hannah marveled at the tasteful wicker furniture and the breathtaking view of the terraced parkland dotted with fountains (as well as several new benches that the school council had successfully lobbied for the previous year).

She was also delighted to see three sheep grazing in a small meadow at the far end of the park. Dolly, Dolly II, and Miss Velvetnose belonged to Miss Whitfield, who taught deportment, etiquette, and English and lived in a small cottage on the edge of the meadow. After we'd inspected the tennis courts and the brand-new sports hall, which housed a swimming pool with competition lanes and spectator seating, we couldn't resist paying a visit to Stolzenburg's woolliest residents.

Hannah tickled Dolly II under the chin while Dolly and Miss Velvetnose grazed a little way from the gate, occasionally lifting their heads and fixing us with a skeptical glare. Miss Whitfield had shorn her three darlings just before the holidays, and their fleeces were still short and smooth.

"You've got the same haircut as my grandma," Hannah told

Dolly II, then lowered her voice to a whisper. "But it suits you better."

It was a while before I could pry Hannah away from the sheep. But I was keen to show her the woods and the ruins before lunch.

Stolzenburg, like many castles in the Rhine Valley, had been built on top of a hill so the inhabitants could see their enemies coming for miles around. But the woodland surrounding the castle was so dense that I wasn't sure how well this concept could have worked in practice. You had to fight your way through almost impenetrable undergrowth for about five minutes to get to the ruins of the old monastery, which was only a stone's throw from the park as the crow flies. And you couldn't even see the ruins until you were right on top of them. It was the same with the Rhine. Directly behind the ruined monastery, the rocky ground fell away steeply and the river rushed past so close to the old stone walls that it always surprised me how quiet it was. The approach to Stolzenburg was so thickly wooded nowadays that no knight worth his salt would have had any trouble sneaking up to the castle walls and taking everybody by surprise. I didn't know whether or how often Stolzenburg had been attacked in the past, but I thought it must have been a pretty easy target.

The ruins were one of my favorite places at Stolzenburg. Only a handful of the abbey walls were still standing, and a few Gothic arches that had once formed part of the nave. They were overgrown now with moss and lichens. Between them stood a few broken pillars and solitary buttresses. There was an acrid smell of wet leaves and soil, and the wind sighed in the treetops. There was something peaceful about this place—something magical.

The other students didn't often come here. The Year 7s were scared of the gravestones in the floor of the old crypt, which for the most part lay hidden under a layer of rotting leaves. The older students weren't particularly interested in the remnants of the old church, and it was true that there were a lot more famous, more impressive ruins in the world. But despite, or maybe even because of this, I liked our ruins. I liked the fact that they weren't perfect. I liked sitting on a weathered old piece of wall and looking through the glassless vaulted windows into the woods and listening to the wind. I liked tipping my head back and seeing the sky above me instead of a buttressed ceiling.

Hannah, however (like Charlotte), did not share my fascination with the old monastery. She gave a cursory glance to the crumbling walls and the Rhine beyond, without even seeming to take in the earthy tang of the woodland. Then she pointed to a clump of ferns at the foot of a headless statue. "Do you think Dolly II would like those?"

"No idea," I replied, but Hannah had already started pulling up handfuls of fern.

A moment later, two things happened that made me jump: The first was that now, with the ferns gone, I could see the low pedestal and the feet of the statue for the first time. It was carved from soft sandstone and stood in an alcove of what had once been the nave, and I'd always assumed it was an angel or a saint—Saint George, for example, after whom the monastery had been named. But now I could see it had stone hooves, and its ankles and legs, however much their contours had been eroded by centuries of wind and rain, looked distinctly nonhuman. As I went closer there was a rustling sound beneath my sneakers and an eddy of little silver leaves swirled around my feet. For a fleeting moment I remembered the paper dragonfly wings. . . .

The other thing that made me jump was the warm voice that sounded suddenly from behind me as I bent to take a closer look at the statue—a voice I'd missed over the past few weeks, more than I cared to admit. "That's bracken. I wouldn't give that to the sheep, unless you're trying to kill them."

I spun around.

"It's poisonous." Frederick had tied back his dark blond hair in a ponytail and was wearing his usual green work trousers and heavy boots. He was still limping slightly from a cycling accident he'd been in. He must have been on his way to the compost heap, because he was pushing a wheelbarrow full of garden waste. He gave me a lopsided smile. "Hello, Emma."

"Hi," I said, as nonchalantly as I could manage. "This is Hannah. She's fallen in love with Dolly II."

"Then I *definitely* wouldn't recommend feeding her that stuff." He held out a hand to Hannah. "Frederick."

"Thanks for the tip." Hannah tossed the ferns into his wheelbarrow and shook Frederick's hand. "Are you the gardener here?"

"Only part-time. I'm actually studying biology in Cologne: This is my weekend job."

"But Frederick was a student at Stolzenburg, too, till last year," I explained. "He's like us." Frederick had never boarded at the castle (his parents lived in the nearby village) but other than that we had a lot in common. There weren't many students at Stolzenburg like him, Hannah, and me. Students who didn't come from ridiculously wealthy families—students who'd gotten a place at the school because they'd been awarded a scholarship, or because they lived nearby, or because their father happened to be the headmaster.

"Huh?" said Hannah, not sure what I was getting at.

"Not rich," I explained.

"Thanks," said Frederick.

"I mean that in a good way, of course."

His pale blue eyes sparkled, and only now did I spot a little smudge of dirt on his left cheek, which gave him a slightly bohemian look. "Well, that's all right then. I'm pleased to meet you, Hannah, and I can confirm that I am indeed as poor as a church mouse and forced to slave away on the estate here for a few euros an hour. I don't like to boast, but every holiday while most of the other Stolzenburgers are off sailing their yachts, I'm here pulling up weeds, clipping hedges, and tending to the compost heap. And to top it all off, my car broke down last week, which means I have to walk everywhere and I'm not entirely sure how I'm going to make it back to Cologne once term starts again. Cool, huh?"

"Er . . . ," said Hannah.

"Can't your car be repaired?" I asked.

He shook his head. "It's a total loss—nothing they can do. So for the moment I'm stuck here, looking forward to many a fun evening in front of the TV with my beloved parents."

I looked at him. "Well," I began, and I felt my heart start to beat faster. I'd just had a brilliant idea, and I was going to have to pluck up all my courage in order to see it through. "You could always come and spend the evening with us. We've set up a literature club—we're meeting at eight o'clock tonight in the west wing library. You could join us if you like?"

"A *literature* club?" He smiled his lopsided smile again—a specialty of his. "And . . . what do you do at this literature club?" he asked.

Oh wow, he was actually considering it! Unfortunately, since I'd only come up with the idea a few seconds earlier, I didn't really have an answer to his question. "We, um . . . well, obviously it's all secret and, er, only members are allowed to know. So—do you want to join?" I improvised, forcing myself not to chew my lower lip.

Frederick looked at me for a moment, then nodded slowly. "It all sounds a bit crazy, Emma, but yes. Yes, I think I will come along. See you later, then!" He picked up the wheelbarrow and continued on his way to the compost heap, whistling softly as he went. I hoped he hadn't seen the stunned look on my face as I stared after him. I couldn't believe it!

I sent Charlotte a text on our way back to the castle to tell her what we were doing that evening and why, and when we entered the dining hall twenty minutes later she beckoned us over happily. She and Toby had spent the morning together and were already sitting in our usual spot, at one of the best tables by the window.

"There's spaghetti Bolognese today," she said, beaming. Usually it took more than a pasta dish to send Charlotte into such raptures. I shot a glance at Toby. Was it the sauce that had made his lips so red?

Hannah and I went to get our plates and joined the line at the serving hatch. Berkenbeck the younger was dishing up her special mincemeat-and-carrot Bolognese sauce, and I noticed that she was particularly generous to Dr. Meier, our history teacher, who was in front of us in the line. She tipped three whole ladlefuls onto his plate and launched into an anecdote in which the words "athlete's foot" featured far too many times for my liking. Oh, please—not when we were about to eat!

But instead of grimacing like any normal person would at the mention of a fungal skin complaint just as they were about to tuck into their spaghetti, Dr. Meier smiled and seemed genuinely interested.

"Poor girl," he said. "Has she been to see her doctor yet? He was so good when she had that bout of tonsillitis last year."

For quite some time, the pair of them continued to talk avidly about antibiotics, Marie, doctors in general, and, of course, Marie. It was sweet the way Dr. Meier hung on Miss Berkenbeck's every word, and the way she gazed at him raptly once he finally managed to get a word in edgewise. After a while, I completely forgot that I was actually waiting for my food, so it gave me a bit of a shock when somebody suddenly pushed past me and Hannah, shoved Dr. Meier roughly aside, and thrust a plate under Miss Berkenbeck's nose.

"The girls seem to have lost their appetites," said Darcy with a nod in our direction, as he watched Miss Berkenbeck dish him up an extra-large portion without batting an eyelid. What a jerk!

Couldn't he have waited his turn like everyone else? And surely he could have just let Dr. Meier and Miss Berkenbeck have their little flirtation without barging in like that. I was starting to get the impression that Darcy de Winter was a bit of an idiot.

And what happened later that evening proved just how right I was.

Deciding to set up a secret society and actually doing it were, as I realized that afternoon, two different things. Particularly when you were working on a very tight deadline. The first thing we had to decide was what to call ourselves. I wasn't particularly creative when it came to things like this, and my first suggestion ("The Library Club") met with furrowed brows from both Charlotte and Hannah. So I turned to good old Google for inspiration. I still liked the name "Skull and Bones," but that, of course, was taken: Yale had already nabbed it. And "Bone and Skulls" just sounded silly.

In addition to a name, we needed a concept: What should we do at our meetings? It couldn't be anything too embarrassing or childish—after all, Frederick was going to be there.

Charlotte had eventually saved the day by suggesting "Westbooks" as a working title. And the members of Westbooks, we decided, would meet every Sunday evening to talk about poems and novels and generally broaden our minds (like in *Dead Poets Society*). There would also be tea and snacks, and the whole thing would be effortlessly cool and sophisticated.

Unfortunately, none of us had read any books recently. (We'd all been too busy over the summer holidays.) But we managed to solve this problem in the end, too.

By five to eight, the transformation of the library into our secret headquarters was complete. We still hadn't managed to move the chest of drawers from the middle of the room, but that hadn't proved to be too much of a problem—in fact, it had turned out to be the perfect place to stand the flat-screen TV we'd borrowed from the computer room. Charlotte had connected up her laptop while Hannah and I had gone round the library lighting candles. On the table were bowls of potato chips and candy, as well as tea and lemonade. The DVD menu was already up on the screen. Everything was ready: All we needed now was Frederick.

I was wearing my favorite top, the one with a pretty scoop neckline. I checked my lip gloss and mascara in the glass of the window pane. The courtyard outside was still and silent in the evening twilight. "I don't see him," I murmured. "I hope he hasn't changed his mind."

"He's just running late," said Charlotte. "Don't worry. Come here and sit down." She and Hannah had made themselves comfortable on one of the velvet sofas, and were tucking into some licorice snails.

With a sigh I settled down next to them and snuggled into the cushions. Twenty minutes and a third of our food supply later, we decided to start the DVD. If only to stop ourselves from snacking.

I pressed play and the film began. It had been Hannah's idea to start off with literary films, and as far as I was concerned it was an excellent plan. This way we'd acquire a great mass of knowledge in no time, without having to spend hours poring over complicated vocabulary and antiquated dialogues. We'd decided to start with Shakespeare.

But we didn't get very far, because fifteen minutes into the film somebody came bursting into the library. For a moment I hoped it was Frederick, and my pulse quickened at the thought. But it wasn't Frederick. It was Darcy. And he hadn't come in through the door, but through one of the bookshelves, which had suddenly swung open from a hinge in the wall.

"Can you keep it down?" he asked.

Behind him I could see the corner of an antique bathtub.

"Um . . ." I pressed pause. "What do you mean?"

Darcy sighed. "The music is annoying. The actors' voices are annoying. And you lot giggling the whole time is not helping," he said. "If you don't mind, I'm trying to sleep."

"At eight thirty in the evening?" Hannah asked.

"In the bath?" I added, peering past him into the dimly lit bathroom, the existence of which I had never even suspected. "That's dangerous. You could drown."

Darcy brushed his tousled hair out of his face. He was barefoot, and he was wearing an old-fashioned pair of striped flannel pajama bottoms with a dark-colored T-shirt that showed off the contours of his upper body. He exhaled slowly.

"*Ob*viously I'm not sleeping in the bath. But my bedroom is right next door." He pointed past the claw-foot bathtub to another doorway I hadn't noticed before. I could just about make out the curtains of a four-poster bed. My dad had clearly given Toby and

Darcy the least modern of our guest rooms. The fact that Darcy's bedroom had an en suite bathroom was quite normal, of course—but I'd had no idea there was a secret door leading into and out of the library. What on earth was that for? In case guests needed to stock up on reading material in an emergency or something? Oh, well: It didn't really matter either way, as long as Darcy made use of his weird little secret door to go back where he came from—ASAP.

"Sorry, we're having a meeting of our literature club," I informed him. "We're broadening our minds."

He raised his eyebrows. "Really?" Seriously, what was up with this guy? Could he *be* any more arrogant?

"Yes," I said. "But if we're disturbing you that much then of course we can turn the volume down a bit. No problem." Wow—I had definitely matured over the past few weeks.

Darcy glanced at the screen. "You're a literature club and you're watching films?" he asked. A moment later he spotted the DVD case on the table in front of us and picked it up. "*Shakespeare in Love?*" he snorted.

"What's wrong with that?" I said. It was a pretty good introduction to Shakespeare, in my opinion.

"Nothing," said Darcy, but he was still smirking. "It's just . . . you're sitting here watching romantic comedies, and you say you're broadening your minds?"

"We read books as well. We will do, anyway. Starting next week. Or the week after. Depending how much free time we have—we haven't planned out all the details yet." I cocked my chin defiantly. Why was I even justifying myself to him?

"Would you like a jelly bean?" offered Charlotte, evidently feeling the need to defuse the situation.

"Why are you in bed at this time, anyway?" asked Hannah.

"No, thank you," said Darcy, pretending not to have heard Hannah's question. "But I'd appreciate it if you could find somewhere else to have your girlie night."

"This is not a *girlie night!*" I sniffed. "This is a library, and we happen to meet here regularly to talk about books."

"You can do that somewhere else," Darcy retorted, and he chucked the DVD case back down on the table. Again I was struck by his aristocratic nose. It was long and straight, and perfectly complemented by his dark eyebrows. The eyebrows had a supercilious air about them as they arched toward Darcy's hairline, as if they thought themselves far superior to all the other eyebrows in the world. Admittedly, there were dark circles under Darcy's eyes and he did look as if he needed to catch up on his sleep. But that wasn't my problem.

He sighed again. "I just want some sleep. Is that so difficult to understand?"

"Yes," said Hannah. "Seeing as how you're not an eighty-year-old man."

"Have you considered earplugs?" I asked.

Darcy took a step toward me and drew himself up to his full height. "Go. Somewhere. Else," he said, enunciating each word with cold clarity. Who did he think he was?

"No."

"Now." His voice had become quiet, even a little threatening.

But I wasn't going to let him intimidate me. Ha! This was my school and my library.

A few minutes later Charlotte, Hannah, and I found ourselves standing on the stairs clutching bowls, cups, candles, the laptop, and half my DVD collection. (We hadn't had time to pick up the TV.)

It was unbelievable! Unbe*liev*able! I was fuming. The owner of the castle, he'd said. *The owner of the castle!* This was ridiculous!

But unfortunately Darcy's claim was not as ridiculous, and his arguments not as easy to dismiss, as I would have liked. It was true that the school was a charitable foundation set up by the de Winter family. That was common knowledge. And it was also true that nobody had ever said anything about the castle itself being part of that foundation.

By now I'd also remembered that a few weeks ago, when the computer room was being converted, the workmen had needed to knock down a wall and my dad had had to write to Derbyshire for permission. That permission must have come from Darcy's father, I now realized, since Darcy had coolly informed me that we were standing on his family's property and he was well within his rights to lay claim to the west wing library whenever he saw fit. And right now he saw fit to ensure he could sleep in peace. *Idiot!* Then he'd ushered us out into the corridor and slammed the door behind us! It had to be said that my negotiating position was not as strong as it could have been, given that I hadn't actually asked my dad for permission to use the library yet. But still!

I was so furious that I didn't see the person coming round the corner at the bottom of the stairs until it was too late. Tea slopped over the edge of the tray I was carrying, soaking my sweater, as Frederick and I bumped into each other. Several mugs fell to the floor and shattered on the marble steps.

"Oops." He bent down and helped me pick up the pieces. "I thought we were meeting upstairs."

"Something came up," I said darkly. "But it's nice that you could make it, anyway. I thought you'd forgotten about us."

"We'll, um . . . we'll see you later," said Charlotte, dragging Hannah away with her.

"What happened?" Frederick asked.

While we collected up as many of the china fragments as we could see in the dim light of the hallway, I told him what Darcy had done. Frederick didn't seem particularly surprised. "That's typical of him," he said. "Now I remember why I was so happy when he left Stolzenburg."

"He's the most arrogant person I've ever met," I said.

"And he's only happy when everyone does exactly what he wants," Frederick added. "No wonder his sister made a break for it."

"Mhm," I said. We'd picked up all the broken china by now, and I realized that Frederick's eyes were fixed on a point somewhere below my chin. I suddenly became painfully aware of the tea stain spreading across my sweater, and I stood up and folded my arms across my chest. "Anyway, I can't believe how rude he was, chucking us out like that—we'd only just cleared out that library! It was a complete mess before we went in there and tidied it up. Nobody's used it for years, and suddenly along comes Darcy de Winter, mouthing off because he *can't sleep!* He should try counting sheep or reading himself a bedtime story. Or he could just go back to where he came from and save himself the trouble!"

Frederick raised his hand as if to tuck a stray lock of hair behind my ear. I held my breath, but halfway to my face his hand fell back again and instead he said, "I can talk to him if you like."

"Thanks," I murmured. "It's nice of you to offer. But I'll sort it out myself." I'd made a resolution over the holidays, after all, that I was going to learn to deal with things myself. Though it was sweet of Frederick to offer to help. Very sweet, in fact. But first of all I was going to talk to my dad. I'd do it first thing tomorrow. At the end of the day, he was the headmaster, and it was up to him to decide how the rooms should be used.

Frederick smiled at me. "Fair enough," he said. Then his face darkened again. "But I'm still going to pay a little visit to our princeling upstairs. He and I have some unfinished business of our own."

"Oh, really?" I wondered what Darcy had done to annoy Frederick. But he'd already turned to go.

"Good night, Emma. See you around," he called and hurried up the stairs to disturb Darcy's sleep once more.

August 1758

My labors consume me. I spend many hours in my laboratories. I neither sleep nor eat. It is a week since I saw the sun. Although I cannot say with any certainty what date it is, for I have lost all sense of the passage of time.

It is better that way, perhaps. The passage of time, after all, is what I am seeking to conquer.

I know there is much talk among the servants. The villagers, too, trade rumors about the machinations of the lord of Stolzenburg. They believe I have lost my wits; some even say there are ungodly forces at work in my castle. But I care not. I care only for my creature.

He is the son I have never had.

# 4

IN HISTORY LAST YEAR WE'D TALKED ABOUT HISTORICAL SOURCES and the power of chroniclers. Dr. Meier never tired of pointing out how much influence these people had on what became part of history and what did not. His argument had been convincing: Aside from buildings, and objects such as coins and pottery shards, most of our knowledge of the past—of ancient Rome, for example— came from the documents left behind by eyewitnesses. Things that had been recorded in writing were still remembered today; things that had never been written down were quickly forgotten. (I assumed so, at least: I didn't know what the ancient Romans had omitted to write down. And that in itself was proof of Dr. Meier's theory.)

These discussions had motivated Charlotte and me to start writing more frequent blog posts for the school website. Charlotte also liked to document her life in the form of photos and social media posts. Her grandchildren would have no trouble finding out what their grandma had been like when she was younger (although they would never hear about the *incident*, of course. Charlotte would take that secret with her to the grave, like any self-respecting chronicler).

The memory of this inspiring history lesson came back to me when—after Hannah and I had returned to our bedroom and had another little rant about Darcy de Winter and the way he'd sabotaged our meeting—I happened to glance at the book lying on my bedside table. The things the chroniclers had written there about the history of Stolzenburg dated back to a time long before the invention of the Internet. The book contained thoughts that were several hundred years old and would probably still be legible in another four hundred years' time as long as the book didn't meet with some kind of accident. Those eyewitnesses had determined what would be remembered and what would be forgotten.

Hmm . . .

Wasn't it a tempting thought, to join their ranks and record something of my own—something that would define future generations' knowledge about life at Stolzenburg in 2017?

I leafed through the book.

The last entry was a few years old, and was followed by lots of blank pages. The paper looked as though it would be lovely to write on. I picked up the pencil case from my desk and fished out my fountain pen.

Obviously I wasn't going to write about trivial things like the colors of people's dresses or the menu of a buffet supper. But wouldn't future generations be interested to know when Westbooks had been founded, for instance?

I lowered the nib of my fountain pen slowly onto the paper and wrote *August 2017*, carefully and very neatly, at the top of the next blank page. Yes, it looked good. And it made me feel important. Important and grown up.

I wrote a short paragraph outlining the founding of our club and describing the idea behind it, the cleanup operation in the west wing library, and our first meeting there. Like a proper diarist. Like somebody writing history. It was wonderful. My fountain pen flew across the paper, filling line after line, and before I knew it I was at the point where our soirée had come to an abrupt end.

I hadn't been intending to mention Darcy's ignoble behavior: Nobody would be interested in that a hundred years from now, would they? But my pen carried on writing as if of its own accord, and in the end I couldn't resist devoting a couple of sentences to Darcy. Probably because I was still furious with him: so furious that I found myself wishing that he would choke under the weight of the books in the library he'd taken from us. Oh, dear—that was definitely not something a professional diarist would write!

I started a new paragraph, forcing myself to be a bit more positive. I wrote a few sentences about how happy I was that all the teachers and students were back from their holidays safe and sound. There were plenty of lovely people at Stolzenburg, after all—people who didn't steal other people's libraries. People who were nice to one another. Like Miss Berkenbeck and Dr. Meier, who'd practically kissed in the dining hall today (okay, so I was exaggerating a little) before Darcy had so rudely butted in.

I closed the book and put it back on my bedside table. I really needed to stop getting worked up about Darcy: He was turning me into a bad writer, fountain pen or no fountain pen. I took a couple of deep breaths and tried to get back to the meditative state I'd achieved over the holidays, until my rage finally subsided and my heartbeat returned to normal.

That was better. I snuggled down under my duvet, closed my eyes, and made a conscious decision not to give Darcy de Winter another thought. Darcy who? Never heard of the guy.

On Monday morning we put on our school uniforms for the first time that year and went off to our *actual* first lesson, followed by our second, third, fourth, and fifth lessons. I did my best to help Hannah settle in at Stolzenburg by introducing her to all the students and teachers we met over the course of the day. I wanted her to feel at home as quickly as possible and to enjoy her first day at the school. Like me when I'd arrived at Stolzenburg four years ago, Hannah was somebody who really needed a place to call home.

When she was ten, Hannah's parents and her little brother and sister had been killed in a car crash. Since then she'd lived with her grandma. I felt she'd more than earned a warm welcome from all of us. So I made sure that one of the other students took Hannah under their wing in all the subjects where we weren't in the same class. And whenever Sinan was anywhere near, I laughed extra hard at Hannah's jokes.

By lunchtime I was almost certain that Hannah was going to love Stolzenburg as much as I did. When I entered the dining hall and saw her sitting at a table with Jana, Max, and Giovanni, chatting away to them without a hint of shyness, I took it as a sure sign that my plan was working. (I'd asked Jana to keep an eye on my roommate and make sure she was okay.) It probably helped that Hannah was so good at explaining the difference between alkanes, alkenes, and alkynes: The boys were hanging on her every word.

Charlotte and I, meanwhile, sat at the next table congratulating ourselves once again on having chosen French instead of chemistry. Not only was it a more useful subject, we felt, but significantly better for our stress levels. And French always sounded so sophisticated, no matter what you actually said.

*"Il a porté la petite chouette dans ses bras,"* I said solemnly. ("He carried the little owl in his arms.")

*"Mais oui, la pauvre chouette,"* Charlotte concurred. ("But yes, the poor owl.")

We grinned at each other over our plates. And then, all of a sudden, events took a very bizarre turn. One minute there was a buzz of loud chatter about lessons, schedules, and homework; the next minute silence had descended abruptly on the room.

The reason for this was that Dr. Meier had just dropped his plateful of stew. Or rather, from what I'd seen out of the corner of my eye, he'd *thrown* his plate of stew. Just like that. He'd drawn back his arm and hurled the plate like a discus. It hit the wall behind the teachers' table with a dull thud and left behind a smear of lentil stew as it slid to the floor. (Oh, *mon dieu!*)

Miss Whitfield and Mrs. Bröder-Strauchhaus ducked, narrowly

avoiding the flying plate, and everyone turned to look at Dr. Meier, who was now climbing up onto the counter of the serving hatch with a strangely vacant look in his eyes. He swung himself onto the countertop with an elegance I wouldn't have thought possible at his age, kicked aside the large pan from which Miss Berkenbeck had been dispensing the stew, and pulled Miss Berkenbeck herself up onto the counter beside him. The whole thing happened so quickly that she didn't even have time to protest. A moment later, Dr. Meier put his arms around her, tipped her backward, and . . .

. . . *kissed her!*

It was a very long and a very thorough kiss.

It was such a bizarre sight that my brain had trouble processing it. I watched as though hypnotized as Miss Berkenbeck lay suspended in Dr. Meier's arms and their lips met. . . .

After a while several of the students began to clap hesitantly. This seemed to distract Dr. Meier for a moment. He must have loosened his grip on Miss Berkenbeck, at any rate, because she finally managed to extricate herself and, scarlet-cheeked, slapped him hard in the face. Then she jumped down off the countertop and ran out of the room.

"*La pauvre chouette,*" murmured Charlotte.

Dr. Meier blinked and looked around the dining hall in bewilderment. The outline of Miss Berkenbeck's hand was clearly visible on his face.

That afternoon, Dr. Meier's passionate display was the talk of the school. Miss Berkenbeck was said to have locked herself in the utility room, deeply embarrassed, and insisted she was never coming out again. Dr. Meier, on the other hand, didn't seem to know what had come over him, and sat in my dad's office looking thoroughly befuddled.

So while my dad was (presumably) persuading our poor history teacher that he was suffering from some kind of psychological disorder, Hannah, Charlotte, and I assembled on one of the sofas in the student conservatory for a crisis meeting. We'd been planning to do our homework and discuss how (with my dad's help, if necessary) we could get our library back. But for some time now Charlotte had been constantly glancing at her phone, seeming a little distracted. And it was hard to concentrate because one of the younger girls was practicing something that bore a vague resemblance to an ancient Britney Spears song on the piano in the next room. On top of all that, Helena von Stein and her friends were sitting on the sofa next to ours, giggling at something on Helena's tablet.

At the tables around us, meanwhile, rumors were flying like Dr. Meier's plate of stew. The students were shocked by the incident in the dining hall. Nothing like this had ever happened at Stolzenburg before. And to think it had been Dr. Meier, who'd always seemed so quiet and straightlaced. I'd been taken aback by the projectile stew and the kiss, too, of course—although . . .

"I kind of predicted that was going to happen," I told Charlotte and Hannah.

"Sure," said Charlotte. "How could anyone not have seen that coming?"

"No, I mean it. I was thinking yesterday that it looked like there might be a bit of a romance blossoming—"

"It was more like an ambush, if you ask me. I don't think there was any blossoming involved." Charlotte was still staring down at the smartphone in her lap.

"But still," I said. "I just had this feeling yesterday that the pair of them . . ." I thought about what I'd written in the diary. "You know what—I can prove it."

"You what?"

"Yes, I can pr—"

"This definitely has to go on the homepage," I heard Helena say. "This is amazing—our first scandal, and on the very first day of term! We have to edit this and upload it ASAP. . . ." I suddenly realized what Helena and her friends had been watching on the tablet. Poor Miss Berkenbeck! There must have been loads of people who had recorded the incident in the dining hall on their phones.

"Don't do that," I interrupted, in the loud, firm voice I used when my dad started panicking about one of his imaginary illnesses and had to be dissuaded from calling for an ambulance. He'd once been absolutely convinced he was having a heart attack, when in fact he'd merely had a stitch from running up the stairs too fast.

Helena looked up. "Are you talking to us?"

"Yes, I am," I said, still using my ambulance voice. "I don't know why Dr. Meier did what he did. But don't you think it's embarrassing enough for everyone involved without you posting it online?" I thought of Miss Berkenbeck closeted away in the utility room, and prayed there wasn't any Wi-Fi signal down there.

"Whether it's embarrassing or not is beside the point. As a journalist, I have a *duty* to report it," said Helena. "And I'm going to post that video."

"Please, Helena. Think of how it'll affect them both. It was probably just a moment of madness. If you post it, everyone will see it and people will be making fun of them for months."

"Well, I'm sorry, but that's just the way it goes. I know you and Charlotte think you can just cover up embarrassing stories and pretend they never happened, but the carpet at Buckingham Palace says different." She fixed Charlotte with a meaningful look, causing her to blush to the roots of her hair. "It happened. And if *we* don't upload the video, somebody else will."

"But what about the school's reputation?" I persisted.

"What about it?"

"Well, a video like that might go viral. It might give people the wrong impression of Stolzenburg. I think we should discuss it at the next school council meeting. As the school council rep, I believe—"

"Oh, Emma, would you get off your high horse for once? This is not about school politics—it's about the freedom of the press."

"Or perhaps it's just voyeurism," said Darcy from behind me. "Excuse me, could I come past?"

As we'd been talking, Helena and I had both leaned forward into the gap between our two sofas. We moved apart now to let Darcy through. I'd had no idea he was in the conservatory, too. But he must have been sitting at one of the tables behind us talking to some of the Year 12s there. "If anything does come back to you, let me know," he called back to them over his shoulder. Then he turned to Helena. "Emma's right: You should delete that video," he said, and pushed past us toward the door.

A few moments later, whoever was mangling Britney Spears songs in the next room stopped playing, and another, much more talented pianist launched into a rendition of the *Moonlight Sonata*.

But, of course, Helena did not delete the video. Instead she pointedly turned her back on me and set to work editing the file on her tablet. Her friends watched and made suggestions about music to accompany the video ("What about 'Hit Me Baby One More Time'?—No: 'I Was Made for Lovin' You.'")

I leaned back against the sofa cushions and sighed. "Okay," I said at last to Hannah and Charlotte. "What are we going to do about the library?"

"I still reckon we should get hold of a crowbar, break in, and start squatting in there," Hannah declared. Charlotte stared down at her phone without a word.

The problem was that although my dad had promised to look into the matter of the library for us, he was always super busy during the first few days of term. When I'd told him that morning about our plight, he'd said he'd deal with it over the weekend. The thing that had worried me most about his reaction was that he hadn't seemed at all taken aback by Darcy's behavior—instead he'd admitted that the de Winters did retain certain proprietary rights over the castle. And when we went to the library at break time to retrieve the TV and take it back to the computer room, we discovered that not only did the de Winters still own the building: They were also apparently in possession of the odd key. I assumed it was Darcy, anyway, who'd locked the door to the west wing library (and all the other doors in the corridor) overnight. It was alarming how quickly he and Toby Bell had commandeered hundreds of square feet of the castle for their own use. And what were they planning to use it *for?* I wondered.

Toby had told Charlotte that Darcy had been determined to come to Stolzenburg all along, and that the supposed European road trip had just been a cover to hide the real reason for the trip from his parents. Darcy had wanted to stay at Stolzenburg for a few weeks to give himself time to *reflect*, as Toby had put it. About his twin sister, and about her disappearance four years earlier. I was surprised to hear that Darcy's parents had no idea where he was. In my math lesson I'd toyed with the idea of sending Lord and Lady de Winter a message. ("Dear Lord and Lady de Winter, you probably don't know this but your son is not currently in Rome admiring the Colosseum: He's here at Stolzenburg. I'm sure you'd prefer it if he came home. And we'd quite like our library back. . . .") But then I thought better of it—perhaps it was a little childish to go running to Darcy's parents behind his back.

"We're bound to find something in the caretaker's workshop that we can use as a crowbar," Hannah mused. "Although it would be a shame to damage the carved oak doors."

"My dad would have a heart attack," I said. Possibly even a real one.

"Perhaps we should look for a different place for Westbooks, then?"

"No. We were there first. This is our school." I felt anger rising up in me again. But since I'd vowed not to let Darcy de Winter get to me anymore, I decided to change the subject. I turned to Charlotte, who still wasn't saying a word but was now typing something into her phone. "Is your phone okay? Has it frozen again?"

Charlotte shook her head. "No," she said. "It's just that I messaged him hours ago and he hasn't replied." She showed me the chat she'd been having with Toby over the past day and a half. It was already hundreds of messages long.

"Wow, he must really like you," I said. The messages he'd sent the night before were seriously romantic, full of over-the-top metaphors. But then, at about half past seven this morning, the chat had come to an abrupt end. *I'm off to Cologne for a few days, not sure when I'll be back. Bye!* he'd written, followed by a surfer emoji.

Charlotte had replied: *Oh, that's a bit out of the blue*, and then a little later: *What are you up to in Cologne?* But Toby hadn't replied, not even an hour later when Charlotte had asked him if there was a reason why he was ignoring her.

"That's weird," I murmured, while Charlotte carried on staring at her phone as if convinced she could conjure up a message from Toby through sheer force of will. "Maybe he's got an important meeting in Cologne. Maybe his battery's just dead," she said. "I hope nothing's happened to him."

And I hoped for his sake that he wasn't about to break my best friend's heart.

July 1794

When a girl is destined to be a heroine, Fate will lead her to the very thing that makes that heroism possible.

# 5

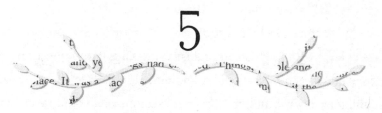

THE FOLLOWING DAY EVERYTHING BECAME CLEARER—AND AT the same time more complicated. It was a day that started off just like any other. But by the evening, events had taken a positively bizarre turn. At dusk, as Charlotte and I walked across the grounds on the way back from our swimming lesson (we were in a bit of a hurry because we wanted to get back to our rooms in time to dry our hair before dinner), there was nothing to suggest that in a few moments the world as we knew it was going to be turned upside down. But as we were passing the largest of the fountains in the center of the park, somebody burst out of the undergrowth and came sprinting toward us.

"Run!" shouted Toby. "Come on, quick!" He looked panic-stricken, his gaze darting in all directions. His clothes were dirty and torn as if he'd come crashing through the woods at full speed. His face was spattered with mud, and he was bleeding from a scratch on his left cheek. His hair was full of leaves and twigs. And he was wearing only one shoe. All in all, he was in a pretty bad way. Like someone who was running for his life. Although, of course, that couldn't be the—

"Or hide!" he yelled. "Come on!"

"Toby!" cried Charlotte. "What's happened?"

We'd come to a halt as soon as we'd spotted Toby, and now he drew level with us. Instead of answering Charlotte's question he grabbed us each by a shoulder and hurled himself to the ground, pulling us down with him. My knees slammed into the gravel and I hit my chin on the edge of the fountain.

"Ow!" I shouted. "Are you insane?"

Charlotte groaned in pain. "My elbow!" she muttered.

"Shhhh!" said Toby, trying to press our heads closer to the ground.

Was he out of his mind?

I tried to wriggle out of the headlock he had me in. The gravel crunched under my grazed knees.

"Quiet," Toby said again through gritted teeth, and tightened his grip on me. I gasped for air as he peered over the top of the fountain toward the trees at the edge of the wood, where (as far as I could see, with my nose wedged in Toby's armpit) nothing was moving.

Toby was clearly delusional. If we didn't want to make him even more berserk, we had to resist the temptation to panic at all costs. "Excuse me," I said in a polite but muffled voice. "I'm having a bit of trouble breathing down here." (And what little air I was getting wasn't particularly fragrant.)

"*Shhh!*" Toby repeated, but he did loosen his grip enough for Charlotte and me to edge away from him a little.

"What's going on?" asked Charlotte under her breath. "Who are we hiding from?"

"We thought you were in Cologne," I whispered.

Toby put a finger to his lips without taking his eyes off the outskirts of the wood. But after several minutes had gone by without any kind of movement in the trees, he seemed to relax a little. "Do either of you have a phone on you?" he asked, in a barely audible voice. "My battery is dead, and we need to call the police."

"Why?" I asked.

"Here," said Charlotte, passing him her smartphone.

We listened as Toby explained to the emergency services that he had been pursued from the village to the castle by a full-grown lion. A *lion*!

Interestingly, the lady on the other end of the phone did not seem particularly surprised by this information. I heard her say that we should stay calm, then something about an old and toothless but still dangerous animal and a specially trained team being on its way. "Thanks," Toby whispered, and hung up.

Charlotte gaped at him. "A lion? Really? Here in the woods?"

I, too, was shocked by the news. Possibly more shocked than Charlotte and Toby put together.

"Yes," said Toby. "From what that woman was saying, it's escaped from the circus a few miles away. I stopped at the gas station in the village on my way back, and it suddenly jumped out at me. It must be quite old, not used to hunting in the wild anymore— it tried to pounce on me and missed. But there was no way I could get back to my car, so I made a run for it and it chased me all the way up the hill."

A shiver ran down my spine. This was one of those stranger-than-fiction situations. It was too surreal to be true, and yet it was actually happening. In fact, it was happening exactly the way I'd . . .

"Are you sure it was a real lion?" asked Charlotte.

But I had no doubt whatsoever that it was a real lion. And I didn't even cry out when the big cat appeared at the edge of the wood and started prowling up and down among the trees.

I was starting to realize what was going on.

We ducked down behind the fountain and waited for the specially trained task force from the police or the fire brigade or whoever the emergency services lady had sent us. The lion slipped out of the shadow of the trees, padded across the neatly trimmed lawn, and lay down under a rhododendron bush, where it appeared to doze off. Its mane was dull and matted, and its skin hung in loose folds from its skinny body. It was true that the poor creature didn't exactly look to be in peak hunting condition. But I was sure it would still have been perfectly capable of killing a human being if it wanted to. And by now it was so close that we hardly dared breathe. Charlotte pressed closer to Toby's side while I, despite my good intentions, finally started to panic. Not because I was afraid of being eaten by the lion, but because I'd finally figured out why it had turned up here in the first place.

The most bizarre thing about this whole bizarre situation was that I had foreseen it. No, more than that: *I had described it.* I'd written about it yesterday evening, in my latest entry in the book.

In a fit of pique. Or madness. Or a mixture of the two. I couldn't quite remember.

First of all I'd described what had happened between Dr. Meier and Miss Berkenbeck in the dining hall—only I hadn't named names, and I'd made it sound much less embarrassing than it actually had been. In my version it was a romantic kiss in a secluded corner behind the drinks machine, far from prying eyes. And then I'd thought of Charlotte, still waiting patiently for a message from Toby. I was in a strange mood (I think I was still high on sugar from all the sweets I'd eaten that evening while watching the rest of *Shakespeare in Love*) and I found myself writing something in the diary about Toby. It was just a throwaway remark, a couple of sentences saying he'd better come back to Stolzenburg soon or I was going to feed him to the lions.

Now, as I crouched beside Charlotte and Toby, listening to the quiet snoring of a real, flesh-and-blood lion, an impossible idea began to take shape in my mind. It wormed its way into every corner of my brain until—despite having a *lot* of unanswered questions and serious doubts about my own sanity—I started to believe it.

However crazy it might seem, I had to face the facts: I'd written about this. And what I'd written had now come to pass. Just like the kiss between Dr. Meier and Miss Berkenbeck, which I'd written about in the diary the day before it had happened. Both events were too surreal to be coincidences. And I'd never been much good at predicting things, especially bizarre things like this. So there was only one explanation, even if it seemed wildly improbable—no, *impossible*. The kiss and the lion could mean only one thing: The book was more than just a diary.

In fact, it now started to dawn on me that it was exactly the opposite: The entries in the book did not describe things that had already happened; they *made* things happen. The things I'd written in the chronicle had miraculously come true *because* I'd written them.

*Oh my God! I must be mad!* Was I seriously considering this as an explanation? My whole body was trembling now, but I couldn't deny it. Yes, I was considering it. And not only that—I believed it. I felt sick.

"Emma," Charlotte whispered. "The lion's asleep." She patted me reassuringly, while I clutched her arm with icy-cold fingers. The book in my bedroom was . . . No, I had to stop this. It was impossible. End of story. But the lion . . . and Toby . . . I couldn't . . . I stared past Charlotte into one of the bushes. My heart was racing. Beads of cold sweat stood out on my forehead.

"I think she's in shock," said Toby.

Charlotte hugged me tighter. "Don't worry, Emma. The lion's asleep. And help is on the way."

A few minutes later, as promised, a police van pulled up in the courtyard, and it wasn't long before a vet had put the slumbering lion into an even deeper sleep with the help of a tranquilizer dart. The creature looked almost cuddly as it was lifted into a transport crate.

My dad, of course, was absolutely beside himself. A dangerous predator had made its way onto the school grounds and had almost attacked several students, including his own daughter! He became so agitated at the thought that he ended up having an asthma attack and retired to bed around eight o'clock. Charlotte and I still felt a little frazzled, too, even though hours had passed since the lion had been taken away and the circus manager had apologized profusely for what had happened. We'd skipped dinner and taken long, hot showers to try to calm ourselves down a little. Now we were on our way to Miss Whitfield's etiquette lesson, which was held in her cottage on the edge of the woods, and we ran part of the way so as not to have to be outdoors any longer than strictly necessary. Who knew what kind of wild beast was going to come prowling out of the undergrowth next? Although, technically . . .

"Do you think he's annoyed with me?" asked Charlotte as we passed the fountain. After we'd been rescued, Toby had left us standing in the middle of a throng of curious students who'd been watching the lion out of the window, and he'd disappeared into the west wing. It would have been the perfect opportunity to take Charlotte in his arms and apologize for his mysterious trip to Cologne and his radio silence. But Toby had done nothing of the sort—he'd simply vanished. Again. What was wrong with the guy?

"No," I replied firmly. Whatever the reason for the sudden change in Toby's behavior, it surely didn't have anything to do with Charlotte. "You haven't done anything wrong."

"I really thought he liked me."

"I thought so, too," I said. I stroked Miss Velvetnose's back as we passed. "And he does. It'll sort itself out, you'll see. I'll help."

Miss Whitfield's living room was small and very British-looking. The curtains were the same pale pink color as the climbing roses outside the window and the crocheted cushion covers on the sofa. On the mantelpiece stood a row of family photos, and the shelves were full of beautifully bound books. There was an elegant bureau in one corner, and beside it an old gramophone was perched on a spindle-legged stool. To make sure all fifteen students taking the course had somewhere to sit, there was also an assortment of armchairs, dining chairs, and occasional tables, giving the room a cluttered look.

The etiquette course was one of a number of elective modules that pupils at Stolzenburg could choose to study alongside the main curriculum. The purpose of this particular module was to prepare us for a life in the highest echelons of society, and teach us all the social graces we would need when attending formal dinners, balls, and official receptions. A world where I felt completely out of place, in other words. But Charlotte's family had insisted that she take the course, so I'd immediately signed up, too, in order to provide moral support. I also happened to like Miss Whitfield, and it couldn't hurt to know how to hold a teacup properly, could it?

"And then you raise your little finger ever so slightly," Miss Whitfield was explaining. Charlotte sipped daintily at her Earl Grey. (Contrary to the claims of the British tabloid press, Charlotte had impeccable table manners. When she wasn't barfing, that is.)

"Oh, man," said Hannah, who was sitting with us at one of the tiny tables. (We'd managed to persuade her to come along to the etiquette class, too.) She'd wedged her thumb through the handle of the teacup and seemed to be having trouble getting it out again. "I think I'm stuck."

Miss Whitfield smiled benignly. "If you should ever have this problem while taking tea with a lord, you could always smash the cup over his head and shout 'Down with the aristocracy!'" she suggested. Miss Whitfield was a tall woman with an ageless face. Her hair was shot through with silver strands, and I'd never seen her in anything other than an ankle-length dress or skirt. She eyed Hannah's trapped thumb with a sigh. "I'm afraid that even if you were to raise your little finger, my dear, you would struggle to look elegant holding your cup like that. Come through into the kitchen and we'll pour out that tea before you scald yourself. And we'll see if we can't use a little soap to set you free without breaking my favorite teacup."

Hannah and Miss Whitfield disappeared into the next room. I looked around surreptitiously, but everybody else was completely preoccupied with their own teacups and with conversations about lords and lions. Jonathan and Tom, the boys at the next table, were engrossed in a battle between swallows made out of folded napkins, so I pulled the book out of my bag and slid it across the table to Charlotte. "Remember this book? I found it that day we were tidying up the west wing library."

Charlotte nodded. "Yes. What is it?" She flicked through the first few pages. "An old diary?"

"Sort of." I bit my lower lip, then opened the chronicle to my latest entry. I'd written it about three-quarters of an hour earlier, with the intention of testing out my theory. "Look—this is what I wrote just now."

Charlotte skimmed my paragraph. It wasn't very long. Then she looked at me uncomprehendingly. "So . . . ," she said, "you knew we were going to be learning how to drink tea today?"

I shook my head. "No. I made it up."

Charlotte frowned. "And the bit about my scone?"

"I made that up, too. But I think if you . . ." I pointed to the cake stand in the middle of the table, which held four scones and a little pot of clotted cream.

"Are you serious?" Charlotte looked from me to the scones and back again.

"Trust me. I have a theory about . . . well, about this book. So, which scone are you going to pick?"

"Are you sure you're okay, Emma?" said Charlotte gently. "Toby did say you might be in shock, after what happened with the lion."

"I am in shock," I said. "But it's more to do with this book than the lion. So please, do me a favor and pick a scone."

I gnawed my lower lip again as Charlotte's hand hovered over the cake stand. After lingering by the bottom tier for a moment, she eventually selected a scone from the top tier. She bit into it gingerly, chewed it for a moment, and stared at me.

"I don' beweeve it," she mumbled with her mouth full. "Tha's . . ."

I nodded. "But next time you take tea with a lord, I recommend you don't speak with your mouth full," I said. Charlotte took my advice and swallowed everything that was in her mouth apart from the black trouser button that had been baked into her scone. The button was exactly as I'd described it. It lay between us on the tablecloth, dark and shiny.

"Emma," said Charlotte, "are you telling me . . ." She paused, presumably finding the idea too ludicrous to say out loud.

"Exactly," I said, stroking the cover of the book in my lap. "I don't know how or why. It goes against all the laws of physics. But it's a fact: The things you write in this book come true."

"No way!" Charlotte exclaimed. She reached for the cake stand and crumbled the remaining scones between her fingers one by one. "Miss Whitfield must have baked a little object into each scone, to see how we'd react. To see if we could keep our composure."

But, of course, none of the other scones had anything inside.

A moment later, Hannah and Miss Whitfield came back into the living room. Miss Whitfield eyed the crumbled scones with a sorrowful shake of her head. "That isn't very good manners, Charlotte. And you were drinking your cup of tea so beautifully a moment ago."

"Make there be chocolate cake for breakfast tomorrow," Hannah suggested. "And world peace."

It was already past midnight. The three of us were sitting on my bed leafing through the book. Charlotte was still skeptical, but Hannah was bursting with excitement. Since hearing about my amazing discovery, she'd been full of suggestions for things we could write in the book. But so far I'd hesitated to act on any of them. Now that there was conclusive evidence for my theory, in the form of an unassuming little black button, I was suddenly awestruck at the thought of the power this tatty old book possessed. Again I felt as though I was holding a living thing in my hands, something more than paper, ink, and glue. Something *magic*. Although I still hardly even dared think that word, let alone say it out loud.

And besides, my sudden hesitation was surely justified: It was one thing to suspect that the book had incredible powers and even to prove it; it was quite another to embrace those powers and start using them as if it were the most normal thing in the world. If there was one thing this chronicle was *not*, it was normal.

The events of the last two days had also made me realize that I needed to think carefully about what and how to write in the book, given that the real-world consequences were not entirely predictable. It was probably best not to conjure up anything too outlandish, anyway, which was why I'd provisionally vetoed Hannah's request for a unicorn.

"We have to find out where it comes from," said Charlotte firmly. "Where did you say you found it again? In the west wing library?"

I nodded. "In a secret compartment in the bottom drawer of that chest we couldn't move."

"Mhm."

"Hang on, go back a few pages," Hannah said.

We'd spent the past few hours perusing hundreds of the entries in the chronicle, but we'd still managed to read only about a quarter of them. Some were penned in microscopically tiny writing and were barely legible; others featured handwriting so old-fashioned that none of us could read it. And some contained nothing more than mundane details (and a few flowery, rather overwrought poems about dark nights). As we'd flicked through the pages, I'd scanned the text for information about the book itself. Had all the "chroniclers" understood how it worked? Had they left any hidden clues? And why couldn't I shake the feeling that the further I leafed through the book, the more pages there were?

"Stop." Hannah pointed to the drawing of the strange faun-like creature I'd come across a few days earlier. "I know it's not a unicorn," she said. "But couldn't we—"

"No," said Charlotte and I together.

"Why not?"

We bent over the paper. The ink drawing and the accompanying text were dated 1758 and had clearly been penned by one of the de Winters' ancestors, because the author kept referring to himself as the "lord of Stolzenburg." His first few entries, from the beginning of 1758, showed that he must have been a very lonely man. Again and again he lamented his solitary life and the fact that he had no wife or children.

But as time went on, his entries started to change. They grew darker, more purposeful and . . . more unbalanced. Not only had the lord of Stolzenburg been a lonely man, but a paranoid one, too. He'd had several secret passages built into the castle, as well as concealed rooms he referred to as "laboratories," in which he'd shut himself away with increasing regularity throughout the spring of 1758. After a while he started mentioning a son, or a creature, who would outlive him and carry his words into the future. A creature that would transcend the barriers of time and mortality. Huh?

I began to suspect that the lord of Stolzenburg had been a few sandwiches short of a picnic. From October 1758 onward his entries became completely incomprehensible, and were frequently illustrated with the same ink drawing. We stopped reading. This wasn't getting us anywhere.

But Hannah was still pointing triumphantly at one of the sketches. "Look: He *did* create a unicorn!"

Charlotte snorted. "That's enough now. We have no idea what we're getting ourselves into. Lion or no lion, we have to be sensible about this. It's all getting way too weird." She took the book out of my hands, snapped it shut, and slid it under my pillow. "Let's go to bed and talk about it tomorrow, okay? There's no such thing as magic."

*Really?*

"Good night," I said.

Charlotte was almost at the door. Before she went out of the room she checked her phone for what must have been the millionth time that day. But it seemed she still hadn't had a reply, because she shoved the phone straight back into her pocket. Hannah went through to the bathroom to brush her teeth, and I was left alone. There was a slight bulge in my pillow where the book lay.

I closed my eyes for a moment and leaned my head against the wall. What on earth was going on? I was sixteen years old: almost an adult. Next spring I planned to stand for election as head girl, and once I'd finished my A-levels in three years' time, I was going to travel the world. After that I would go to university and pursue a career. Possibly as a lawyer or a journalist. I was a sensible person, for heaven's sake. Was I seriously sitting here with an antique book wondering whether there was really such a thing as magic?

On the other hand there was the button in the scone, the lion, and Dr. Meier's bizarre behavior in the dining hall. I'd managed to set a full-grown lion on Toby Bell! The thought still made me shiver. That had been a very reckless thing to write. The way events actually unfolded after being written about in the chronicle seemed to be pretty unpredictable in general. Although the button baked into the scone had gone exactly to plan—perhaps because my description had been very precise?

I listened to the sound of running water and Hannah's electric toothbrush. My hand slipped under the pillow as if of its own accord and pulled out the chronicle.

Knowledge—as I'd heard John attest some forty-two times that summer—was not about simply believing things to be true but about establishing hypotheses and testing them. Either I'd completely lost my marbles today, or I'd made a groundbreaking discovery. And either way, wasn't it safest to take a logical and scientific approach? To test my hypothesis? If I wanted to find out what was really going on here, surely there was nothing for it but to experiment a little. . . .

I looked at the embossed creature on the binding, the madman's creature, which looked—even now that I knew the impossible was possible—like something out of a fairy tale. I had to know how the book and the diary entries worked. I had to find out more. And fast.

Of course, I would have to be extremely cautious and start off with small things, like the button. But I was going to come to grips with this thing and I was going to do it tonight. Emma Magdalena Morgenroth was a woman of action.

I went over to my desk, fished out a pencil, and started writing very faintly on the next blank page. When Hannah emerged from the bathroom and saw what I was doing, she grinned. "Am I getting my unicorn?"

"No," I said, and carried on writing, hoping against hope that I was not going crazy. "But how would you feel about having Sinan in your group for the biology project?"

Hannah tilted her head to one side, then the other—and then she nodded. "Forget the unicorn," she said.

December 1758

My strength has deserted me. For weeks now I have been confined to my bed. I feel that Death is near, and I welcome it. My time on this earth is drawing to a close. Soon I will be no more. But something of me will live on, even after my body has returned to dust. Now, at last, I am certain of it.

The same is true of my words in this book. They will last forever, I know it, for I have tried many times to undo or to change them.

But always in vain.

# 6

T HE NEXT FEW DAYS WERE A DROP IN THE OCEAN COMPARED
to the castle's long history.

But they changed everything.

I'd always wanted to be able to change things. Ever since I was
a child I'd hoped, someday, to become somebody who made a difference; somebody who helped people and made the world a better
place. And because I knew those things took a lot of effort, I'd
always been a trier. I'd studied hard for my exams, and last year I'd
even been elected school council rep. But so far I hadn't really managed to change anything (unless you counted the part I'd played in
the long-drawn-out negotiations over our school uniforms). Now,
however, with the help of the chronicle, I suddenly had opportuni-
ties I could never even have dreamed of before, and which were only
gradually starting to dawn on me.

A few of my efforts had already borne fruit: Hannah and Sinan, for instance, had been put in the same group for our biology project and had spent Thursday afternoon planning the wetland habitat they would be creating and observing over the next few weeks. And with just a few strokes of my pen I'd done what no doctor had ever been able to do: For days now my dad had been fit and healthy, plagued neither by migraines nor asthma nor imaginary tropical diseases. His mood had improved markedly as a result. I'd even seen him jogging in the park yesterday and could scarcely believe my eyes. He was also smiling a lot more.

To cap it all, Dr. Meier and Miss Berkenbeck were now officially a couple. At dinner a few days ago, some of the students had seen the two of them disappear into the corner behind the drinks machine. Since then they'd been spotted several times holding hands on the castle grounds. Nobody knew quite what had persuaded Miss Berkenbeck to forgive our history teacher for the kissing-on-the-countertop incident. Hannah and I, on the other hand, had a pretty good idea.

Charlotte and Toby had also happened to run into each other in the corridors more than usual lately. But unfortunately they hadn't ended up rekindling their romance. Whatever had happened between them, it looked as though Toby's interest in Charlotte had faded as quickly as it had begun. Eventually, Charlotte (who'd guessed that I was incapable of leaving the book alone) asked me not to write anything else about her. And she didn't seem to like talking about the chronicle in general, either. In the evenings, while Hannah and I chattered away about the book and its powers and decided what to write about next, Charlotte did everything she could to stay out of our conversations. She confined herself to repeated warnings that we should be careful, but she would have preferred it if we'd simply put the book back in its secret compartment and forgotten all about it. "Why do you want to interfere in the course of events, anyway?" she'd asked us more than once.

But I knew there was no going back. Not now that I knew the kind of power that lay within the book's well-thumbed pages. I couldn't and didn't want to forget what I'd found out—I was too enthralled by it.

By now I'd gotten very good at using the book to influence minor events. I knew how to describe things so that they would happen in an inconspicuous, seemingly coincidental way. I still hadn't mastered the chronological aspects of the book's powers, though. Some of the things I wrote about would happen immediately, almost before the ink was dry on the page. Others could take several days. Two days ago, for example, I'd written an entry about us getting the west wing library back from Darcy. But it hadn't happened yet. Darcy still hadn't left the castle, nor had he unlocked the door to the library.

It was now Saturday and my dad had promised to deal with the issue that morning. We were due to meet in the west wing in half an hour to negotiate with Darcy—who would have to back down eventually, surely. *Surely he must see that?*

I yawned widely as I swung my legs out of bed and skimmed the parquet floor with my toes, trying to find my slippers. Hannah had gotten up much earlier than me, as had everyone else in the castle, I imagined. I'd missed breakfast, at any rate. And still I was dog-tired, having stayed up late reading the chronicle and not slept very well afterward.

Not for the first time, I'd been tormented by nightmares full of paper dragonflies with rustling wings. They seemed to be following me. And recently the creature with the curled horns and the goat's legs—the faun—had also started to appear in these dreams, creeping through the castle, scurrying down secret passageways that everyone had forgotten existed, and lurking in the shadows of the ancient halls. Although I never came face-to-face with the faun, I knew it was him.

In the last few hours I'd woken up several times, heart pounding, and quickly checked that the book was still there under my pillow. Every time I'd woken up I'd been afraid someone had stolen it while I slept.

Now, by daylight, these fears seemed a little ridiculous. Apart from Charlotte, Hannah, and me, nobody even knew of the book's existence, let alone the powers it possessed. So who would think of stealing it? I was getting myself all worked up about nothing.

I finally located my slippers, put them on, and shuffled into the bathroom. I stood under the shower and started to feel more awake as the stream of hot water and the scent of my favorite shower gel (lemon and mint) banished the last of the nightmares from my mind. Then I pulled on a pair of jeans and a T-shirt, brushed my teeth, and tied my hair back in a bun. I dabbed a little concealer on the dark circles under my eyes, but there was no time for mascara—it was already five to eleven.

I hurried over to the west wing, where my dad was already in conversation with Darcy de Winter. They were both standing outside the library door, with Darcy clearly refusing to hand over the key.

"I'm aware that your family does retain certain rights of owner-ship over the building itself," my dad was saying as I joined them. "And I apologize for any inconvenience this may cause. But, as headmaster, I am entitled to act as the representative of the owner of the castle. Which is why I must ask you to please unlock this door!"

Darcy folded his arms across his chest. He was wearing a white shirt with the sleeves rolled up, and already looked a bit like the lawyer he would probably become in a few years' time. "As far as I know this library is no longer used for the day-to-day running of the school," he said.

"Where did you even get the key?" I asked.

"Ah, Emma, there you are. Good morning," said my dad.

Darcy greeted me with a nod, then turned back to my dad: "That's right, isn't it? This wing is no longer used for staff or stu-dents? There are no regular events here, nothing like that?"

"Yes, that's true," my dad replied. "But my daughter has been given permission to host a . . . er . . ."

"Literature club," I supplied.

"She has my official permission to use this library for a litera-ture club. So I would be much obliged if you'd open the door. Other-wise, of course, we can always come back with the caretaker and his set of master keys."

"That won't be necessary," said Darcy, but he still didn't move. He wrinkled his nose and exhaled. "It's open."

*Oh, please.* I grabbed the door handle and turned it. The door swung open. We'd been checking the doors on this corridor every day for a week, and yesterday afternoon every single one of them had still been locked. And now . . .

We entered the west wing library—or what was left of it.

I heard my dad give a sharp intake of breath behind me as I burst into the room.

"It . . . I found it like this ten minutes ago," said Darcy.

I cast my eyes over the library.

Heaps of books lay scattered around us: There was not a single book left on the shelves. Some of the shelves themselves had also been pulled off the walls and lay broken on the floor, surrounded by bits of splintered wood and ripped fabric. The curtains had been torn down and the upholstery on the sofas and the armchairs slashed open. The drawers of the desk and the chest had been wrenched open, and their contents lay strewn across the floor. Someone had even managed to pull up some of the floorboards—perhaps in search of something hidden underneath.

"Didn't you say you and your friends were going to tidy up?" asked my dad.

"Yes," I said through clenched teeth. "We did . . . we . . ." I broke off and glared at Darcy. "Were you looking for anything in particular?" I spat. I balled my hands into fists. I was absolutely livid at the sight of my beautiful library in ruins.

"No," he said, "I—"

"Then why did you do it? To stop us from meeting here and disturbing your sleep?"

"I already told you: It wasn't me."

"The room was locked," I retorted. "You were the one with the key."

"So all this chaos is new?" asked my dad. He'd taken a few steps across the room, picking his way between the heaps of books, and was prodding at the loose springs sticking out of one of the arm-chair cushions. "It is important to give children the space to find their own place in the world," he quoted from his book. "But I'm really not sure this is the right place for you and your book club, Emma. Look, one of the windows is broken. You'd catch cold."

Darcy and I rushed over to the window, where there was indeed a fist-sized hole in one of the leaded glass panes.

"Maybe somebody got in from outside," suggested Darcy, but I was having trouble believing in his innocence. Wasn't it much more likely that he was the one responsible for the destruction? He was the one who'd banished us from the library, after all, and locked all the doors. He'd taken over the whole corridor. And for what . . . ?

My reflections were interrupted by Darcy saying: "Even if they didn't get in through the window, there's dozens of secret passages in this old place. There must be plenty of entrances other than the official front door."

"They? Who's they?"

"The intruders."

"Of course, the *intruders*. Strangers came and broke into the castle specifically in order to trash this room. And pigs might fly."

"It does seem unlikely," my dad agreed. He was still looking warily at the rusty springs, as if afraid they might come pinging out of the cushion at any moment and take someone's eye out.

Darcy shrugged. "I'm sorry I threw you out of the library. That was . . . very rude of me."

"Yes, it was," I said. I could think of plenty of less polite words than *rude* to describe Darcy de Winter.

"I apologize," he said, and I wondered if I'd heard him right. "I shouldn't have behaved that way. Of course you can meet here and watch your films—er, sorry, I mean read your books."

"Because you've found whatever it was you were looking for in the library, and now that you've finished ransacking it you've got no more use for it? Wow, thanks. That's big of you."

"Emma," he said, taking a step toward me, "we de Winters always admit when we've made a mistake, and I'm genuinely sorry, okay?" I blinked. Well—I had written an entry in the chronicle to this effect, hadn't I?

Darcy lowered his voice out of earshot of my dad, who was now examining the other chairs for deadly springs. "I wasn't in a very good mood that evening," he said quietly. "I was tired and . . . and stressed. I was out of order to you. But this"—he gestured at the devastation around us—"is not my doing. After you left the library, I locked the doors and I didn't set foot in here again until a few minutes ago. That's the truth. Over breakfast this morning I decided I should stop behaving like an idiot and give you your library back, and then I came up here and found it like this. I'm surprised I didn't hear anything, to be honest—my bedroom is practically next door, and whoever did this must have made a lot of noise."

I studied him for a moment, looking for an indication somewhere in his chiseled face that he was lying. But I found none. He genuinely looked as though he meant what he was saying. Hmm. Assuming Darcy really was innocent, what on earth had happened here? Who else could have done this? And why? Had someone been looking for the chronicle? My fears of last night suddenly didn't seem so unreasonable after all . . . and I started to wonder whether there was something weird going on at Stolzenburg—something other than my experiments with a magic book, that is.

I looked suspiciously around the room at the jumble of broken furniture and books. The drawers from the immovable chest had been pulled out, but the secret compartment didn't seem to have been touched. The intruder must have overlooked it. When I crouched down to take a closer look, I spotted something else amongst the chaos of books and loose floorboards. Strewn across the floor was a cloud of tiny silver leaves that weren't much bigger than my thumbnail.

They were exactly like the ones I'd found in the woods the previous weekend.

I pressed them gently with my fingertips. Some of them crumbled at my touch, and the rest I gathered up and put in my trouser pocket. Then I stood up again.

"We need to talk," I said to Darcy. Even if he'd had nothing to do with the trashing of the library, I'd started to think that his sudden appearance at the castle was as strange as that of these little leaves. "Why did you come to Stolzenburg?" I asked. "And please spare me the story about your European road trip. I know it's something to do with your sister."

He seemed to reflect for a moment, then slowly nodded. "All right," he said, "but not here." He glanced at my dad, who was attempting to reassemble one of the broken drawers. Then the ghost of a smile flitted across his face. "How about we go for a walk?"

The woods around Stolzenburg were dense and wild. They consisted mainly of spruce trees, and their fallen needles formed a soft blanket on the ground. When you left the path and walked among the trees it felt as though you were walking on a thick carpet, and it gave the woods a cozy feeling even in the iciest depths of winter.

That morning, however, Darcy and I took one of the paths that led in a broad curve around the estate. It was less a path, really, than a set of tire tracks, and we each walked in one of the two ruts. Ferns sprouted on the green strip in between. The sunlight slanted through the treetops and bathed the tree trunks on either side of the tracks in a golden light.

I waited for Darcy to start speaking. But he contented himself with kicking a pinecone along the ground in front of him.

It was only when a startled fox burst out of the undergrowth, ran up the hillside, and disappeared behind a rock that Darcy emerged from his reverie. It was as if a curtain had been drawn back from his face. "Gina and I both attended Stolzenburg from age eleven," he explained. "It's a tradition in my family. After my ancestors moved out of the castle and the school was set up, all the de Winters came here for their education. Only Gina and I didn't get to finish ours."

"I heard about that," I said. "About Gina, I mean. How she went missing four years ago. People say she ran away."

He was silent again, as if he didn't trust himself to speak. For a few minutes the only sound was our muffled footsteps and the occasional burst of birdsong. "She didn't run away," he said at last. "She disappeared. There's a difference. Gina would never have run away. Not without telling me."

"Of course not."

"We're twins."

"Of course," I said, but I did wonder whether Darcy's confidence might be misplaced. Sure, it was often said that twins had a special connection. But was it true? There was a pair of identical twins in Year 8 (Robb and Todd) who hated each other's guts and whom Mrs. Bröder-Strauchhaus had had to put in separate rooms to stop them from killing each other in their sleep. Those two definitely took things to the opposite extreme.

"Sorry, but I don't think you can really understand it," said Darcy. His voice was quiet and cool, and he stared straight ahead into the dense thicket of tree trunks.

"Well, anyway—so now you've come back to find out what happened to Gina?" I ventured. He nodded.

"The police searched every inch of the woodland," he said. "They told us she must have fallen in the river and drowned, and my parents accepted that explanation. They mourned Gina's death and took me out of the school and said they didn't want me to dwell on it anymore. They thought I was just reopening old wounds." He kicked the pinecone a long way away and suddenly looked so sad that I felt an urge to touch his arm, comfort him. I didn't, of course. "But I can't just accept it. I won't accept it. I don't believe Gina's dead. I . . . I can sense she's alive," he went on, and then added tonelessly: "Particularly the past few nights. I can just feel that she's still here, you know?"

Goose bumps crept up the back of my neck. "Do you think

she's somewhere nearby?" I murmured. I looked warily at the tree trunks around us and the crumbling remnants of the monastery wall, which were now coming into view. Were these woods really as cozy as I'd always thought?

Darcy shrugged. "I know the whole thing sounds completely mad, and to be honest I'm not sure why I'm even telling you about it. But I just knew I had to come back to Stolzenburg if I ever wanted to see Gina again."

"I see."

We clambered over a fallen tree, which must have been brought down in a recent storm. I, too, was a little surprised that he was telling me all this. But only a little. The fact that Darcy was being so open with me and had even apologized for his past wrongdoing was, of course, the direct result of one of my entries in the chronicle. I'd written that he should apologize and let us back into the library, and it had worked like a dream. Darcy had handed over the library and apologized to me—and to cap it all, here we were having a conversation like two normal people!

We'd reached the ruins by this time, and the spot where the path bent around to the left and followed the riverbank for a stretch. But Darcy didn't seem any more bothered about walking along the Rhine this morning than I was. Without saying anything we both stepped off the track at the same moment and carried on toward the ruins.

"I'm not going to do anything stupid," Darcy continued, running his left hand along one of the old stone archways. "I just want to find out a bit more about what was going on with Gina before she disappeared."

"You were at the school then, too."

"I know," he said. "But at the time . . . for a few months we'd sort of been going our separate ways. Gina had changed—she spent a lot of time out here in the woods, and she suddenly developed an interest in old ghost stories. I thought it was all a bit stupid and just a phase she'd grow out of, so I . . ." He broke off and blinked at me, bewildered. It was almost as if he was waking up from a dream. He looked a bit like Dr. Meier in the dining hall a few days ago. . . . Oh, dear, was the book's effect wearing off already?

"What kind of stories?" I asked quickly.

"Oh, something about our ancestors and this monastery," Darcy murmured distractedly—then he suddenly turned his back on me and moved with long strides down what had once been the nave. I followed him hesitantly. I didn't like that self-assured stride: With every step, he seemed to be turning back into the haughty lord of the manor I knew him to be. His shoulders were rigid now, and his jaw was set.

"That's a funny-looking angel," he said at last, pointing to the statue of the faun as we passed it. "The stonemason can't have been very good at his job."

"It's not an angel," I said, but Darcy had already turned to one of the faded gravestones and was scraping off some of the moss with his shoe to reveal the inscription. "Still ugly, though," he muttered.

"Is that one of your ancestors?" I asked, coming to stand beside him.

"Yes." He removed his foot from the gravestone and looked at me. Then he frowned, and a furrow appeared on his forehead. "Er . . . sorry, but what are we doing out here again?"

The effect of the chronicle must have completely worn off. "You wanted to apologize for kicking us out of the library and to explain why you came back to Stolzenburg in the first place," I said helpfully.

Darcy seemed lost in thought. "Well, I don't know what I was thinking, but . . . as far as I can recall, I've now done both."

I nodded. "But I'd still like to know more."

"About what?"

"About you and Gina, and what you plan to do next. About what you mean when you say you can sense she's still alive." I could see the shutters coming down, but I carried on. "Oh, yes, and about Toby. Do you know why he suddenly seems to have lost interest in Charlotte?"

"Well—that's because she's already got a boyfriend, and he's not into playing games," said Darcy impatiently.

"*What?*"

He shut his eyes for a moment and took a deep breath. "Look, I don't feel very well today for some reason," he said. "I've felt really weird all morning—I'm just not myself. I'm afraid I'm going to have to go and lie down." He did look a bit green about the gills, to be fair.

"Charlotte doesn't have a boyfriend," I exclaimed, but Darcy had already turned away and was hurrying back toward the castle.

I sank down onto one of the old walls and rested my chin in my hands. Thoughts were whirling around my head like a flock of startled sparrows. What Darcy had told me about Toby was a surprise, but it was still by far the least bizarre thing that had happened today. There was no doubt that my entry in the chronicle had affected

Darcy's behavior. I wasn't sure why or how, but my words had obviously caused him not only to hand over the library as planned but also to confide in me, in an almost friendly way, for at least half an hour. No wonder he was feeling nauseous.

I, on the other hand, had got what I wanted, and you might have thought I'd be feeling very pleased with myself. But I suddenly felt a bit subdued. The seriousness of what had just happened—of the things Darcy had confided in me, despite the fact that we usually couldn't stand each other—hit me hard. Suddenly I wondered whether what I'd written about Darcy had really been such a good idea after all. It would have been nicer to get a real apology than one conjured up by the book, wouldn't it? Although I'd probably have been waiting a very long time.

Trying to change Darcy's character had definitely been a step too far, I decided. A few scribbled lines in the chronicle had manip- ulated him into telling me things he'd probably never told anyone else in the world, and that shocked me. I'd made Darcy tell me something he wouldn't have chosen to tell me of his own free will. And I'd been given an insight into his feelings that I had no right to. I bit my lower lip and decided that in the future I would be a lot more prudent, and choose my words with greater care. I didn't want this kind of thing to happen again, especially not to people I liked. Eavesdropping on my friends was not my style.

What a morning it had been! I tipped my head back and gazed up at the little patch of bright blue sky that shone through a gap in the leaves. I couldn't stop thinking about how Darcy de Winter had come here hoping to find his twin sister and how he still believed she might be somewhere nearby, after all this time. True, he wasn't my favorite person in the world, but surely there must be a way I could help him in his search for Gina. Perhaps I could write something about it in the book? Or was that too dangerous?

I pondered for a while. The truth was, I knew nothing about Gina de Winter or why she had gone missing. And that would make it very difficult to find the right words. Something like "And so Gina de Winter reappeared after a four-year-long walk in the woods" would be far too risky. From what I knew of the book, a line like that could easily result in a rambler stumbling across Gina's dismembered corpse in the woods the next morning. What I'd have to do was find out a bit more about the circumstances of her disappearance, and then perhaps . . .

The other problem was that there was still so much I didn't know about the chronicle itself. I was learning new things about its powers every day. For example, Hannah and I had discovered that its magic only applied to Stolzenburg land and the people who lived on it. As soon as you tried to describe anything non-Stolzenburg-related, your pen would simply stop working. The book's pages seemed to reject the ink.

And my conversation with Darcy had shown me that the book did not have the power to alter people's personalities, at least not permanently. Unfortunately, this meant that sooner or later my dad's hypochondria would be back with a vengeance.

The fact that we'd gotten the library back, however, was a step in the right direction—even if it was in a terrible state and needed a huge amount of work to restore it to its former glory. But we'd think of something. Now that we had the chronicle . . .

Yes: The chronicle might be complicated and a little unpredictable at first.

But it was definitely a good thing.

The summer at Stolzenburg is doing me a world of good. I take great pleasure in my long walks in the woods and the untamed beauty of the Rhine Valley. I miss my family, of course, especially dear Cassandra. Oh, if only my dear sister were here with me! I am impatient to see her again when I return to England in the autumn. But until then I plan to take full advantage of these weeks with Father's friends in Germany.

In the village they tell strange tales about the castle. It is rumored to be haunted. Although cannot the same be said of any grand house? There are eerie tales that tell of an ancient creature living in the catacombs beneath the castle, like the Minotaur in the Labyrinth. They please me: I have a mind to write them down. Perhaps they will even become my first real novel.

# 7

THE SCHOOL COUNCIL MEETING THAT EVENING WAS A DISASTER. Helena, without my knowledge, had put the school uniforms back on the agenda *again*. And when I objected that we had more than enough on our plates with the upcoming open day, the alumni reunion, and the Autumn Ball (which were all due to take place the following weekend), nobody listened. The school reps were still refusing to compromise on the school-uniform issue, and they'd even found some new allies in the Year 9 boys. The way I saw it, it made absolutely zero difference whether we wore navy trousers, skirts, and blazers with white shirts or black trousers, skirts, and blazers with light blue shirts. So why create unnecessary expense for our parents?

During the hour-and-a-half-long discussion about the sample fabrics somebody had ordered over the summer holidays, I cursed myself for not having thought to write about this in the chronicle.

When Clara in Year 13 pointed out for what must have been the hundredth time that the school crest had light blue in it and would go *so* well with sky blue shirts, I decided that resistance was futile and leaned back in my chair. I would deal with the matter that evening, in my own way.

In my head I composed a few sentences that I hoped would solve the school-uniform problem once and for all. I kept my eyes down, gazing intently at a mark on the tabletop and pretending not to notice the glances—some curious, some envious—that I'd been getting from the other students all day. By now, everyone had heard that I'd gone for a walk in the woods with Darcy de Winter.

Ten minutes later the majority of the school council voted in favor of the new uniforms, and Helena declared the meeting over. I left the room quickly and hurried outside.

The sun was already sinking behind the treetops, and in the meadow on the edge of the parkland, the archery club was gathering up their equipment. I watched them for a while, enjoying the feel of the last rays of sunshine on my face. It had been stuffy inside the meeting room and I'd started to feel a bit sleepy, but the fresh air soon perked me up again. I decided to take a walk around the castle before going back to my room, since I'd probably be up half the night writing in the chronicle.

As I passed a trellis covered with climbing roses, Frederick suddenly appeared in the archway. He was wearing his gardening overalls and holding a pair of hedge clippers, and he had a little twig stuck in his hair. He smiled when he saw me.

I pointed to the twig. "Um, you've got something—"

"Where?"

"There, in your hair. A twig."

"Can you get it for me?" Frederick bent his head toward me.

"Of course," I said, hoping my fingers weren't trembling. He looked up at me and grinned as I picked the twig and also a few leaves out of his dark blond hair.

"I'm about to finish up for the day," he said. "What do you reckon, Emma, do you fancy a drink in the village?"

Waaah!

*Okay, stay cool.*

I plucked one last leaf out of his hair. "Um, I dunno . . . ," I said (though my voice came out a little more high-pitched than I'd intended). Then I shrugged. "Yeah, why not."

The walk from the castle down to the village had never felt so short. It felt as though we'd barely had time to say two words to each other (Frederick told me about his broken-down car and all the repairs it needed, and I told him about the frustrating school council meeting) before we found ourselves approaching the houses on the outskirts of the village.

Stolzendorf was a tiny village, which had stood nestled in the hollow at the foot of the hill for centuries. It only had about a hundred inhabitants, and it was made up of half-timbered houses and a few cottages built from the same sandstone as the castle. There was also a little market square in the center with a hairdresser's, a nail salon, and a pub called the Golden Lion. A few years ago a supermarket had opened up on the edge of the village, and Stolzenburg students were frequently found there stocking up on sweets and other necessities.

Frederick led me inside the Golden Lion and we found a

snug spot in an alcove by the window, as far away as possible from the bar and the TV on the wall beside it. There was a football match on.

"Champions League?" I asked, evidently revealing my footballing ignorance, because Frederick laughed and didn't answer. His laugh was as quirky as his smile. I realized I was staring at him and quickly looked down at my lap.

I suddenly remembered I was wearing my oldest sweater and almost no makeup. But that didn't seem to bother Frederick. He beamed at me. "I'm having a beer," he said. "Same for you?"

"Sure," I said without a moment's thought. I didn't actually like the taste of beer—I wasn't keen on any kind of alcohol, really. But now was not the time to appear boring or uncool.

Frederick nodded. "Back in a minute." He made his way to the bar and returned a few minutes later with our drinks. I took a sip of my beer and swallowed it hurriedly, before my taste buds could properly register the bitter flavor.

Frederick watched me with a twinkle in his light blue eyes. "Emma," he said at last, softly. "I'm really glad you came out for a drink with me. It's so nice to be able to spend a bit of time together, just the two of us."

"Yeah," I said, as a warm feeling spread through my stomach. "I think so, too."

Frederick took a sip of his beer. His hands were still slightly muddy from gardening—and was that a little caterpillar crawling up his shoulder? So cute!

"I heard what happened to the west wing library," he said.

"That was awful. All those precious books just pulled off the shelves and chucked on the floor! It's an outrage!"

"I know." After my conversation with Darcy I'd gone back to the library that afternoon for a more thorough inspection. The extent of the damage was heartbreaking. It would take days to turn the library back into a comfortable meeting place for Westbooks.

"Did you know my family made those bookshelves?" said Frederick. "The Larbachs have been running the joinery here in the village for generations, and at some point in the mid-eighteenth century the lord of Stolzenburg got my ancestor Johannes Larbach and his brothers to refurbish the west wing library. They also put in a whole load of secret doors and passages all over the castle." He grinned and made the cuckoo sign. "The lord was a little paranoid, by all accounts."

I thought of the splintered bookshelves. "Well, you're not going to be very happy when you see what your ancestors' shelves look like now," I said.

"No, I don't doubt it. Did Darcy say how it happened?"

"No. He said he had nothing to do with it."

"Sure."

"I actually believe him, to be fair," I said, surprising even myself.

Frederick frowned. "Why? Because he went for a walk with you? Because he's been flirting with you?"

The rumor mill at Stolzenburg really *was* working overtime. For some inexplicable reason, I felt my face turn red as Frederick looked at me. I quickly lifted my glass to my lips and took another swig of beer, which to my surprise didn't actually taste that bad. At least it seemed to be helping with my shyness. After the next gulp I felt much less flustered in Frederick's presence, and I thought I would soon be back to my usual articulate self. (I hoped so, anyway—I really didn't want to mess this up.) I cleared my throat. "Why would Darcy have trashed the library, though?" I asked. "Do you think he's looking for something? Whoever did it obviously searched the place from top to bottom."

"Hmm, I don't know. I mean, what could he be looking for?" Frederick leaned back slightly and stretched out his bad leg (his ankle still hadn't fully healed) beside the table. "I have to admit I can't stand the guy, personally."

"Ditto."

Frederick sighed. "It's so unfair the way these rich kids carry on, isn't it? They get an amazing education handed to them on a sil-ver platter and during the holidays they swan off all over the world without ever having to think about getting a job or earning money. A de Winter can do whatever the hell he likes—he can take over an entire wing of a castle and trash a library and everyone will still kiss his arse. I bet he was just bored so he decided to smash the place up like some rock star in a hotel room." I was struck by the bitter-ness in Frederick's voice.

"No," I said slowly. "I do think Darcy's rude and arrogant, but I don't think he would do that. He hasn't come here just to have a good time." Darcy had looked so sad in the woods that morning. And what he'd said had seemed genuine.

Frederick rolled his eyes and muttered something about things being unfair and car parts not growing on trees, but then he seemed to regain his composure. "Okay, I'm done ranting. But I'm still intrigued to hear about your walk with Darcy. Did he say anything about Gina?"

"Er—that's his sister, isn't it? The girl who went missing?" However much I liked Frederick, sharing other people's secrets was not my style.

"Yes," said Frederick, looking me squarely in the eye. "Did he mention her?"

"Why do you want to know?"

Frederick shrugged. "It was awful, what happened. And me and Gina—well, we were friends. So I just wondered whether the family had heard from her," he said quietly. His thumb brushed the back of my hand as he reached for his glass. I took another sip of my drink. "Darcy hasn't changed. He was a jerk back then, too," Frederick went on. "Gina was really unhappy, but he just ignored her. And he had a huge go at me for taking it seriously and trying to help her."

"Really? What do you mean?" I had time to take two or three more sips before Frederick finally came out with a rather confusing explanation. "It was a long time ago," he said. "She started having these nightmares. Nothing too disturbing, but she took them to heart. But her brother thought she was just making a fuss about nothing and . . . well, he's always been an idiot, basically. Do you want another drink?" He pointed to my empty glass.

"Yes, please," I said. Frederick hobbled over to the bar to get our drinks just as a cheer went up among the men watching football—someone had obviously scored an important goal.

"Tell me about Gina. What was she like? Do you think she

might still be alive?" I asked Frederick when he returned with our beers.

He gave me a strange look. "They never found a body," he said, putting his head to one side. Had he realized I was staring at his lips? I blinked, suddenly feeling a bit dizzy, and took a large gulp of beer to try to shake off the fuzzy feeling in my head.

"Some people said she might have gone to America," said Frederick. "But why would she do that?"

Why indeed? Had she been running away from something, or someone? I closed my eyes for a second, then asked: "Whawascheena afraid of?" *Come on, Emma, focus.* "What was Gina afraid of?" I repeated, crystal clear this time. Ha! I rewarded myself with more beer.

"Are you okay, Emma?" asked Frederick.

"I'm *fine*," I said, nodding a little more energetically than usual. The room started spinning. Oh, man. The beer must have gone to my head. Perhaps because I'd missed dinner to go to the school council meeting, and I hadn't eaten much at lunchtime, either. Or perhaps because I just wasn't used to alcohol. I put my head in my hands, but the room carried on spinning and I realized that I was going to have to face facts: a) I was drunk and b) I'd just finished my second pint of beer. Damn it. How had that happened?! "I'll be fine. Could I have a . . . a glass of water, please?" I asked, staring at Frederick's lips.

"Of course."

He was still grinning when he returned with the water a moment later.

Was he laughing at me?

No, he was laughing *with* me, I was sure of it. I liked Frederick so much. He was so caring, the way he came and sat down next to me and put his arm round me. I rested my head on his shoulder. And he smelled so good, of the woods and the soil and the rosebushes he'd been trimming that day.

"I don't make a habit of getting girls drunk. But you're definitely a little worse for wear!" he said, holding a bowl of nuts under my nose. "Here, have some peanuts." But I shook my head, while Frederick smiled to himself.

"D'you blieve in ghosshtories?" I slurred, when the room stopped spinning for a moment.

"Ghost stories?"

"Yeah, he said shomething about ghost shtories."

"*Darcy* believes in ghost stories?"

"No," I said, "but Gina . . . he thinks she . . . Oh, crap, I think I'm going to be shick."

Frederick dropped the bowl of peanuts back onto the table and hauled me to my feet. "Right," he said. "Time to head home."

"All right," I said, and let him maneuver me outside into the cool night air. "But I'm not drunk, okay? Or jussa liiiittle bit."

"You're as drunk as a skunk," said Frederick. "It's gone straight to your head."

"Whatchoo mean?" I protested. "I'm *fine*. Shall I shay a twongue tister?"

"What?"

"I shaid shall I shay . . . Oh, never mind," I said, and promptly began reciting all the tongue twisters I knew as we climbed the hill to the castle. After a while I was so engrossed in Peeper Piper, sorry,

Peter Piter, er, no, hang on . . . that I found it a bit rude when Frederick eventually changed the subject. "Emma, if you keep saying them till you get them right we'll be here all night," he said, dragging me up the hill. "Come on. Why don't you tell me some more about those ghost stories? Does Darcy think there's some kind of supernatural explanation for why Gina went missing?"

"Peeper Piter," I muttered, and I barely noticed as Frederick heaved a sigh and started humming to himself, lost in thought. Then he began telling me a spooky story about his ancestors, the lord of Stolzenburg, and a statue he had commissioned shortly before his death. I was only half listening, probably because I was talking to myself the entire time. I babbled away about this and that and managed to come up with a few fairy stories of my own (which clearly weren't all bad, since they made Frederick laugh out loud several times) as I tried valiantly to walk in a straight line. And then, quite suddenly, I found myself alone.

I felt as though one minute Frederick had been standing there beside me chuckling at something I'd said, and the next minute he was gone. It was as if he'd vanished in the blink of an eye, leaving me on my own in a castle courtyard that seemed to be spinning faster and faster with every second that passed. But in my alcohol-induced daze I probably just hadn't noticed him saying good-bye.

I leaned back against the wall by the gate and took a deep breath. It was okay—I wasn't far from my bed.

But despite the walk from the castle to the village having felt so short, the walk from the gate to the front door seemed to go on forever. I shuffled across the gravel at a snail's pace, quite proud of myself for crossing the first half of the courtyard without falling over. It wasn't until I was within a few yards of the front steps that I stumbled over a flowerpot (which seemed to have popped up out of nowhere) and fell face-first into the gravel. Once there, I decided to take a little nap.

I rolled over onto my back and lay with my arms and legs outstretched, gazing up at the sky. The wind murmured in the treetops. It whispered a lullaby that sounded just like the tune Frederick had been humming on our way up the hill. The stars twinkled at me in a friendly way, and I almost felt like waving to them. Unfortunately, I seemed to have forgotten how to use my arms, and before I could recall how to do it I was fast asleep.

"Emma?" said a voice from somewhere above me. "What happened?"

"Darcy?" called another voice from farther away. "Where are you?" I heard footsteps in the gravel, then the second voice again, directly above me. "That's Charlotte's friend. Wow, she's completely wasted."

"Give me a hand."

I felt myself being hauled up into a sitting position, and blinked warily. It was dark and I was outdoors. In front of me I could see the blurred faces of Darcy de Winter and Toby Bell, and behind them the towers of Stolzenburg silhouetted against the night sky.

"Emma," said Darcy again.

"Hi." It was less than ideal that Darcy, of all people, should be the one to find me in this unfortunate state. And my head was still spinning and I was tired. So very tired. "Good night," I murmured, closing my eyes and trying to lie down again—but there was an arm in the way. Never mind. I let my head flop to one side; that was the next best thing.

"Oh my God!" Darcy exclaimed. "Has she passed out?"

They were both silent for a moment.

"Toby?"

"Mm?"

"What's up?"

"Nothing. I'm just waiting for you to begin your lecture," said Toby.

"What lecture?"

"The one about the youth of today, how immature they are, how sad it is to see kids who don't know their limits getting hammered. . . ."

"I hope she hasn't gone into a coma."

"Of course she hasn't. She's snoring like a trooper."

"I don't snore," I grunted. "It must be Hannah."

"What's she doing out here? We have to get her back to bed," said Darcy.

"Yes, obviously, but . . ."

Darcy sighed. "But *what?*"

"You're seriously telling me you're not even going to pass comment on this? You're not going to take the piss even a tiny bit? Or are you saving it for later?"

Another arm slid under my knees and suddenly the ground fell away beneath me. I found my head resting on a chest that smelled of fresh laundry, and Darcy's voice was much closer to my ear now as it said: "She's freezing cold. God knows how long she's been out here."

"You liked going for that walk with her, didn't you?" Toby mused. "Perhaps there's actually something in these rumors I've been hearing all day."

Darcy snorted. "Please. She hates me."

"Please just go away and let me sleep," I said as if in confirmation of his remark, and snuggled deeper into the arms that held me.

Darcy didn't say anything for a while, and at first I thought he'd done what I'd asked and made himself scarce. All I was aware of was a slight rocking motion and the crunching of the gravel beneath me.

"We'll take her in through the old coal cellar. That way we won't set off the alarm." Darcy's voice again, vibrating against my ear.

"Good idea. But watch out, the steps are very steep."

"I know."

The gravel stopped crunching and the rocking motion became more pronounced.

"You could try being a bit nicer to her. Then maybe she wouldn't hate you anymore," Toby suggested.

"What would be the point of that?"

"Just think about it."

I felt the air around me getting warmer and I let out a contented sigh.

"Okay, this is the girls' floor. Now we just have to find her bedroom," whispered Toby.

"No problem," Darcy murmured. "I happen to know which one it is."

"Ah, that's . . . handy." Toby was silent for a moment. Then he changed the subject: "Do you still want to show me that ugly angel thing? Only it's just started raining and I don't really fancy going back out there. . . ."

"Fine, we'll go tomorrow," said Darcy. "And by the way, it's not actually an angel. But for now just open this door for me, would you?"

In my dream the paper dragonfly fluttered in through the window of the Golden Lion, flew a lap of honor around the light above the table, and landed on the rim of my glass. Its translucent wings shimmered as it cleaned its front legs, one of which it had accidentally dipped into the foam on my beer. Then it took off again and started flying around in circles close to the ceiling. I tipped my head back and watched it.

"I'm dizzy," I murmured after a while.

"That's because you keep flying around in circles. Why don't you come down?" said Frederick.

I wanted to reply that I wasn't flying, I was sitting right there next to him, but I couldn't: I realized I couldn't speak and that I was in fact flying in circles around his head. I was also surprisingly small, and there was a rustling noise coming from behind me. When I looked over my shoulder, I saw that I had a pair of silky paper wings, rising and falling as if by magic. In front of me the dragonfly hung in the air, her eyes glowing like mysterious moons. She stretched out an antenna toward me and beckoned to me to follow her.

"Wait! Emma!" Frederick called after me. "Come back and tell me a ghost story!" But I couldn't hear what he said next because we'd floated out into the cool night air and away, leaving the roofs of the village far behind us.

It was wonderful.

The little paper dragonfly guided me through the darkness. Together we soared higher and higher, closer and closer to the stars, which were out tonight in their thousands to watch us fly, while the treetops swayed far below us and the Rhine snaked away into the distance like a glittering ribbon.

And Stolzenburg seemed so tiny! It looked like a toy castle— it was hard to believe that up until now it had been pretty much my whole world. From way up here I could see how much more world there was beyond Stolzenburg's walls—the forest stretching away for miles, the faraway lights of towns and highways, and beyond them, other towns, other countries, other continents.

One day I would see all these things for myself. The whole wide world would be my home—I'd known that for a while now. But for now, I belonged at Stolzenburg. For now, my life still revolved around the ancient building below me, and to be honest that was fine by me.

The dragonfly, too, seemed reluctant to stray far from Stolzenburg. It started to descend toward the castle, and I followed, so entranced by the feeling of the wind beneath my gossamer wings that I didn't notice which part of the grounds we were heading for until I landed beside the dragonfly on a mossy stump of wall.

*What now?* I wanted to ask, but all that came out of my mouth was a soft buzzing noise. I cleaned my antennae while the dragonfly stared at me with its moon-shaped eyes. *What are we doing here?* I buzzed after a moment. It was impossible to tell whether the dragonfly had understood me or not. But at last it put its head to one side and blinked. Then it started to speak, in a voice that sounded like rustling leaves. *Emma,* it whispered. *Emmaaa.*

*Who are you?* I asked. *What do you want with me?*

*Emma,* repeated the dragonfly. *Emmaaa!*

*Yes,* I replied. *That's me.* Was my name the only word it knew how to say?

It crawled toward me a little way, blinked again, and made a soft rustling sound that might have been the start of a new word.

But at that moment, a shadow loomed over us and the dragonfly fell silent. At first I thought it was just clouds drifting overhead, but then the shadow leaned forward and a huge hand appeared in between us. Gently, it scooped me up and lifted me into the air.

I flapped my wings frantically in an attempt to fly away, but I suddenly found I couldn't move. *Help!* I buzzed. *Help!*

Then Darcy de Winter's face appeared in front of me, gigantic, his nostrils gaping like dark caves. Every time he exhaled it was like a gust of wind that tugged at my antennae. "Emma," he said. "Come with me."

And he carried me away into the dark wood.

5<sup>th</sup> March 1927

The renovation work is almost complete. It looks as though the new teaching rooms will be ready for use, as planned, sometime before Easter. Some of the students, accompanied by their parents, are going today to view the newly refurbished east wing. The teaching staff have begun moving into their new lodgings on the castle grounds. All in all, we are confident that the day-to-day running of the school will continue as normal when the new term begins.

Fortunately, there have been no unpleasant surprises concerning the building's structural integrity, but we did make one rather odd discovery in the cellars during an inspection of the sewer pipes. One of the workmen from the village happened to come across a concealed door, and when it was opened, thousands of little slivers of paper came wafting out. Nobody is able to explain where they might have come from. The sewer pipes were in perfect condition.

# 8

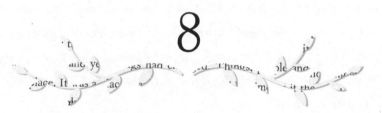

THE NEXT MORNING I DIDN'T FEEL AT ALL WELL. I WAS VERY thirsty, but every time I drank from the bottle of water on my bedside table I wanted to throw up. And I had a splitting headache, and the daylight hurt my eyes. Damn it! When I sat up in bed, I realized I'd slept in my clothes. For a moment I couldn't remember what had happened or how I'd gotten there. Then, bit by bit, it all came back to me, and I felt even worse than before.

What on earth had possessed me to drink that much beer? I knew how sensitive I was to alcohol—even half a glass of champagne was enough to tip me over the edge. So two pints of beer on an almost-empty stomach had been a disaster waiting to happen. Just the thought of Frederick seeing me in that state was enough to make me blush with shame. *I'd recited tongue twisters on our first date!* And that couldn't have been the only stupid thing I'd done. Oh, man— perhaps it was better if I didn't try to remember everything I'd said to Frederick. He'd had a bit to drink, too, so there was always a chance he didn't remember much about last night, either, right? *Right?*

Hannah had been worrying about me all evening and had sent me several messages (until she'd heard from Louisa and Jenny in Year 8 that I was out with Frederick). Now she was impatient for details of our secret date. "So he walked you back to the castle. And then what?" she called through the bathroom door as I brushed my teeth, desperately trying to get rid of the stale taste in my mouth. "Did he kiss you?"

"Dunno. I don' fink fo," I called back through a mouthful of toothpaste. The end of the evening was even more of a blur than the rest of it. But I seemed to recall that I'd met Darcy de Winter and Toby Bell at some point, and that they'd walked me back to my room. That was a bit unfortunate, too, now that I came to think of it. They'd probably look down their noses at me even more from now on. Well, let them. I didn't care. I finished brushing my teeth and rinsed my mouth out, and as I got into the shower I resolved to stop dwelling on the weird evening I'd just had. And never to drink alcohol *ever* again.

"It's nice that Frederick asked you out, though," said Charlotte, as we sat together amid the wreckage of the west wing library a few hours later. It was Sunday, and we were having our Westbooks meeting. Today it consisted of perching on piles of old books and coming up with a plan of action.

"Definitely," Hannah agreed.

"Mhm," I said. My head was still pounding, despite the two aspirin I'd just taken.

I decided to change the subject. "Anyway, have either of you had any bright ideas about what we're going to do with all this?" I gestured at the carnage around us.

"Er—tidy it up?" Charlotte suggested. "Also, I've thought of a book we could read next. . . ."

"I think we should write something in the chronicle about a couple of tradesmen who just happen to be in the area," Hannah piped up eagerly, as if this was just the cue she'd been waiting for. "I was thinking two brothers, Karsten and Jochen. Jochen loves the great outdoors, and Karsten recently got divorced and needs something to take his mind off it. They're hiking across Germany and they've pitched their tent near Stolzenburg. Oh, and they have a friend called Paul with them who happens to be an upholsterer. He's going with them as far as Karlsruhe to visit his great-aunt. But one night, they get attacked by a pack of wolves. It's terrifying—the animals are half-starved and they rip the tent to pieces and nearly bite Paul's leg off." Hannah had leaped up from her pile of books and was now embellishing her story with a series of melodramatic gestures. "The men run for their lives. They think they're about to die, the wolves are so close behind them! But then, in the nick of time, they get to the castle, where Mrs. Berkenbeck serves them some hot chicken soup with croutons. They're very grateful. It's now past midnight, but the men have nowhere to sleep because the wolves are still lurking around outside and their tent is ripped to shreds. So your dad lets them stay the night in the west wing.

"During the night Paul hears a noise. It's only a rat, but seeing as how he's just escaped from a pack of wolves he starts panicking and runs out of his room. The rat follows him, and he goes dashing along the corridor like a headless chicken. Then he throws open the first door he sees and hides behind it. He stays there all night, fearing for his life, no idea where he is. When day dawns he realizes he's ended up in the west wing library. The sight of the slashed sofa cushions breaks his poor upholsterer's heart.

"At that moment the carpenters Karsten and Jochen arrive. They've been looking everywhere for their friend. Like Paul, they're shocked to see the state of the library. For breakfast that morning Mrs. Berkenbeck serves them fresh brioche buns, still hot from the oven, and Jochen . . ." Hannah paused for breath. "Basically, the three of them are so grateful that they offer to repair everything in the library for free. Perfect, right?" She beamed at us triumphantly.

I put my head to one side. "Wow, you've really thought this through. But I don't know . . . starving wolves in the woods. Rats in the castle. That would just create a whole new set of problems. I mean, it would be cool if we could use the library again, but we also wouldn't be able to go outside because of the wolves." And apart from that, the idea of conjuring up three entirely new people gave me a slightly queasy feeling in the pit of my stomach. Or was it just the alcohol making me feel sick again?

Hannah pouted. "Then we'll just write something about a hunter who shoots the wolves. Or a disease. Wolf plague or something. And voilà—no more wolves. Come on, it's taken me all day to come up with that story," she pleaded, determined not to give up her tradesmen without a fight. "Look at this place. We'll never be able to fix it without professional help." She held up a jagged piece of wood, which must once have been part of a bookshelf, and waved it in our faces. "For Jochen, Karsten, and Paul it would be a breeze."

"I still think we should put the book back in its secret compartment and just forget about it," said Charlotte, nodding in the direction of the (now three-legged) intarsia table where the chronicle lay.

For a few hours now I had actually been toying with the idea of not keeping the book in my bedroom any longer, but hiding it in the secret compartment here in the library instead. If somebody really was looking for the chronicle then surely this was the safest place in the whole castle: Whoever it was had already searched the library from top to bottom, and wouldn't come back here again. I'd decided the book wasn't safe in its previous hiding place under my pillow, so yesterday afternoon I'd transferred it to my sock drawer (which wasn't exactly high-security, either). So all in all, the secret compartment wasn't such a bad idea.

But simply forgetting about the chronicle was out of the question. I was fully intending to write in it again today, since I hadn't gotten around to dealing with the new school uniforms last night. I scooped the chronicle onto my lap and was about to open it when Charlotte, guessing what I was up to, suddenly slammed another book down on the table in front of me. This was too much for the rickety little piece of furniture, which now collapsed once and for all.

"Oops," murmured Hannah, but Charlotte acted as though nothing had happened. "*Anyway*, about our next book for Westbooks," she said loudly, and I closed the chronicle for the time being. "How about Eleanor Morland?"

"Who?" asked Hannah.

"Why her?" I asked. I'd heard the name, of course. About forty-two times that summer. And what I'd heard had been very, *very* boring.

"Eleanor Morland," Charlotte repeated. "She's a famous English writer."

"I see," said Hannah.

"Eighteenth century. Romance novels," I added, and turned back to Charlotte. "Please no."

"But she'd be perfect. Didn't your mom's boyfriend mention in his lectures that Eleanor Morland spent time at Stolzenburg?"

I shook my head. Although perhaps I just hadn't been paying attention? John's monotonous delivery had the power to send me into a trancelike state within a matter of minutes. It was entirely possible that I'd slept through the only interesting nugget of information in his entire lecture.

Luckily, Charlotte was better informed than I was. "Eleanor Morland was the daughter of a vicar. She grew up in Hampshire. As a young woman she made several trips to visit relatives and family friends, and on one of those trips she spent a summer in Germany—at Stolzenburg. That must have been around 1794. It was only when she returned to England afterward that she started writing novels and became world famous."

"Cool," said Hannah. "Perhaps she was inspired by the castle."

"She was," said Charlotte, pointing to the book she'd just slammed down on the table. "I thought we could start with *Westwood Abbey*. It just so happens to be about an old monastery and a heroine who investigates a series of mysterious events. So, what do you reckon?"

"Sounds good to me!" cried Hannah, brimming with enthusiasm again.

I could see the appeal now, too. It would be fun to read a story inspired by our castle. And I didn't exactly have time to come up with an alternative. I had more pressing things to think about. For Charlotte's sake, I managed a smile. "Fine by me," I said. "But I can't promise I'm going to have much time for reading over the next few days. I've got some writing of my own to be getting on with."

Charlotte nodded. "Yes. I don't suppose I'm going to be able to stop you, unfortunately," she said, then stood up and went to sit in the window seat with her copy of *Westwood Abbey*.

I flicked through the chronicle on my lap, took out a pen, and wrote *September 2017* neatly at the top of the next blank page.

With Charlotte engrossed in *Westwood Abbey*, Hannah and I spent the next two hours writing a few carefully worded paragraphs in the chronicle. First of all we had the parent governors overturn the plan for new school uniforms at the last minute. Then we thought hard about the best way to fix the library. I still felt that Hannah's tradesmen, wolves, and rats were too dangerous, and getting a team of elves to bring about a miraculous transformation overnight was even more risky—something was bound to go wrong.

In the end we opted for a less dramatic solution to the problem, and we wrote that Miss Whitfield donated a few nice pieces of furniture she'd found in her attic and wanted to get rid of. Then we started tidying up. Together we lifted the books back onto the battered shelves and lugged the broken furniture into one of the rooms across the corridor. After a while, Charlotte looked out the window and saw a light go on in Miss Whitfield's attic.

It was all going like clockwork.

Hannah and I hurried downstairs and across the grounds, and five minutes later we were ringing the doorbell of the little cottage by the meadow.

Then we waited.

It was quite a while before we heard footsteps coming to the door, but eventually it opened and there was Miss Whitfield, wearing a frilly apron and a headscarf and holding a feather duster. "Emma! Hannah!"

"Er, hi," I stammered. "We . . . er, we . . ." In our excitement we hadn't planned what to say to Miss Whitfield so as not to arouse suspicion. Crap!

Hannah was better at thinking on her feet than I was. "We wanted to ask if we could gather some leaves in the woods and give them to Dolly, Dolly II, and Miss Velvetnose," she improvised.

Miss Whitfield stared at us. "Now?" she queried. "In the dark?"

"Why not?"

"Do you know much about plants?"

"A bit."

"Hmm, I'm not sure it's such a good idea," said Miss Whitfield. "But while you're here, do you happen to know whether the school might have any use for a few old bits of furniture? I've just come across some in my attic."

"Really?"

A moment later we were following Miss Whitfield up to her bedroom. The bedspread, pillows, wallpaper, and curtains all featured exactly the same floral design. Just looking at them made me feel slightly dizzy, so I averted my eyes and hurried up the spiral staircase that led from one corner of the bedroom up into the attic.

Bent double, we inched along beneath the rafters. The attic was a square room dimly lit by a bulb hanging from one of the beams. I accidentally knocked it with my shoulder as I shuffled past, and as it swung to and fro it cast a flickering, ghostly light over the boxes and clutter on the attic floor.

Miss Whitfield pointed to a collection of dusty bedsheets draped over what I assumed to be furniture. I could see the arm of a chair poking out from underneath, upholstered in dark red velvet. "I was actually up here looking for some old photo albums," she explained. "But then I came across these." She pulled back the corner of the sheet to reveal yet more velvet upholstery and some tassels made from shiny thread. "I so rarely come up to the attic that I'd forgotten these were here. In fact, I can't even remember how they came to be in my possession. But if a sofa, two armchairs, and a coffee table would be of any use to you . . ."

"Wow!" cried Hannah, and I, too, was delighted. We beamed at Miss Whitfield.

"Thank you so much," I said. "They're exactly what we need. I'll ask Mr. Schade to come and collect them first thing in the morning."

"Wonderful," said Miss Whitfield.

As our teacher went back down the stairs, Hannah and I bumped fists and grinned at each other, congratulating ourselves on our cleverness.

When we joined her in the hallway Miss Whitfield invited us to stay for a cup of tea, but Hannah (keen to avoid another close encounter with Miss Whitfield's best china) politely declined. And I also found myself in a sudden hurry to leave the cottage. I'd just happened to glance at one of the old photo albums Miss Whitfield had mentioned; it was about eight inches thick, with a dark brown cardboard cover, and was lying open on the sideboard by the door. Several black-and-white photographs with jagged white edges had been glued onto the double-page spread. They probably dated from the early 1900s—that was my guess, anyway, judging by the clothes a woman in one of the photos was wearing. She was standing in the forefront of the picture in a pale lace dress, with a matching parasol in her gloved hands.

But I was more interested in what lay behind the woman: a tall, crumbling archway, surrounded by spruce trees. I knew at once where the picture must have been taken. There was no doubt about it: Behind and to the right of the woman I could see part of the faun statue. And at its base (and this was the most remarkable thing), instead of a big clump of ferns, there was a staircase.

A staircase that led underground.

Oh. My. God.

My palms began to prickle with excitement. "I'm afraid we have to get back," I told Miss Whitfield hurriedly before bundling Hannah out the front door and marching her off toward the woods.

"I didn't mean it about collecting leaves for the sheep," protested Hannah as she struggled to keep up with me. This time I didn't bother with the path but headed straight through the trees at a brisk pace, taking the most direct route to the ancient monastery. "I really don't feel like feeding them right now. Shall we just go back to the castle? Emma? Hey, I'm talking to you!"

"Sorry. I just have to check something." The soft needles under our feet swallowed up every sound, the darkness wrapped itself around us like a cloak, and the first wisps of fog were starting to drift up from the river. I had to admit it was pretty spooky out here. Especially when I thought about that pack of hungry wolves. . . . But I was too intrigued to wait till tomorrow morning.

Hannah seemed a little freaked out, too. "In the woods, in the pitch dark?" she whispered. "Can't it wait?"

"We're just going to make a little detour to the ruins."

"But why? It's cold, it's late, and . . ."

"Yes, I know, but I think . . . I think I might have just discovered something important in one of those photos."

"Huh? What photos?"

"Please just come with me, okay? It won't take long."

Hannah sighed. "Okay. As long as it's quick."

We soon spotted one of the ruined walls through the trees and ran the rest of the way to the old church. The statue of the faun seemed to be waiting for us in its alcove, shiny particles in the stone glittering in the moonlight. I crouched down and started scraping at the ground with both hands, sweeping aside rotting pine needles and dead leaves and a thin layer of earth until . . . *yes!* Just a couple of inches down, my fingers touched something hard. It was a stone slab set into the ground.

"Is that a grave?" whispered Hannah.

I shook my head. "I think it's the entrance to a secret passageway."

"Cool!"

"Really?" said Toby Bell from behind us.

Hannah and I spun around to see both Toby and Darcy de Winter standing beside a broken pillar, watching us. Oh, great!

"You again," I greeted them, shuffling from one foot to the other. "It feels like we're always bumping into each other. Are you following me or something?" I hoped they wouldn't notice that my voice was trembling slightly and my cheeks had turned scarlet.

"Of course not," said Darcy, while Toby looked from him to me and back again with a strange expression. My drunken antics last night had clearly turned me into a laughingstock. Damn it! I drew myself up to my full height and tried, in spite of everything, to look cool and self-assured. Darcy walked slowly toward us. "Do you really think it's a secret passageway?" he asked. I nodded and pointed to the metal ring I'd just uncovered at one end of the slab.

"We need to see if we can lift this thing out somehow," I said.

"Okay." Darcy grabbed hold of the ring straightaway and started tugging at it. "Help me, Toby," he grunted, his feet planted firmly on the ground on either side of the slab. Toby quickly came to his aid, and Hannah and I joined in, too. The slab was incredibly heavy and seemed almost to have fused with the ground in places. But together we finally managed to shift it. There was a grinding noise as we slid it slowly to one side.

Underneath the slab was a yawning black pit. A musty, moldy smell rose from its depths.

"What if it's a grave?" asked Hannah in a shaky voice.

"But then why would it have stairs?" Darcy shone the light from his smartphone into the hole, revealing a flight of worn stone steps.

"Exactly," whispered Hannah, taking a step backward.

I, on the other hand, leaned farther forward and peered over the edge, fascinated. The light from Darcy's phone was too dim for us to see to the bottom of the steps. How deep did they go? What was down there? A gust of wind blew through the treetops, filling the air with a gentle whispering sound.

"How about you two go and see what's down there, and Hannah and I will wait for you here," Toby suggested.

"That's a good idea," said Hannah, who'd already taken another step backward and now sat down cross-legged beside the broken pillar. "We'll stay here and stand guard."

"Er . . ." I hesitated. I wasn't madly keen on the idea of entering an ancient tunnel (potentially a grave) with Darcy de Winter, of all people. But Toby had already sat down beside Hannah, quick as a flash. "Off you go," he said.

Darcy glared at Toby. Then he heaved a sigh, stepped carefully into the hole, and began his descent.

I had to follow him, of course. This was my discovery, after all, and I had to know what was hidden beneath the stone slab. Answers, maybe? Clues about the ghost stories Gina had apparently been so interested in, or the little silver leaves I kept finding?

I got my phone out, too, and switched on the flashlight app. (I couldn't help noticing that I didn't have a huge amount of battery left.) Then I waved to Hannah and Toby and stepped onto the stone staircase. I heard Hannah say to Toby, "So tell me, why aren't you talking to Charlotte anymore?" And then the cold darkness swallowed me up.

The steps led steeply downward. They were hewn straight out of the rock. I ran my fingertips over the rough stone walls, and I could feel the jagged edges left by the chisel. There was no handrail, and the steps were covered with a slippery layer of damp moss. Under the circumstances, the sight of Darcy's back ahead of me was actually quite reassuring. If I were to fall, he would make an excellent airbag.

We made it to the bottom, however, without any mishaps. The last step (the thirty-seventh—I'd counted them) gave way to a stone floor. The bluish light from our phones illuminated columns and brick arches. At first I thought we'd ended up in the monastery's old crypt, but then I saw that the three archways were not the entrances to vaults—they were the beginnings of tunnels.

"Secret passages!" I breathed. "I knew it!"

Darcy shone his light through one of the arches. "Looks like it," he murmured. "Which one shall we take?"

I shrugged. "The one on the left?"

"Okay."

The tunnel led uphill a little way, then bent around to the right. There were no forks in the path, which I was glad about—at least we wouldn't lose our way. (I was pretty sure Google Maps wouldn't be much use down here and unfortunately, unlike Hansel and Gretel, we hadn't thought to bring any breadcrumbs or pebbles with us.)

Eventually the tunnel opened out into a room with an empty wine rack, covered in cobwebs, standing against one wall. Was this just an old wine cellar after all? A wave of disappointment rushed over me, particularly when the tunnel snaked around to the right again soon afterward and we found ourselves standing at the bottom of a stone staircase that looked very familiar.

"We've gone around in a circle," I said, pointing to the three brick archways at the bottom of the stairs. We'd just emerged from the middle one. I fought back a yawn.

"Hmm," said Darcy. He scrutinized me more closely. "Tired?" he asked.

"Yes, I—er—thanks, by the way . . . for last night. I've been meaning to say. It was . . . very nice of you," I muttered, looking down at my feet.

But Darcy simply shrugged. "We couldn't exactly leave you lying there."

"Well, I would have gone inside eventually."

"Yes, if you'd been able to walk."

I sniffed. "I wasn't that bad," I said defensively. "Anyway, shall we see what's down the last tunnel?" I tried to slip past him, but Darcy stood his ground.

"Did you have a date last night?" he asked.

"Of course not," I lied. "I always drink alone—I'm classy like that. A few swigs of vodka behind the rhododendrons, you know . . ."

"Very classy." A smile tugged at the corner of Darcy's mouth, then he shook his head abruptly, turned away from me, and strode swiftly down the third tunnel. I stared after him in surprise. Had he accidentally *smiled*? No—my eyes must have been deceiving me, surely?

After a few yards the third tunnel became so narrow that we were forced to walk in single file. The tunnel went on for quite a long way, which was unusual for a wine cellar and gave me a glimmer of hope. There were also metal brackets on the walls every few yards, with burned-out wooden torches still inside them. How long was it since anyone had been down this tunnel? I shuddered at the thought that we might be the first people for hundreds of years to breathe this stale air. Although the thought that we might *not* be the first made me shudder even more.

"What were you and Toby doing wandering around the ruins at night, anyway?" I asked after a while, more to take my mind off my surroundings than anything else.

He didn't answer straightaway, and I sensed that he would rather have said nothing at all, but eventually he stopped and turned to face me.

"I wanted to show Toby the statue," he said, so confiding all of a sudden that I thought for a moment I must have written about him in the chronicle again. But I couldn't for the life of me remember doing so.

"The ugly angel?" I asked.

"Yes," he said. "Although it's not actually an angel. It's some other kind of creature. But I have no idea what."

"I think it's a faun. Judging by its legs and feet, anyway."

"A faun? Like in ancient mythology? Hmm . . . you might be right."

"I didn't know you were interested in the statue. Apparently your ancestors had it put there in the mid-1700s." I vaguely remembered Frederick saying something like that last night.

"In the middle of a church? That's a bit weird, isn't it?"

"The monastery must already have been abandoned by then. I reckon the statue was put there to mark the location of something. The entrance to the tunnel, for example."

Darcy pressed his palms against the ceiling of the tunnel. Only now did I realize how silent it was down here.

"Some of her classmates said Gina used to spend a lot of time out here by the ruins. So I wanted to find out what's so special about them," said Darcy softly. "And the statue does seem a bit unusual, doesn't it? It fits with the weird stories Gina used to tell me about a creature with cloven hooves. Maybe she got hold of some old legend, and . . . I don't know . . . took it too much to heart."

"So you're hoping that if you find out what that old legend was, you'll find her," I surmised.

Darcy lowered his eyes. "Let's go," he said, turning away again.

We walked on in silence. The tunnel ran in a straight line for a while, then suddenly swerved uphill. The roof was now so low that Darcy had to stoop, and even I had to duck my head a little. Every now and again we heard a rustling beneath our feet. When I shone the light from my phone on the ground, I saw lots of tiny little silver leaves. In fact, I got the impression that the farther on we went, the more of them there were. But I couldn't say for certain.

After a few minutes, the tunnel bent around to the left. For a split second I was afraid that the vaulted space that opened up before us as we rounded the corner was nothing more than another empty storage room and that this tunnel, just like the other one, was leading us in a big circle back to the ruins. But then I spotted the apparatus. An enormous set of bronze scales on a workbench, surrounded by weights, measuring jugs, and corked glass flasks containing the dried-out remnants of liquids and powders. On another bench stood various old books, candlesticks covered in dried wax, and, of course, leaves.

Thousands upon thousands of little silver leaves.

They were everywhere. They filled the huge copper basin in the middle of the room. They dangled from the cobwebs above our heads. And with every step we took we sent little flurries of them swirling up into the air, along with thick clouds of dust.

"The *laboratory*," I breathed.

"The what?" asked Darcy.

"The lord of Stolzenburg," I began, "kept talking about these secret laboratories in his notes from 1758. Saying he wanted to create an heir." I moved closer to the copper basin. It was larger than the average bathtub. A creature the size of the statue would probably have fit inside it. . . . Seriously? What was I thinking?

The basin drew me toward it like a magnet. I leaned over the edge and was about to plunge my hand into the leaves—they were already tickling my fingertips—when my phone battery finally gave up the ghost and the flashlight went out.

Taken by surprise, I took a step backward, tripped over my own feet, and lost my balance. I would have fallen over if Darcy hadn't caught me.

"Th-thanks," I stammered. He smelled of fresh laundry. I quickly extricated myself and stood up again.

"No problem," said Darcy. Now he, too, leaned over the edge

of the basin and shone his flashlight onto the leaves. "What do you mean, he wanted to create an heir?"

"Well," I said, "as far as I know, he had no children and had never been able to accept that fact. And he was probably losing it a bit, too. Anyway, he tried to create 'a creature of paper and ink'—I think that's how he put it. Something that would live on after his death. And it looked very much like the statue."

Darcy frowned. "That sounds completely insane."

"I know. But I do wonder . . ." I was still staring at the copper basin, and in my mind's eye the ink drawings in the chronicle melted into the sweeping handwriting of the lord of Stolzenburg. "I do wonder—what if he actually succeeded?" I whispered.

Darcy squared his shoulders. "That's ridiculous," he snorted. "Yes, I know there was an eighteenth-century earl in our family who lived alone in the castle and apparently went a bit bonkers toward the end of his life. But he definitely didn't leave an heir. That was why the British branch of the family took over the castle, along with the lands and the title."

"I know it sounds crazy, but . . . oh, I don't know. Frederick said he didn't think you took those old legends seriously enough four years ago, and if we wanted to find Gina—"

"Frederick," Darcy broke in sharply, "has no idea what he's talking about. You should stay away from him."

A few seconds earlier, in a moment of madness, I'd actually been considering mentioning the chronicle to Darcy. But now— seeing his rigid posture, his wrinkled nose, the hint of scorn that was always present in his dark eyes, the way he was looking down his nose at me again as if I was a stupid kid—I thought better of it.

"Well, something must have happened to your sister; otherwise, she wouldn't have disappeared." I looked at him with a hint of defiance. "And you must think those old legends have something to do with it, too; otherwise, you wouldn't have taken such an interest in all this stuff in the first place."

He took a step toward the basin, so abruptly that it made me jump. Then he began to stride up and down, his feet making a dull thudding sound that echoed around the room. "The *stories* might be important," he said. "But not the mythical creatures *in* the stories, Emma. That's just ridiculous!"

I leaned back against one of the workbenches and watched Darcy pace the length of the room and back again. "I see," I said slowly. "So you're not even prepared to consider it. Because you're so vain that you can't think of anything worse than looking even the tiniest bit ridiculous."

"I'm not prepared to consider it because I'm a rational pers—" He paused, stopped pacing, took a step backward, and squatted down on the ground.

"What is it?" I asked. What had he found? I hurried across the laboratory to join him. Darcy was shining his flashlight beam over the ground. "They're not ours, are they?" he murmured.

In the light from his phone I could see yet more silver leaves, and a thick layer of dust. Clearly imprinted in the dust was a set of footprints. The feet that had made them must have been small and delicate: smaller than Darcy's feet and smaller than my size seven sneakers.

The footprints ran alongside the wall for a few yards before turning off into the middle of the room, where they approached the copper basin and were lost in the muddle of our own footprints.

I gulped. So we were not the first people for hundreds of years to breathe this air. Someone had been here not long ago. A girl, judging by the size of the footprints. Darcy and I looked at each other.

"Who—?" I whispered.

"Gina?" called Darcy. "Gina?"

August 1794

# A Faun's Dream

## A Fairy Tale by Eleanor Morland

Once upon a time there was a faun. He lived in a castle in a faraway land and he often dreamed of what it would be like to be human.

For the faun was big and ugly and terribly lonely. From his head grew a pair of long, curling horns, and his legs were like those of an enormous goat. Anybody who had ever laid eyes on him had been frightened half to death. They had thought him a monster; they had shouted at him and struck him and chased him away, and not even the melancholy little tune he had played for them on his flute had been enough to change their minds.

And so the faun had kept himself out of sight for many, many years, hidden away in the tunnels beneath the castle like the Minotaur in his Labyrinth. It was dark and lonely in the tunnels and the faun would surely have died long ago, had he been any ordinary faun. But he was not an ordinary faun: He was a product of his creator's imagination, born of words on paper. Ink ran through his veins, and it was the magic of words that kept him alive and that, one night, would help to make his dream come true.

A storm was raging that night; lightning rent the sky and rain thundered down onto the battlements and dripped into every nook and cranny of the castle, even into the secret underground tunnels where the faun lived, and where he now sat eating his supper. Because he was no ordinary faun, he ate words from books instead of food; and tonight's book was a particularly tasty one. The words tasted serious and slightly salty. As ever, the faun longed for nothing more than to share these words with somebody else. If only he had somebody to talk and laugh and cry with, he thought as he chewed on the beginning of a juicy sentence. If only he had been human!

And as he sat there, big and ugly, dark and lonely, something happened that only ever happens once in a hundred years: All of a sudden, one of the thunderclaps high in the sky created a fairy.

The fairy's tiny body glinted as the lightning lit up the sky and she plunged down, down, down through the clouds and the rain and the wind, past the rooftops of the castle, past turrets and windows, past gates and walls. She flapped her gossamer wings wildly as she fell through the night, but she went on falling. Even when she came to stone and roots and earth, she fell straight through them until at last she landed in the faun's lap.

"Ugh!" cried the little fairy, shaking herself. "Ugh, what a wet night!" Little droplets flew off her in all directions.

"Who are you?" asked the faun, staring at this strange creature. Just like him, she was made of paper. She was slender and delicate and looked a little like a dragonfly, cleverly folded from the page of an old book. Letters were printed on her dainty body, and her eyes shone like pearls in the moonlight. She did not answer; instead she fluttered her wings and looked at him so intently that it was as if she could see into his soul.

"Who are you?" the faun said again. "Where do you come from? What are you doing here?"

"Not an easssy matter," whispered the fairy. "Not an easssy wish to grant. But"—she nodded sagely—"you can become human, if you wish. Yesss, you can. Yes, yesss."

She flew up into the air, buzzed around his head, and landed on one of his large horns.

"How?" asked the faun. "I would give anything to be human. Please, tell me what I must do."

"I will ssspin you a cloak made from ssspiders' sssilk," said the fairy. Then she crawled across his face, touching his nose, his eyes, and his lips, then farther down his neck, across his chest, over his shoulders, and along his arms. And wherever she touched him, silver threads sprang up and began to weave their way across his skin. They formed a web, which quickly grew thicker and thicker, enveloping him, binding him tighter and tighter until he could scarcely breathe.

"As long as you wear this cloak, nobody will be able to sssee your true nature. They will think you are human, just like them," the fairy explained, seeming pleased with her handiwork. "But if you want to become human, you must do more. You must find sssomebody to whom you can reveal your true nature. Sssomebody who lovesss you just as you are. Sssomebody who is willing . . . ," the fairy hissed, flying very close to his ear. She lowered her voice to a whisper that sounded like a delicate piece of paper being torn in two.

The faun listened. He could barely breathe inside the cloak of spider silk that bound him like an icy cloth. "But," he whispered at last, "what will happen if I choose the wrong person? If I take off the cloak too soon?"

The fairy crawled up onto the tip of his nose and looked him squarely in the eye. "Then," she said, "you will belong to me. You will pay with your life. So choose wisssely."

# 9

"I WANTED TO ORDER THE FLOWERS FROM THE SAME FLORIST the Swedish royal family uses. They looked so beautiful at Sofia and Carl Philip's wedding. . . ." Miss Berkenbeck had settled herself on the edge of our table by the entrance to the dining hall, dislodging most of the name tags that Hannah, Charlotte, and I had spent the last fifteen minutes sorting into alphabetical order and laying out in rows. We dived off our chairs and started collecting them up off the floor. But Miss Berkenbeck was in full flow, and went on without missing a beat: "The delivery costs wouldn't have been a problem: They said on TV that the florist lives in Heidelberg and is a close friend of Queen Silvia. But unfortunately our budget still wouldn't stretch to . . ." Only now did she realize that the three of us were scrabbling around on all fours at her feet. "Goodness gracious, what are you all doing down there?"

I held up a fistful of name tags.

"Oh, dear, did I knock them off? I'm so sorry!" Miss Berkenbeck started fiddling with the name tags that were left on the table, trying to line them up again. But she only succeeded in making things worse, because now they were all in the wrong order. Luckily she soon gave up and declared: "I'm going to give you all some doughnuts to make up for it. Just a minute, I'll go and fetch them. They're still warm. Dr. Meier tried one earlier and he said it was delicious. . . ." She hurried off, still talking (though nobody was quite sure to whom).

"Er," said Hannah, "weren't those doughnuts meant to be for tomorrow? For the parents and the new students?"

"Yep," said Charlotte. "You could try telling her that. Or you could just not ask any awkward questions, and help yourself to a free doughnut. They're still warm, you know."

Hannah grinned. "Okay. It was just that I thought everything had to be perfect for tomorrow. . . ."

"It will be, don't worry. Every time we have an open day, the Berkenbecks make three times as many doughnuts as there are guests," I reassured her, and returned to my task of allocating name tags to welcome packs.

The next day was Saturday, and it was a very important day—one of my favorite days on the school calendar. Tomorrow morning we would be showing the families of prospective students around the school, and there would be all sorts of sample lessons, tours, speeches, and activities, as well as plentiful supplies of cake (naturally). From the late afternoon onward, ex-students would start arriving for the school's 190th alumni reunion, and the climax of the festivities would be on Sunday evening at the annual Stolzenburg Autumn Ball.

Charlotte, Hannah, and I were to be in charge of registering the visitors and giving them their name tags, school prospectuses, and event schedules. I'd also volunteered to show small groups of parents and children around the grounds and tell them a bit about the castle. I'd been looking forward to it all week. All the more so since I'd come across a fairy tale in the chronicle by Eleanor Morland, which she must have written while she was staying at Stolzenburg. I was planning to read out excerpts from the story as a special highlight of my tour.

Preparations for the open day had kept me busy most of the week. What was more, our teachers had really started to pile on the work recently—the school year was in full swing now, and next week we would have our first exams. I was also doing extra swimming training in preparation for an interschool competition in November. So, what with one thing and another, I'd been so busy that I hadn't had time to write in the chronicle all week. I'd had to content myself with flicking through past entries written by other chroniclers (I always ended up discovering new pages when I did that) and looking back at my own entries to see whether they'd taken effect yet.

I'd managed to use the chronicle to avoid running into Frederick for a few days after our date at the Golden Lion. I'd been so embarrassed by the state I'd gotten myself into that it had seemed a good idea to steer clear of him for a while, until it had all blown over. I'd finally decided to lift the ban that morning, but it still took me by surprise when I saw him come staggering into the dining hall carrying an enormous vase. Our eyes met, and he smiled his crooked smile.

"Where d'you want this?" he grunted, and I pointed to the opposite corner of the room where some of the older boys were carrying in tables one by one and some younger girls, directed by Helena, were decorating them with elaborately folded napkins. That was where the cake buffet was going to be laid out the next day, and the huge vase of roses would make the perfect centerpiece (even if the flowers had only come from the castle grounds, and not been handpicked by a royal florist).

"Okay," said Frederick, lurching off toward the other side of the room with the vase. I forced myself to stop gazing at him and, before Hannah could ask when Frederick and I were finally going to get around to having our first kiss, I hurried over to Miss Berkenbeck. She'd just returned from the kitchen with a plateful of steaming doughnuts. "You really didn't need to do this," I said out of politeness, though I knew full well that resistance was futile. "The name tags are already back in order, look."

"Now, Emma, I won't take no for an answer!" Miss Berkenbeck said firmly, gesticulating wildly with her free hand. "Somebody's got to test them, haven't they? As they always say on the *Bake Off*..."

A heavenly aroma wafted through the dining hall. The doughnuts were plump and golden-brown and dusted with icing sugar that looked like the first snow of winter settling on the castle battlements. My mouth started to water as I imagined the sugar melting on my tongue.

Miss Berkenbeck held the plate under my nose. "Here," she said, and I breathed in the delicious fresh-baked smell.

"No awkward questions sounds good to me," said Hannah, reaching for a doughnut. "Fanks," she mumbled with her mouth full.

I couldn't resist any longer. With a sigh, I, too, picked up a doughnut and bit into it. The sweet, buttery flavor was incredible— they tasted even better than they smelled.

While we chomped away happily on our doughnuts, something happened that caught everyone's attention and even succeeded in distracting Hannah from the fascinating topic of me and Frederick. In amongst the stream of boys carrying tables into the dining room, Toby and Darcy appeared, holding a heavy claw-foot desk between them and advancing inch by inch across the room. It was a miracle that they'd managed not only to lift the thing, but to lug it all the way down here from the west wing. Red-faced from the effort, they finally reached the corner where the cake buffet was to be served and set the desk down. But Helena did not look at all pleased to see it. "What's *that*?" she asked with a hint of irritation.

"We couldn't just stand by and watch while two twelve-year-olds nearly killed themselves dragging this thing along the corridor," said Toby. "So we took pity on them and brought it down here ourselves. We didn't want you to have to serve your buffet on the floor."

"Well, there must have been some kind of misunderstanding," said Helena, putting her hands on her hips. "This is much too high and too wide, we can't possibly use it. Anyway, we've got enough tables already."

Darcy and Toby exchanged a glance that said there had been no misunderstanding whatsoever: The twelve-year-olds had clearly played a trick on them, and a pretty blatant one at that. And they'd fallen for it hook, line, and sinker. I grinned into my half-eaten doughnut.

"We were only trying to help," said Darcy.

"Well, thanks," said Helena, "but what would really help me is if you'd take that desk away and put it back where it came from."

Toby snorted.

While the two boys went on talking to Helena, I watched Charlotte out of the corner of my eye. Every time she'd run into Toby over the past few days, she'd plastered on a smile that was presumably supposed to look happy and carefree, but which couldn't hide the fact that she actually wanted to burst into tears. Today was no exception. Something really did seem to have gone badly wrong between them. The night we'd run into him at the ruins, Toby had told Hannah that for a few days he'd been under the (false) impression that Charlotte was playing games with him—that she was already Frederick's girlfriend. He wouldn't say where he'd gotten this ridiculous idea from, or why he still didn't want to go out with Charlotte even now that he knew the truth.

Charlotte had told me everything was fine and that what had happened with Toby really wasn't a big deal, but I didn't believe a word of it. She never mentioned him anymore, and most of the time she acted as though he didn't exist: That alone was a sure sign that it *was* a big deal. In fact, it was almost on a par with "the incident."

"Take it away! It's blocking the fire exit!" Helena was saying.

"Do you have any idea how long it took to get this thing down the stairs?" Toby demanded. His blond hair was plastered to his face with sweat.

Darcy looked exhausted, too; there were dark circles under his eyes again. He'd pointedly turned his back on Frederick and was now looking gloomily down at the heavy desk in front of him. I'd hardly seen him since last Sunday, the day we'd found the lord of Stolzenburg's secret laboratory. For almost an hour we'd searched every inch of the laboratory and the secret tunnels for Darcy's sister. But there had been no sign of Gina, nor any clues as to her disappearance, and eventually Darcy's phone battery had run low, too, and forced us to give up. Since that day, he'd been even more elusive than before, and I increasingly found myself wondering what exactly it was that he and Toby were up to in the west wing.

"Taking it upstairs will probably be even harder," said Helena, smiling sweetly. "But at least it'll keep you fit."

The napkin-folding girls, meanwhile, had been busy moving the other tables around to try to make space for the enormous desk, casting shy glances at Darcy as they did so. When he looked up at them, two of the girls blushed to the roots of their hair and a third tripped over a table leg and fell onto the display of folded napkins, squashing most of them flat. Darcy seemed to feel he'd been caught out, and immediately resumed his usual expression of sullen aloofness. "This desk is not moving," he told Helena, folding his arms across his chest.

"I think you'll find it is," said Frederick, coming to stand beside Helena. "Otherwise we might all die in a fire, or the inevitable stampede when the food starts running out."

"Don't you have some flowers to arrange?" said Darcy, taking a step toward him.

Frederick drew himself up to his full height. He was half a head shorter than Darcy, but much stockier—all that gardening work had left him with a pretty impressive set of muscles. "The flowers are all done, thanks," he hissed. "But you guys carry on; I'm sure the twelve-year-olds have a few more tricks up their sleeves. Now get out of here and take your massive table with you!"

Darcy glared at him, his face scarlet with rage. But Frederick merely grinned. "Touched a nerve, have I?" he snorted, and now he, too, took a step forward. "You think I ought to show more respect to a spoiled little prince like you?"

Darcy stared at him silently for a moment. "Get out of my sight," he said at last, in a quiet but menacing voice. His fists were clenched, and he looked dangerously close to punching Frederick.

Frederick backed off a little, but probably only to position himself for the counterattack.

"Perhaps we could use the desk as our registration table?" called Hannah. She hadn't caught much of what had passed between the boys: She'd been too busy polishing off another of Miss Berkenbeck's doughnuts.

"That's a great idea," exclaimed Toby, laying a hand on Darcy's shoulder. "Come on, Darce, give me a hand."

Darcy glared at Frederick a moment longer, then turned on his heel and lifted one end of the desk so roughly that it gave a loud creak. He and Toby lugged it across the room toward us at the same snail's pace as before, while Frederick grinned again and started distributing single red roses to Helena and the napkin girls.

Although I was glad the boys hadn't ended up having a fight and that nobody had been hurt, I was surprised to find that part of me felt a tiny bit disappointed.

Anyway, Hannah's idea had been a good one: Ten minutes later, once we'd moved everything over onto the stately desk, our registration table looked a lot more impressive.

"Th-thanks," said Charlotte to Toby.

He nodded. "No problem." He shifted his weight from one foot to the other with the same I-feel-like-crying-but-I'm-pretending-everything's-fine smile as Charlotte.

Charlotte lowered her eyes.

Toby cleared his throat.

Oh, man, what was going *on* here?

I'd just opened my mouth to tell the pair of them to stop beating around the bush and go and talk about it over a cup of coffee, and Hannah, too, had piped up, "Seriously, you two?" when Toby heaved a sigh and shook his head. He glanced over to where Darcy was standing. "I—I'm sorry," he said. "Have fun with the heaviest desk in the world, yeah?" And he hurried out of the dining hall.

I looked at Darcy, who was clearly in a world of his own. Had he not even noticed Toby leaving? "You're forgetting to frown again," I called over to him.

Darcy started, looked around for his friend, muttered something unintelligible, and followed Toby out of the dining hall.

"What was all that about?" said Hannah.

I shrugged. "Strange," I said, while Charlotte, still trying to muster a smile, started humming to herself in a quavering voice as she laid out the last of the name tags.

"Typical Darcy," said Frederick, sauntering over to us. "Would any of you ladies like a rose?" He held out three long-stemmed flowers. The bunch of roses in the big vase was now looking somewhat depleted.

"Thanks," I said.

"I just don't understand why Toby's being such a douche," Hannah murmured.

"Oh, Toby's all right," said Frederick. "It's just the company he keeps. You'll never guess who it was that told him to stay away from Charlotte."

"No way!" I exclaimed.

Frederick nodded.

The next day, Stolzenburg played host to more than two hundred families from all over the world who were thinking of sending their offspring to the school the following September. The place was crawling with children, and their parents subjected my dad and the other teachers to a constant barrage of questions. Prospective students trotted along beside their parents as I led them on guided tours of the school. I'd been allocated five different tour groups throughout the day, and I showed each of them around the classrooms, the bedrooms, the dining hall, the sports hall, the swimming pool, the tennis courts, the imposing ballroom (which was already being set up by an events company for tomorrow night's ball), and, of course, the grounds. Each of my tours was better than the last: I embellished them with anecdotes about the school and the castle and, for my grand finale, I recited Eleanor Morland's story about the lonely faun. All in all, it was a triumph.

Until the last tour of the afternoon, anyway.

Up to then everything had gone so smoothly. I'd been feeling positively jubilant when I'd set off with the final group. And right up until just before the end, it had been the most fantastic tour any visitor to Stolzenburg had ever had (in my opinion). But then, out on the lawns beside the fountain, everything started to go wrong. I'd just finished the part of the tour where I talked about the landscape architect who'd restored the fountains fifty years earlier, and the visitors were hanging on my every word, when a group of alumni came streaming out onto the lawn. Most of them were young men who'd probably left the school only about three or four years ago. Now they were milling about, laughing, greeting each other with funny handshakes, and generally making lots of noise. I raised my voice to make myself heard above the din as the ex-students drifted closer and closer to our little group.

"The writer Eleanor Morland," I said loudly—I was getting to the highlight of my talk now—"stayed here at Stolzenburg for several months. During the summer of 1794 she often went walking on the castle grounds, and they inspired her to write one of her first short stories, a fairy tale that I recently . . ."

The ex-students suddenly roared with laughter—one of them had just told a hilarious joke, by the sounds of it—and I had to shout even louder to drown them out as I launched into the tale of the faun and the fairy. But it didn't matter—my listeners were enjoying the story. Weren't they?

". . . and so the faun set off in search of his true love. Some say he still hasn't found her, and that to this day he wanders the secret tunnels beneath the castle looking for her. At midnight, if you are very quiet, you can still hear his footsteps echoing through the walls. And that is the end of our little tour."

I waited for the customary applause, but instead I heard an angry voice right by my ear exclaim: "What are you talking about, Emma?"

Startled, I took a step backward, tripped over the base of the fountain, teetered, and lost my balance.

Damn it!

For a fraction of a second my arms flailed wildly as I tried to stop myself from falling. A hand shot out and tried to catch my elbow, but I slid out of its grasp and toppled backward into the fountain. I tried to grab hold of the edge of the basin, but my hands slipped on the algae and I sank farther into the water. My head went under.

Icy cold water enveloped me, soaking through my clothes, blinding me, filling my ears and nose. I opened my mouth as I thrashed around, accidentally swallowing a mouthful of water. I'd lost my bearings now—I didn't know which way was up. The fountain was no more than about three feet deep. It couldn't be that difficult to get out of, surely? Unfortunately, my body seemed to have other ideas. My lungs screamed for air, my eyes blinked helplessly in the murky green water, my limbs were paralyzed by the cold, and I was seized by the irrational fear that I was going to drown.

But all this lasted only a few moments: Then I felt somebody climbing into the fountain beside me, grabbing my shoulders, and pulling me back up to the surface.

Gasping for breath, I coughed and spluttered for a moment as the shocked faces of the families around me came into view. I heard the ex-students chuckling, and I could clearly make out Helena's tinkling little laugh.

The hands grabbed hold of me once more and lifted me onto my feet. I slipped again on the slimy bottom of the basin, but this time the arms wrapped themselves around me and held me up.

"Are you crazy? You nearly made me jump out of my skin!" I yelled, wrenching myself free. The water sloshed and gurgled as I waded to the edge of the fountain.

"How was I supposed to know you were going to go down like a sack of potatoes?" said Darcy, clambering out of the water behind me. He, too, was drenched: His shirt was plastered to his body, his trousers were dripping wet, and he had half a waterlily stuck to his shoulder. And I looked even worse; my shirt was coated in a layer of slimy green stuff, I'd managed to lose my left shoe, and I was pretty sure my mascara was running all over my face. Shivering, I wrung out my ponytail.

"How about a thank-you?" Darcy had the audacity to ask.

I glared at him.

Helena's giggles grew louder. "Looking good, Emma!" she cried. "That would be a nice color for the new uniforms, too!" The families from my tour group allowed themselves a little grin at this, and even Darcy looked as if he was trying not to smile.

I sniffed. "Thanks for listening," I said to the families. Water ran off me in rivulets as I took a bow. Then I turned on my heel (the one that still had a shoe on) and stormed off.

In hindsight it probably would have been better to storm back to the castle rather than into the woods, so I could've had a hot shower and changed into some dry clothes. But I was too irate to think clearly. I went striding off into the trees and I didn't stop until I reached the ruins. Shivering and gasping from the cold, I leaned against one of the broken pillars and gazed into the undergrowth for a while, trying to calm myself down.

A moment later, I got another shock—Darcy had followed me into the woods and was now walking toward me through the trees.

"I'm sorry," he said. "You know I didn't mean to make you fall in the water."

"Oh, right," I said. "Maybe you shouldn't have pushed me, then."

"I didn't—"

"I know." I folded my arms across my chest and tried to stop myself from shivering, while Darcy stood there shifting his weight from one foot to the other.

"Listen," he said at last, "I didn't mean to make you jump, either."

"Right," I said again.

"Do you want to put my shirt on?"

"No, thanks. Your shirt's wet, too."

"Fine. Whatever." Darcy came to lean against the pillar beside me. For a minute or two we both stared angrily into the trees without saying a word. Then Darcy said, "What was that ridiculous story you were telling them? It sounded like the sort of story my sister used to have nightmares about."

"You sound like one of those people who think we should ban fantasy novels in case kids start thinking magic is real."

"Of course not." He made a dismissive gesture. "It's just . . . I was talking to some of the guys who were in my year here, and they'd just started telling me what they remembered about the night Gina went missing, when *you* came along and—"

"When I came along and gave an informative and entertaining speech to the next generation of Stolzenburg students? How rude of me! You were quite right to tip me into a fountain full of icy water."

"I told you: I didn't mean to. And I'd been standing behind you for ages, I thought you'd noticed." Darcy ran a hand over his face and massaged his temples for a moment. "Oh, I don't know what's wrong with me. Perhaps I'm just finding it hard to come to terms with . . . with the fact that those legends about the faun *must* have had something to do with Gina going missing," he murmured. "It's a ridiculous idea. I thought so at the time, too. But my sister's been gone four years. And I've spoken to so many people over the past few days who've told me that . . . that before she disappeared, she kept talking about a 'creature' living in the cellars of Stolzenburg. I can't ignore it any longer." He sighed. "Where did you come across that story about the faun?"

I bit my lip. "Oh, in amongst all that stuff in the west wing library," I lied, but even as I said it I wondered whether I should perhaps be telling Darcy the truth. We'd discovered one of the lord of Stolzenburg's secret laboratories together, after all; we already shared one secret. But on the other hand, he was still Darcy de Winter, and most of the time he treated me like a stupid kid.

I pulled my soaking wet blazer more tightly around me. My clothes felt heavy and icy cold, and the wind blowing up from the river was making my teeth chatter. But Darcy's wet clothes couldn't have been much more comfortable than mine, and yet here he was leaning against the broken pillar beside me, trying to apologize.

"I'm sorry," he said again, and this time I nodded.

"Th-thanks for pulling me out of the fountain," I muttered.

I looked up a moment later to find Darcy giving me a rather odd look. He wasn't looking down his nose at me as usual. There was a softness in his eyes.

"No problem," he said. "No problem."

I stared at him.

"Emma." The warmth with which he said my name was almost enough to make me stop shivering. "I wish I could protect you from everything and everyone—I . . ." He cleared his throat. "I like you, okay? Even I don't understand how it happened, but I think I . . . I really like you."

*What?*

"Er . . . ," I said. My mouth opened and shut again like a goldfish, and I felt a kind of warm glow in my chest that I couldn't explain. Was Darcy de Winter saying that he . . . No, he couldn't mean it. Anyway, the only person I'd ever thought about in that way was Frederick, and I . . .

My mind suddenly went blank as Darcy put out a hand and tucked a lock of wet hair behind my ear. I looked up into his dark eyes, the color of hazelnut caramel.

"This kind of thing doesn't normally happen to me," he murmured. "I mean, Toby and I are only here for a few weeks—I'm going back to England soon. There's no way this could ever have a future. And you're only sixteen, you're still at school. Stolzenburg is your whole world. You have your little secret society, you go on dates and get so drunk you almost pass out. . . ."

EXCUSE ME?!

"We're completely wrong for each other, and over the past few weeks I've been desperately trying not to think about you all the time. But it's no good." He leaned toward me. "I can't get you out of my head, Emma Morgenroth," he whispered, and I felt his breath on my lips. His right hand was resting on the pillar beside my face, his left hand was still playing with my hair, and his perfect lips were almost touching mine. . . .

Quick as a flash I jerked my head aside, dodged out from under his arm and took a step backward.

Darcy stepped back, too. "What is it?" he asked, puzzled. "What's wrong?"

"Nothing," I said, scraping my wet hair back into a ponytail.

He looked at me in bewilderment. The fact that I wasn't yearning to kiss him seemed to be beyond the bounds of his comprehension.

I sighed. "I'm . . . well, I'm very surprised and flattered but I'm afraid . . . I don't want to go out with you. But thank you, anyway," I said formally.

Darcy's face instantly resumed its usual arrogant expression. He raised his eyebrows and squared his shoulders and pressed his lips tightly together. "I see," he said. "Might I ask why?"

I shrugged. By now I was shivering uncontrollably, and I knew

I had to get out of these wet clothes as quickly as possible. "If a simple *no* isn't enough," I retorted, "firstly: We'd have no future. Secondly: I'm only sixteen and still at school and *so* naïve. And thirdly: Do have you any *idea* how you come across?"

Darcy blinked at me uncomprehendingly and I could see I was going to have to spell it out for him. "It's not just the fact that you swagger around here as if you own the place. You also start acting really weirdly whenever there's any mention of Gina. You're out of order to Frederick, who was her friend and actually tried to *help* her. And as if that wasn't enough, you told Toby not to go out with Charlotte!"

He gave a slow, jerky nod. "So that's what you think of me?" he said quietly.

"You're not denying that you tried to keep Toby and Charlotte apart?"

"I advised him to steer clear of her, yes," said Darcy. I was speechless. Who did this guy think he was?

"But . . . ," I stammered. "But *why*?"

"It's a long story."

"Aha."

"I know it's hard to understand, but it's nothing to do with . . ." He was visibly embarrassed. "Let's just say I had my reasons."

I scoffed.

The wind had turned even colder in the past couple of minutes, and I felt as though I was about to turn into an icicle. "Oh, I'm sure you did," I hissed, drawing myself up to my full height. "Perfectly good, made-up reasons that you're going to guard like state secrets because everything you do is so mysterious and important." I had to tilt my head back a little in order to meet his eye. "Well, I'm sorry, but I don't have time for your mind games anymore. I'm freezing my arse off here."

Darcy gritted his teeth. "Me, too," he growled. His teeth were chattering now, and his shoulders were shaking.

For a moment we stood there looking at each other and shivering, both so furious that it wouldn't have taken much for us to come to blows. We were like two chemical elements drawn together by the force of attraction, but bound to cause an almighty explosion if they ever did come into contact.

At last I turned my back on Darcy and stomped off toward the castle, breaking the strange tension between us.

October 2013

Some mornings I wake up and wonder if I'm going mad. No, I don't wonder, I know. For a moment I'm sure it's all just a dream. That this book is just an old book and the stories are just old stories.

But then, the next moment, I remember his face.

# 10

WHEN I GOT BACK TO MY ROOM I HAD A VERY LONG, VERY hot shower to clear my head (and to stop my toes falling off). By the time I emerged from the bathroom forty-five minutes later in a cloud of fragrant steam, my mind was made up—I'd had enough of this whole stupid business. I was in no mood to deal with it.

As I dried my hair in a towel and shuffled across the room to open the window, a stream of thoughts ran through my head over and over again, as if on a loop: the things Darcy had said, the way he'd looked at me, his breathtaking arrogance—he'd obviously thought he was paying me such a compliment by telling me he liked me that I wouldn't mind him saying, in the same breath, that I was a naïve little schoolgirl! And then there were those ridiculous legends about the faun. How could I possibly have believed they were true? I was *not* just a naïve little kid. I didn't believe in mythical creatures, nor did I allow myself to be kissed, out of the blue, by stuck-up aristocrats. And I wasn't afraid of the chronicle, either. . . .

"My poor little Emma!" cried my dad.

I spun around and saw him sitting on Hannah's bed holding a scruffy toy rabbit. "Helena told me about your accident," he said. "Oh, my poor little girl! It doesn't bear thinking about! You could have drowned, or broken your neck! And in these freezing temperatures . . . !"

"It wasn't that bad. Really," I said, trying to downplay the incident. "I didn't even get that wet. Just a little bit."

My dad raised his eyebrows. "I heard you were completely submerged."

"You know what rumors are like. Every time someone tells the story they make it sound that little bit more dramatic. . . ."

My dad wasn't listening. He pressed the stuffed rabbit to his chest. "My poor little Emma," he moaned. "Are you sure you're not hurt?"

I nodded, and Dad gave a sigh of relief. But he went on clutching the toy rabbit tightly. "Isn't this the little fellow you used to carry around with you everywhere when you were small? You took him to the nursery and to the dentist and . . ."

"Er—no, actually. I had a teddy bear. And that's Hannah's bed. I sleep over here."

"Oh." My dad stood up hastily, but before he could return the rabbit to the pillow where he'd found it, the door opened and in walked its rightful owner.

"Has Mr. Fluffball been misbehaving again?" asked Hannah.

"No, I . . . er . . . I do beg your pardon," Dad stammered,

thrusting the rabbit into her arms. Then he turned to me. "Perhaps we should drive over to the hospital and get your head X-rayed, just to be sure. Or should I call an ambulance?"

"No," I said. "Definitely not."

"All right, I'll drive you myself. But—"

"No!" I said more firmly, steering my dad toward the door. "I feel fine, I don't need to go to the hospital. There's absolutely nothing to worry about. And I know how important it is for modern parents not to wrap their children in bubble wrap," I added, reminding him of one of his favorite maxims. "I'll be fine."

"Really?" he asked again, just to be sure. When I nodded, he cleared his throat and tried to banish the worried expression from his face. "Well," he said, patting me on the shoulder, "it's true, Emma, you do need to learn how to deal with some of the less pleasant aspects of life." He put on his most educational voice. "Falling into a fountain is not the end of the world—it's an experience you can learn from." With those words he stepped out into the corridor, at last, and I hurried to close the door behind him. I flopped down onto my bed with a sigh.

"You're not really fine, are you?" asked Hannah.

But I didn't answer. I pulled the duvet up over my head and wrapped myself up in it like a cocoon. My thoughts whirled faster and faster, melting into a jumble of images and dragonfly wings and eventually into dreams.

When I woke up, it was the middle of the night.

Hannah was snoring softly and, as I so often had in the past few weeks, I reached for the book. (I'd found I couldn't bring myself to return it to the secret compartment in the library.) By the light of my bedside lamp, I leafed through the delicate pages. I didn't feel like reading any of Eleanor Morland's entries today, or her fairy tales—today I wanted to write in the chronicle myself. My urge to take control, to change the course of events, was suddenly stronger than it had been for a long time. I was still Emma Magdalena Morgenroth, sixteen years old and practically an adult. I wasn't going to let life pass me by—I was going to take control of my destiny. And I certainly wasn't going to let Darcy or Frederick or some stupid legend or fairy tale make me think I was going crazy. Pah!

I pulled out my pen and launched into what was to become my most detailed entry in the chronicle so far.

First of all, I decided to restore order to the castle: I got the ex-students to abandon their usual drinking binge in favor of a games night, and I got my dad to stop worrying about my dip in the fountain. Then I decided it was time to think a little bigger. I still felt a certain awed respect for the chronicle's powers, but somehow my previous strategy of cautious experimentation just didn't appeal to me anymore. I had a magical object in my possession, and I was going to use it.

What if, for example, a couple of our outrageously wealthy alumni were to announce at the ball tomorrow night that they were donating some money to the school, to be used for the long-awaited riding stables? That would be brilliant. And my dad would be over the moon if he were to receive a special award for his work as headmaster of Stolzenburg. And wasn't it about time *dear* Marie came to visit her aunt and great-aunt in person, instead of bombarding them with email after boring email?

Oh, yes, and the faun . . . If the faun really did exist, then I wanted him to show himself. I wanted to meet him face-to-face, damn it! And I wanted him to tell me what had happened to Gina. If he didn't exist and I was simply suffering from an overactive imagination, that was fine. I just needed to know one way or another. I needed some clarity, or I was going to go mad. That was all.

Although . . .

As I finished the final paragraph, I started to have misgivings about what I'd just written. Hmm—those last few lines were the opposite of cautious! Had I gone too far? After a few seconds I decided to cross out what I'd written about the faun, just to be on the safe side.

I tried to put a line through the words.

But the nib of my fountain pen slid across the paper without leaving a mark. It wasn't that the ink cartridge was empty: When I drew a squiggle in the margin to test it, it worked fine. But the moment I tried to change or cross out one of the words I'd already written, the paper seemed to reject the ink.

Interesting.

Also a little creepy.

For a while I doodled randomly all over the page, drawing dots and dashes, wavy lines and zigzags. The words I'd already written were not obscured in the slightest. In fact, by the end they seemed to stand out even more clearly than before against the sea of scribbles. It didn't matter how many times I drew over them. Not even ink eraser or correction fluid could get rid of them, and my attempts to rip out the whole page also failed miserably. Damn it! Eventually I gave up, closed the book, hid it (under my mattress this time), and hoped for the best. Then I switched off the light and sank back into the maelstrom of my dreams.

I was woken the next day by the chaos that always descended on Stolzenburg on the morning of the Autumn Ball. The atmosphere was as feverish as you would expect in a castle full of teenagers getting ready for a prom. Some of the students had been dreaming about the perfect outfit for months, and had spent the summer holidays trawling the most exclusive boutiques in Paris, London, and Berlin, armed with Daddy's credit card. Others were less keen on the idea of a formal dance and grew more and more irritable as the event approached.

This year, like every other year, pandemonium broke out in the corridors as preparations for the ball began. Hair straighteners and huge makeup cases were carried from room to room, dresses were tried on with different hairstyles and different shoes, eyebrows were plucked to within an inch of their lives, and in the common rooms, those who had no interest in the ball sat around looking grumpy and greeting any mention of ball gowns and curling tongs with rolled eyes and sarcastic remarks.

Charlotte and I were somewhere in between. We liked getting dressed up occasionally and doing our hair and makeup. But we certainly didn't treat the ball as a matter of national importance like Helena, who bought her outfit at Berlin Fashion Week every year. Our dresses were at least three seasons old: I'd bought mine (a backless dark-red gown with a high neck) in a department store, and I'd already worn it to last year's ball. Charlotte was wearing a midnight-blue dress that had once belonged to her mom. And half an hour before the ball Hannah had rifled through the pile of clothes in her wardrobe and produced an extremely crumpled, strapless, black-and-white polka-dot garment that she insisted was a ball gown. It didn't actually look that bad once she had it on, apart from a few creases in the skirt.

I thought the three of us looked gorgeous, anyway, as we joined the throng of students making their way to the west wing shortly before seven o' clock. We certainly looked better than Helena, who swept past us in a sort of feathery sack full of holes. (Haute couture or no haute couture, the thing was hideous.)

The ballroom on the first floor was already filling up when we arrived. Every student in the school would be at the ball that night, as well as all the teachers, the rest of the school staff, and over a hundred alumni. Everyone was standing around looking very smart in the light of myriads of candles. The candlelight was reflected back into the room by the mirrored walls, casting a warm glow over the faces of the guests, and the crystal chandeliers sparkled with rainbow-colored light.

I spent a few minutes, as I did every year, just marveling at the splendor of this room—its gleaming parquet floor, its high windows, the ornate furniture around the edges of the dance floor. For the rest of the year, the ballroom lay in the same deep slumber as all the other rooms in the west wing, and when you hadn't set foot in it for twelve months it was easy to forget how beautiful it was.

"Wow!" Hannah exclaimed as we edged through the crowd toward the Berkenbecks, who were waving at me with great excitement.

"Emma, love!" called Miss Berkenbeck, beaming at me. I didn't think I'd ever seen the two of them looking so happy. "Guess who's coming to see us next week? Marie! We got an email from her today. . . ." Berkenbeck the elder waggled a piece of paper under my nose. They'd obviously printed off Marie's email and planned to spend the evening reading it out to as many people as possible.

"Wow," I cried. "That's great news! I can't wait to meet her! But I can't stop, I'm afraid—I was just going to go and wish my dad good luck."

"Of course, pet, of course! But you two have a minute, don't you? Charlotte? Hannah?"

They both nodded obediently, while I turned away with an apologetic smile and carried on across the room. My dad, armed with a microphone, was just stepping up onto the little podium, but when he saw me he climbed down again and gave me a quick hug. "You look lovely," he said.

"Thanks," I replied, trying to straighten his tie without anyone noticing—the knot was so askew that he looked as though he'd been in some sort of accident. "So do you." I gave him a kiss on the cheek and stepped back into the expectant crowd. The string orchestra at the other end of the ballroom struck up a little overture, drowning out the noise the caterers were making in the next room as they put the finishing touches to the finger buffet.

I let my eyes wander for a moment until I spotted Frederick standing nearby. He appeared to be trying to compliment Helena on her dress (no mean feat, in my opinion). He was gesturing toward the holes and the feathers, at any rate, and whatever he'd said had clearly put a smile on her face. He also scrubbed up pretty well in a suit.

After a while the orchestra fell silent, and my dad began his welcome speech. "Dear Stolzenburgers—students, colleagues, and alumni," he announced, "it gives me great pleasure to welcome you to our annual Autumn Ball, which is now in its 164th year. Tonight we come together once more to celebrate the outstanding education with which this school has been providing its students for the past 192 years."

At this point there was a burst of applause, and Dad had to pause for a moment before continuing. "Not only are we one of the best and most famous schools in the world: We also take the health of our students extremely seriously. Particularly during the autumn and winter months, when outbreaks of cold and flu are rife, our standards of hygiene are . . ."

I raised my eyebrows at him; Dad got the message and cleared his throat. "Anyway . . . I am very glad so many of you have been able to join us this evening, and I hereby declare this year's Stolzenburg Autumn Ball officially . . . open!" He clambered down onto the dance floor, where Mrs. Bröder-Strauchhaus was waiting for him to make his customary old-fashioned bow. "May I have this dance?" he asked.

The orchestra was already playing the first waltz, and the two of them went gliding off across the floor (as they did every year) in perfect synchrony. After a few minutes, lots of other couples joined in, and soon the room was full of twirling dancers. I'd decided to leave Frederick hanging for a while, and I was about to step in and ask Mrs. Bröder-Strauchhaus if I could take over from her, when suddenly all hell broke loose on the dance floor. My dad's secretary, Mrs. Schnorr, came barreling across the room like a charging bull;

Sophia in Year 9 (who was wearing a Versace gown—I knew this only because she'd been telling everyone about it for weeks, whether they wanted to hear it or not) was forced to leap out of the way, and only just managed to rescue her train. Completely out of breath, Mrs. Schnorr held out a phone to my dad. "It's the European Commission!" she panted, in a voice so high-pitched it was practically a squeak. "They want to give you the International Educational Achievement Prize. *You!* For your work here at Stolzenburg!"

My dad took the phone. "Dr. Morgenroth speaking," he said, and paused for a moment. As he listened to the voice on the other end of the line, his eyes filled with tears. "What a . . . what a very great honor," he stammered. "Would you . . . would you excuse me for one moment? I'll be with you in just a second, and then we can discuss the details."

He quickly handed his dance partner over to Dr. Meier and hurried out of the ballroom. I, meanwhile, had decided not to keep Frederick waiting any longer. He was still standing with Helena on the edge of the dance floor, grinning at me over the top of the dancers' heads. I smiled back and nodded, waiting for him to make his way across the room toward me . . . but instead he turned back to Helena and said something that made them both giggle.

"Would you like to dance?" asked a voice from beside me.

"Sure," I said without thinking. I was still staring at Frederick and Helena, who were now making themselves comfortable on a little sofa. . . .

"Nice dress, by the way," said Toby as he led me out onto the dance floor.

"Thanks," I replied. "Have you seen Charlotte's?" Toby didn't answer; instead he started to whisk me across the floor in a series of complicated steps that I found very difficult to follow. Usually I wasn't a bad dancer, but at this speed it was all I could do not to trip over my own feet. "Um—you know this is just a waltz, right? It's not about who can get around the room the fastest," I informed him, as Sophia in her Versace gown was obliged to leap out of the way again.

"I know that," said Toby. "What I don't know is why, since yesterday afternoon, Darcy has suddenly turned into the most antisocial person in the world."

"Well, perhaps you didn't *notice* it until yesterday afternoon, but—" I got no further, however, because Toby suddenly gave me a shove that sent me staggering off the dance floor. What did he think he was doing? That was no way to treat a lady!

"You two should talk," said Toby, and I didn't even have time to ask him what on earth he was playing at before I collided with a tall, dark-suited figure wearing an even bigger scowl than usual.

"What are you doing?" growled Darcy, but Toby had already turned his back on us and was fleeing the scene as quickly as he'd arrived. Oh, *great*!

"I don't know what you said to Toby, but—"

"Nothing," Darcy interrupted me, his face darkening still further.

"No?"

"I'm guessing he's put two and two together and made five. We don't need to talk—we've already said everything we had to say."

"I agree."

"Good."

"Well then." I turned to go, but suddenly we found ourselves boxed in by a crowd of waltzing Year 7s, and I had to stand there and wait for them to disperse.

Darcy sighed. "At first it was just a misunderstanding," he said from behind me.

"What was?" I asked without turning around.

"Charlotte," said Darcy. "Do you remember the night I threw you out of the library?"

"You really think I could forget?"

"After you'd gone, Frederick turned up and—well, he threatened me, tried to get me to leave Stolzenburg. He said he'd heard me yelling all the way from the tower room in the east wing, where he'd been waiting for his girlfriend. Which was ridiculous, obviously—I wasn't *that* loud."

"I don't know about that," I said, then shook my head and turned to face him. "I ran into Frederick on the stairs—I told him what you'd done. We were supposed to be meeting up that evening." The Year 7s around us had now embarked on what looked like some sort of synchronized group dance.

"I see," said Darcy, putting his hand on my elbow and steering me through the Year 7s and out onto the dance floor. As he turned toward me, his left hand slipped automatically into my right and he put his right arm around my waist. "Anyway, I thought Frederick was talking about Charlotte—that is her room, isn't it, the tower room?" he continued, as if the fact that we were now gliding slowly around the room in a close embrace was completely normal. "I thought she was his girlfriend. So I felt I should warn Toby and tell him to be careful." He sniffed. "I know now that it was a misunderstanding, and that you shouldn't believe everything Frederick says. He talks a lot of crap, if you ask me, and—"

"Hang on—first of all, I'm curious as to how you know where Charlotte's bedroom is," I interrupted him. "And second of all, why are you still trying to keep her and Toby apart, even now that you know she's not with Frederick?"

Darcy pressed his lips together for a moment. "First of all," he replied, "I happen to know this old place like the back of my hand, and second of all, Charlotte's been acting rather strangely these past few weeks. She's been doing some detective work."

"Detective work? What do you mean?"

"Well, I've run into her in the west wing quite a few times recently. She seems very interested in the paintings in the portrait gallery. And the books in the library. She's been sneaking in there at night and looking through them one by one and . . . to be honest, I wouldn't be surprised if she was the one who trashed the place."

I gasped, furious, but before I could say anything, Darcy went on: "I know she's your best friend, Emma, but she was here four years ago when Gina went missing. I can't help feeling she might be mixed up in it all somehow. So I told Toby to keep his distance until we knew whether we could trust her or not."

"That's ridiculous. How could you not trust Charlotte? She's the nicest, most honest person I know. She would never have trashed the library. And I very much doubt that she abducted Gina at the tender age of twelve!" I shouted. I tried to pull away from Darcy, but he held me tight. "What are you doing?" I hissed. "And would you kindly stop insulting my friends?"

"Fine," said Darcy. "If Charlotte's as honest as you say she is, I'm sure she's already told you what she's been looking for in secret all this time."

"Not exactly," I admitted. "But I'm sure she has a perfectly good explanation." I bit my lip. Why on earth was Charlotte keeping secrets from me all of a sudden? What was going on? What was she doing poking around the west wing at night? I needed to talk to her, ASAP.

Darcy nodded. "I hope so," he said, letting go of me at last.

I resisted the urge to run off and find Charlotte immediately. Instead, I studied Darcy for a moment. "Since you're feeling so talkative tonight," I said, "perhaps you could enlighten me: What exactly have you got against Frederick?"

"Frederick," Darcy spat, making it sound more like a swear word than a name, "was a little too friendly with my sister. She had a crush on him, but she was very shy and—well, I think he enjoyed messing with her head."

"What do you mean?"

"I've talked to quite a few people about Gina over the past few days, and some of them said she'd mentioned something about Frederick—something about him being an enchanted prince. A mythical being who needed her help."

My mouth went dry. "She . . . she thought Frederick was the *faun*?" I stammered. "Do you think that might have had something to do with—?"

"Yes. I do," Darcy retorted. "And now I really have said everything I had to say." He bowed, the way I imagined the men here had bowed to their dance partners 190 years ago, and then he disappeared into the crowd.

I found Charlotte standing in a corner with the Berkenbecks. They were reading her the email from their dear Marie for what must have been the fourth time that evening. I grabbed her firmly by the wrist and dragged her away.

"Thanks," said Charlotte, the moment we were out of earshot. "Hannah escaped to the bathroom about ten minutes ago, but I didn't know how to get away from them without being rude. . . ."

"It wasn't you, was it? That trashed the library?" I asked quickly.

Charlotte's eyes widened. "No!" she cried. "Why would you even think that?"

"Darcy says he's seen you sneaking around the west wing at night, looking at the portraits, going through the books. . . ."

Charlotte's sigh told me there must be at least a grain of truth in these accusations. I looked closely at her. "What are you looking for?" I lowered my voice to a whisper. "Another chronicle?"

Charlotte tilted her head. "I have to tell you something," she said at last, slipping her arm through mine. "But not here. Come on."

The huge ballroom took up almost the whole of the first floor of the west wing—the only other room on this floor was a long narrow corridor that also served as the portrait gallery. Generations of the Stolzenburg and de Winter families looked down from the walls, watching the guests come and go. Charlotte led me past

Darcy's great-uncles and great-aunts (who all had the same long, straight nose as him) right down to the far end of the corridor. We stopped in front of a portrait of a man who must have been one of the very first residents of the castle. He was wearing a ruff and what looked like the breastplate from a suit of armor, and he peered down at us over the top of his curled mustache.

"Is that the lord of Stolzenburg?" I asked. He didn't look like a madman. Although with a mustache like that, he couldn't have been entirely sane.

"No," said Charlotte. "That's his great-great-great-grandfather, Earl Clovis of Stolzenburg, born 1566, died 1605. He was the one who built the castle."

"Oh."

Charlotte stepped in between me and the painting and looked me squarely in the face. "Listen," she said, "of course I've been doing some research! You didn't think I was going to sit there and do nothing while my best friend started messing around with what I'm pretty sure is some kind of occult artifact, did you?"

"Hmm," I said. In fact that was exactly what I *had* thought Charlotte was doing when, having warned Hannah and me about the chronicle so many times, she'd suddenly stopped mentioning it altogether. I'd assumed that Charlotte was too rational to accept what the book was really capable of—that she couldn't bring herself to believe in its magical powers—and that she'd found it easier to just ignore the whole thing and bury her nose in *Westwood Abbey* instead.

"So Darcy really did see you in here, and in the library. At night. On your own," I murmured.

Charlotte nodded. "There's all sorts of evidence about the history of the castle: *actual* chronicles, paintings, letters, old maps, and architects' drawings. And most of it's just lying around in the west wing, in boxes and dusty bookcases."

As I wondered why it had never crossed my mind to do some research into the book's origins myself, Charlotte continued: "I spent days (and nights) working my way through piles and piles of the stuff. Most of it wasn't very interesting—in fact, hardly any of it was. That's why I haven't said anything about it till now. But a couple days ago I was reading this old letter, and it mentioned something about a legend dating back to the sixteenth century. Old Clovis's time . . ." She gestured at the painting behind her. "Back then, the monastery in the woods was still up and running and the monks had decided to build a paper mill there, to bring some extra money in. But no sooner had the building work begun than things started going wrong: The foundations collapsed into the mud, wooden beams snapped in half for no apparent reason, some of the builders were injured, and the first time the mill was used, one of the monks fell under the mill wheel and was crushed to death. A few days later, both the mill and the monastery caught fire during the night and were almost burned to the ground. The monks managed to make seven books out of the paper they'd already produced, and they gave them to the Earl of Stolzenburg as a gift."

Charlotte turned to the painting. "See the top right-hand corner, in the background?"

"Yes," I said, stepping back to get a better view of the pile of dark-colored books she was pointing to. (Why were old paintings always so dark? Did the paint change color over the years or did painters in those days just have a thing for doom and gloom?) "But there are only six books there, not seven."

"I know—I wondered about that, too, at first," said Charlotte. "But then I read in another letter that the earl gave the first of the seven books—the prototype, if you like—to his steward, and the other six to his wife as a present when their second son was born. Apparently all seven of the books had the same power: the ability to make anything you wrote in them come true." Charlotte's voice was so soft now that it was almost a whisper. "At first the books brought the earl and his family great power and boundless wealth, but as time went on their luck seemed to turn. They couldn't control the consequences of what they wrote in the books, and they found themselves getting more and more hopelessly entangled in the situations they themselves had created, until one day—so the story goes—it cost the earl's wife and children their lives. After that, the earl threw all the enchanted books into the river to break the curse. But the seventh book, the one he'd given to the steward, couldn't be found and was never seen again."

"You're saying *the books were cursed?*"

"According to the legend, the monks had built their paper mill on top of a hidden palace that belonged to a fairy queen. In revenge for what they'd done, she put a curse on the mill, the monks, and the paper they produced." Charlotte looked piercingly at me. "Now do you see how dangerous all this is? Your chronicle is the seventh cursed book! The steward's book, the one everybody thought was lost!"

I blinked, slowly, then reached for Charlotte's hands and clasped them tightly in mine. "So . . . now we not only believe in magic and quite possibly a mythical faun, but also in fairy queens and ancient curses?"

Charlotte shrugged. "I don't know what I believe," she said. "Perhaps all these stories are just stupid fairy tales. But I'm still worried about you, Emma."

"Thanks," I said quietly, giving her a hug. "Thanks for sitting up at night researching all this stuff."

"I haven't been able to sleep much anyway, the past few weeks," said Charlotte as we moved apart. She was wearing her trying-not-to-think-about-Toby smile.

"I'm sure things with Toby will sort themselves out," I said. "I think it was all just a misunderstanding." A misunderstanding that was entirely Darcy de Winter's fault.

Charlotte blinked back tears. "Anyway. Shall we go back in and have a little dance?" she asked with forced cheerfulness.

I nodded.

The ballroom was heaving. Miss Berkenbeck glided past us in Dr. Meier's arms; the Year 7s had formed a circle and were taking turns dancing in the middle; and my dad was back from making his phone call and was dancing with Mrs. Bröder-Strauchhaus, who wanted to know all about his prize and what the lady from the European Commission had said.

Charlotte and I made a quick detour via the buffet to stock up on canapés and orange juice, then we wandered around the room for a while mingling with the other guests. We talked to Miriam and John in Year 13 about the choice of music (classical, but actually pretty good), the amount of people in the room (definitely too many), and the most bizarre dresses (an imitation snakeskin ball gown, seriously?!). Eventually we ran into Miss Whitfield in the crowd, though I didn't see her at first because she was bending down to pick something up.

"Oh, sorry," I said, rubbing my hip where I'd walked into her.

"No harm done, my dear," she muttered absently, slipping something small and silver into the pocket of her dress. Then she turned away from us and peered into the middle of the dance floor, where a boy and a girl were dancing the Hustle. I followed the direction of her glance, and a moment later I nudged Charlotte in the ribs. Frederick didn't seem to know the steps: He was laughing and making them up as he went along, while his partner tried valiantly to show him how the dance was meant to go.

"There she is!" Charlotte exclaimed. "I was starting to think she was going to spend the rest of the night hiding out in the bathroom."

The girl dancing with Frederick was none other than our good friend Hannah.

September 1794

My stay at Stolzenburg is nearing its end. Tomorrow I will begin my journey back to Hampshire. I am eager to see my home again, my friends and family, my dear sister. And yet I feel a certain sorrow: for all that I must leave behind, for all that has happened here. How I wish I could take this book and its wondrous powers back with me to England. But I have decided to leave it here, hidden in a safe place.

It is for the best.

This, then, is my last entry—these are the last words I will ever write in this chronicle. I will write new words on new pages, new stories on paper that is no more than paper. I will take my leave of this book and return without it to England, where I will live as an ordinary writer forever and always, without recourse to magic. The characters in my novels will do my bidding, but never again will I try to control real people and their real lives.

Farewell!

# 11

"YOU'RE *SURE* YOU'RE NOT ANGRY WITH ME?" HANNAH asked me in biology the next morning, for the third time. "I was so surprised when he asked me to dance that I wasn't thinking straight. And it was kind of fun, and it distracted me from Sinan—I've realized he's not really my type. But I didn't want to come between you and Frederick—"

"It's fine," I assured her, and carried on rummaging through my schoolbag for my pencil case. For some reason, the fact that Hannah had spent half the night dancing with Frederick didn't really bother me. Well—not much, anyway. Yes, I'd expected him to dance with me last night. And I'd been surprised that he hadn't asked me, and that he'd suddenly seemed so interested in Hannah despite the fact that they'd barely said a word to each other before yesterday. But I still hadn't felt jealous. Even I found that puzzling.

Because, for the past year and a half, I'd spent a considerable amount of my time pining after Frederick Larbach. He was good-looking, funny, and charming, and I'd genuinely thought I was in love with him. But this morning I suddenly wasn't so sure. Why didn't it bother me that he'd barely looked at me all evening? When had I last wondered what it would be like to kiss him? I'd been over the moon when he'd invited me out to the pub, but since then . . . Had things changed between us that night? Had I just not been aware of it until now? I suddenly realized that, for whatever reason, Frederick hadn't been on my mind as much as usual. And I felt sure of one thing: I still liked Frederick, but I didn't love him the way I'd thought I did.

All I could think about now was what Darcy had told me about Gina. Had she really believed Frederick was the faun? Might she even have been *right*? Was that why she'd disappeared? The very thought seemed absurd, and yet . . . only yesterday the book's powers had caused my father to win a prestigious award and the Berkenbecks to receive an email from their niece. Perhaps the idea that the faun existed wasn't so ridiculous after all? And if he *did* exist, because he'd been written about in the chronicle, then surely there must also be some truth in the story of the fairy who had given him human form? Perhaps Frederick's limp wasn't the result of an accident after all—perhaps that was what happened when cloven hooves turned into human feet?

Mrs. Bröder-Strauchhaus passed along the rows of tables handing out a test on the topic of photosynthesis, but I didn't even attempt to concentrate on the questions. The pictures of leaves and stems just reminded me of the sketches of the faun, who always appeared in the chronicle surrounded by plants and insects. Could such a creature really be hiding in plain sight, passing for a human being? And what *were* those little silver leaves that kept appearing everywhere—including the lord of Stolzenburg's laboratory?

Bent low over my test paper, I pretended to be working on the questions when really I was just doodling—little houses, trees, flowers, stars—and trying to get my head straight.

Okay. However crazy and surreal this whole thing was, I had to approach it logically if I was to have any hope of figuring out what was going on. Logically, and step by step. What did I know about Frederick, first of all?

Well, he'd grown up in the village. He came from a family that had lived here for generations and worked for the various earls of Stolzenburg. He'd been a student at the school and was now studying biology in Cologne. And he seemed to be involved somehow in what had happened four years ago. There'd been a connection between him and Gina, Darcy had said. . . . And now that I came to think of it, that night at the Golden Lion, Frederick *had* seemed very interested in Gina, and her ghost stories, and what Darcy had said about her disappearance. But that didn't necessarily mean Frederick was the culprit, did it? And if Frederick wasn't responsible for Gina going missing, then what *had* happened to her? Where was she? And who—or what—was the faun?

Damn it!

Something told me that the story about the faun and the fairy held the key to the whole mystery, but I didn't know how or why. Perhaps it hadn't been such a bad idea after all to write something in the chronicle about meeting the faun. I felt certain that once I came face-to-face with him, all my questions would be answered. Surely it was only a matter of time?

But time, unfortunately, was relative. As the hands of the clock crept around the dial and the biology lesson ticked by, I felt I was no closer to meeting the faun than I had ever been. I eventually managed to complete three of the ten test questions before the bell rang, but I dreaded to think what grade I was going to get in what was usually one of my favorite subjects.

And the rest of the day was no better. The hours passed completely without incident. Of course, everyone was still talking about the ball, and some people asked me about the few seconds I'd spent dancing with Darcy de Winter. But other than that, absolutely nothing out of the ordinary happened. Tuesday and Wednesday were just as bad. Lessons, homework, and studying for the upcoming tests took up almost all of our time. Charlotte, Hannah, and I spent our evenings bent over our books in the west wing library, now partially restored to its former glory thanks to Miss Whitfield's furniture. My dad, meanwhile, was busy giving interviews to the press (who were keen to speak to the winner of this year's International Educational Achievement Prize) and preparing for his trip to Brussels. The school had also been promised a large donation for the building of a riding stable (though not on Sunday evening as I'd planned; the call had come through on Tuesday morning). So the chronicle still appeared to be working just fine.

The only thing that hadn't happened yet was my meeting with the faun, and the more time went on, the more paranoid I became. On Tuesday I pondered the theoretical question of what the faun would look like, and whether he might perhaps be a metaphor for something else. On Wednesday I looked long and hard at everybody I met, examining them from head to toe. And by Thursday afternoon I'd started getting jumpy, expecting to see a huge horned beast come lumbering around the corner at any moment. That evening I checked for the three-hundredth time exactly what I'd written in the chronicle. Perhaps I would find some hidden clue in my own words, something I'd previously overlooked? But however many times I read the few brief sentences I'd written, their meaning didn't seem to change. All I got for my pains was a thumping headache.

On Friday night, I finally cracked.

I couldn't sleep—the duvet was sticking to me and my mind was racing so fast I felt sick. If I didn't find that stupid faun soon, I was going to have a nervous breakdown. Just lying here in bed tossing and turning wasn't an option anymore. I had to do something.

I sat bolt upright.

It was stuffy in the room—we'd forgotten to open the window before going to bed—but that didn't seem to bother Hannah, who was sound asleep. I swung my legs out of bed and pulled on my socks, sweatpants, jacket, and shoes. I urgently needed some fresh air. And I had a pretty good idea of where the faun might be hiding, didn't I? Perhaps it was time to pay him a visit, instead of just waiting for something to happen of its own accord.

Yes, this was a good plan: First I'd go and check the lord of Stolzenburg's secret laboratory, and if I didn't find him there I could always go down to the village, wake Frederick up, and confront him with my questions.

I tiptoed through the corridors of the castle and out into the darkness. It was refreshing to breathe in the cold night air as I hurried across the lawns. The grass deadened the sound of my footsteps, and its sharp, wet smell filled my nostrils.

The hulking ink-black silhouettes of shrubs and fountains loomed around me like sleeping monsters. The edge of the wood ahead of me was as black as the end of the world. For a moment I remembered the runaway circus lion. Then I entered the woods.

The uneasy feeling in my stomach grew stronger as I approached the ruins. Perhaps the faun was dangerous. Perhaps it was stupid to go looking for an ancient mythical creature alone and unarmed. But tonight my resolve was greater than my fear.

The ruined walls of the monastery were waiting for me, looking the same as they ever had. Could there really be a fairy queen's palace somewhere around here? I stepped through one of the archways and walked slowly along the nave. A gentle wind caressed my skin and the pockmarked face of the statue, its features worn flat by hundreds of years of wind and rain.

Since Hannah, Toby, Darcy, and I had first dislodged the stone slab and cleaned decades' worth of mud off it, it had become much easier to lift. But I still had to tug at it with all my strength to get it to move. I planted my feet on either side of it and leaned my whole weight backward. By the time I'd managed to shift it an inch or so, leaving an opening about two fingers wide, I was dripping with sweat. Panting heavily, I leaned back for a moment against the legs of the statue—and they gave way beneath me.

There was a grinding noise.

I leaped to my feet in alarm and watched as the slab slid sideways all by itself, revealing the entrance to the underground staircase. In the tunnels below, something else seemed to be moving: I heard the sound of rock grinding on rock and felt the ground vibrate beneath my feet. Then silence returned.

I turned around and stared at the statue. The faun's right knee looked odd, as if it had rotated 180 degrees around its own axis. I put out a hand and carefully pushed the stone back into its original position. The hidden mechanism immediately sprang into life again, a barely perceptible shiver ran through the ruined walls, and the stone slab slid back into place. Cool!

Intrigued, I was about to open the secret tunnel again when I heard a voice—a woman's voice—drifting toward me through the darkness. I flinched as if I'd been burned.

"Hello!" it called. "Is anybody there?"

My first instinct was to duck behind the nearest wall and hide. But before I could move a muscle, Miss Whitfield emerged from between the pillars. "Emma?" she asked in astonishment. She was wearing a dressing gown, with the hem of a very frilly nightie poking out from underneath it, and swinging a flashlight in one hand. "What are you doing here? It's the middle of the night!"

"I couldn't sleep," I said. "So I thought I'd go for a little walk."

Miss Whitfield eyed me disapprovingly. "You know that's not allowed—"

"I know," I said quickly. "I'm sorry. I'll go straight back to bed. Did I wake you up?"

She shook her head. "No. I was having trouble sleeping myself. I don't make a habit of wandering through the woods alone when I can't sleep, you understand; I usually do a spot of knitting to help me drop off. It's the dullest thing you can imagine, and it works a treat.

It *almost* worked tonight, too, until I spotted that gardener lad climbing out of one of the castle windows and running off into the woods. And you seemed in rather a hurry to follow him, young lady!"

"Er . . . ," I stammered. "Frederick was here?"

Miss Whitfield gave me a meaningful look.

"I didn't come here to meet him!" I cried. "I've got no idea where he . . . or why he . . . Which window did he climb out of?"

"I'd rather not talk about it here." She turned away from me and started walking. "But what would you say to a cup of lemon balm tea?"

Dolly, Dolly II, and Miss Velvetnose bleated softly as we passed them. (Perhaps they were dreaming about the juicy leaves Hannah had brought them the day before.) I soon found myself sitting in Miss Whitfield's chintz-filled living room holding a cup of steaming lemon balm tea, which apparently had a calming effect. As I sipped it, I tried to raise my little finger in the proper manner (even though it wasn't strictly necessary: Miss Whitfield wasn't an earl, after all).

"Wandering through the woods on your own at night!" chided Miss Whitfield, who'd seated herself in the armchair opposite me and was busy embroidering a handkerchief. "It's dangerous! And you'd do best to put that gardener boy out of your mind, by the way."

"I already have."

"Good."

The golden clock on the mantelpiece behind Miss Whitfield's head ticked quietly. I stirred another spoonful of sugar into my tea and cleared my throat. "Might I ask why?"

Miss Whitfield blinked. "Well. From what I can see, he's no gentleman."

"Because . . . because he's got no manners?" I pressed her. *Or because he's not a man at all?*

"Because the window I saw him climb out of was on the girls' corridor."

"I see." I took another sip of my tea. The hot drink was doing me good: The taste of lemon balm had calmed my nerves, warmed my throat, and caused my panic of the past few days to subside a little.

"Promise me you won't ever go out on your own at night again," said Miss Whitfield.

I would have liked to tell her what she wanted to hear, but I didn't want to lie to her. And now that I'd discovered the hidden mechanism in the statue, and I knew it was connected to the underground tunnels (perhaps it opened up new rooms and passageways?), I was far too curious not to carry on investigating. "The woods aren't that dangerous. It's not like they're full of wolves or ax murderers or anything," I replied evasively.

"No," said Miss Whitfield, looking at me intently. "But people have *disappeared*." Her words seemed to hang in the air between us like a dark cloud.

Then she turned her attention back to a violet she was embroidering in light blue thread, while I sipped my tea again. "I know," I said at last. "You . . . you were at the school when Gina de Winter went missing, weren't you?"

"I was on holiday when it happened, but naturally I was told about it," said Miss Whitfield, without looking up from her embroidery.

"Do you have any idea what could have happened?"

"No. All I know is that it was a terrible time for everybody. Particularly for her family." She laid her embroidery frame aside. "I've known the de Winters a long time—our families have been friends for generations. Gina was such a sweet, quiet girl! She would never have run away, whatever the police might say. She loved her family and Stolzenburg more than anything in the world. As did her brother. Even when they were tiny children, four or five years old, they used to play games about Stolzenburg. They used to pretend they were going to Germany to live in their ancestors' castle." Miss Whitfield sighed. "When she went missing it broke poor Darcy's heart. Gina meant the world to him. And to lose her like that, so suddenly . . . it changed him. Since she disappeared, he's become . . . harder, somehow. Cynical, withdrawn. I suspect it's because he can't stand the thought of being hurt that way again."

"Perhaps he feels guilty that he wasn't there for Gina when she needed him," I murmured.

Miss Whitfield shrugged. "Would he have been able to prevent it? Oh, if only we knew what had happened!"

"Hm." The clock on the mantelpiece chimed softly, and suddenly I realized something. "You said *people* have disappeared. Plural. Is Gina not the only one? Has it happened before?"

"Well." Miss Whitfield cleared her throat. "I couldn't tell you for certain—but as I said, my family has had links to Stolzenburg and the de Winters for centuries, and there have always been rumors about the castle and its inhabitants. As is often the case with old houses. Anyway, in the early 1800s one of the village girls is said to have vanished without a trace in the woods. Of course, this was long before Gina went missing and I don't believe the two cases are connected in any way. But clearly these woods are more dangerous than they seem. Which is why you, my dear, need to get yourself straight back to the castle and safely tucked up in bed. Agreed?"

The tea had made me pretty sleepy, and the thought of snuggling up in bed, pulling the duvet over my head, and closing my eyes was very tempting. But what I'd just discovered at the ruins was even more so. . . .

Feeling slightly guilty, I said good-bye to Miss Whitfield and set off back to the castle: But instead of going inside I looped around the edge of the south courtyard and headed back out into the woods. Taking a sheltered path that couldn't be seen from Miss Whitfield's window, I soon arrived back at the ruins. I marched straight over to the statue and twisted its knee again. I had to know what was down there, and I had to know now. I couldn't wait until morning.

I heard stone grinding on stone, felt the ground tremble beneath my feet, and watched as the slab slid slowly to one side, revealing the dark pit beneath. It finally came to rest with a muffled clank that sounded like a latch clicking into place. Then I climbed down into the hole, and the light from my phone (fully charged this time, thank goodness) danced over the steps and cast bizarre shadows on the rough stone walls. An ancient, musty smell filled my nostrils, and I shivered in the subterranean cold.

This whole thing had been a lot less creepy when Darcy was here. But I wasn't the type to be afraid of ghosts, or fauns. No: I felt cool, calm, and collected as I reached the bottom of the steps.

I was ready for anything. This was basically just a moldy old cellar, wasn't it? What was the worst that could happen?

"Is this a grave?" asked a voice from behind me. I jumped about a foot in the air and hit my head on the low ceiling. Ouch!

"It's only me," said Frederick, laying a hand on my shoulder. "Don't panic."

I rubbed my head. "I'm not panicking," I gasped, turning to face him. "But did you really have to creep up on me like that?"

Frederick was wearing his hair down, and it fell in soft waves onto his shoulders. His pale blue eyes glittered mysteriously, unsettling me more than I cared to admit. Was this it? My first encounter with the faun?

"Sorry," he murmured, taking a step toward me and lowering his voice to a whisper. "I was just so *intrigued*."

"Oh, yeah?"

He smiled his wry smile—the one that, not all that long ago, would have made me go weak at the knees. But now I seemed to be immune to its charms. I took a step backward. "I hear you've been climbing out of windows in the dead of night?" I said.

He raised his eyebrows. "I had to meet someone at the castle," he explained. "And on my way back to the village I decided to take a shortcut through the woods. But then I heard a weird noise coming from the ruins and turned back just in time to see you and Miss Whitfield walking away. Since you left I've been poking around trying to find out where the noise came from. But I'd never have thought of that thing with the statue." He pointed to the three tunnels branching off from the room where we were standing. Nothing about them seemed to have changed since my last visit. "So, what are these?"

"Oh, just some old secret passageways," I said nonchalantly.

"Wow!"

"I thought you said your family built them?" I eyed him suspiciously. Was he really surprised by the tunnels, or was he just pretending to be? Was he about to tear the mask off his face and reveal a pair of horns sprouting from his head?

"Yes, that's true. But I didn't know they still existed! How cool is that?"

Okay, fine. He seemed genuinely surprised to see the tunnels. "Shall I give you the tour?" I asked. Now I was the one to give him a wry smile.

The middle tunnel and the one on the left still formed a loop—no change there, then. But the third tunnel felt broader and higher than the last time I'd seen it. We walked along it in silence until we reached the lord of Stolzenburg's laboratory. Frederick wandered from bench to bench, his mouth hanging open in amazement. "Crazy! It's like an alchemist's laboratory," he marveled, picking up a dusty vial. "Perhaps someone was trying to find the philosopher's stone here hundreds of years ago. Or some other way to make gold."

"Perhaps," I muttered. But I was slightly distracted, because I'd just spotted a tunnel in the wall opposite me that hadn't been there before. The hidden mechanism had opened it up in the exact spot where Darcy and I had found the footprints last time. I turned back to Frederick. "Or perhaps they were trying to create a faun," I said, watching him closely.

Frederick's face darkened. He pursed his lips for a moment. "It does look as though this place might have something to do with the old legends, doesn't it?" he said quietly.

I nodded, and so did he, but slowly—almost in slow motion, with a strange, jerking movement.

I felt a sudden urge to get away from him. Was Frederick the faun, just as Gina had suspected? Had I fallen into his trap? Should I make a run for it, before whatever had happened to Gina happened to me?

But Frederick didn't turn into a faun: Horns didn't sprout from his head and his feet didn't morph into hooves. Instead he sank to the floor and squatted there on his haunches with his head in his hands. "Shit," he said tonelessly.

"What?"

He didn't answer but went on massaging his temples in silence. He kept his eyes closed. Suddenly he looked exhausted. There were frown lines on his forehead, and his shoulders sagged.

I sat down cross-legged in front of him and touched his elbow softly. "Frederick?"

He didn't react. Had he even heard me?

"Frederick!" I tried again, louder this time. "What's wrong?"

He sighed.

"Please, tell me. What happened four years ago? What do you know about all this?"

"Nothing," he said through gritted teeth.

"Come on, don't lie to me. What was Gina afraid of?"

Frederick opened his eyes then, and gave me a piercing look. "I have no idea," he said, enunciating every word a little too clearly, and stood up again. "Let's go, shall we?"

"But—"

"No!"

"You don't seriously expect me to—"

"Stop this, Emma! I don't know what happened to Gina!" he shouted. Then he strode swiftly across the laboratory and disappeared into the new tunnel.

I hurried after him.

I wasn't going to let him off the hook that easily. The uncertainty of the past few days had nearly driven me crazy, and I needed answers. But Frederick seemed determined not to give me any. He remained stubbornly silent as we continued along the tunnel, which led steeply downhill, deep down into the earth. After a while it came to an end just as surprisingly as it had begun, in front of a roughly timbered wooden door.

The door's hinges squealed as we pushed it open, and as we closed it behind us we heard a grinding noise far away, as if the stone slab at the foot of the statue were shifting back into its original position. The opening in the wall of the secret laboratory had probably disappeared, too, I thought.

Ahead of us, my flashlight beam fell on brick walls and a spiral staircase that led upward into the darkness. We climbed the steps without a word. It took longer than I'd expected to get to the top, but at last we came to another door. It looked a bit odd: thicker and heavier than an ordinary door. This was probably because—as I realized when we pushed it open—it was not only a door, but also a bookcase. A door disguised as a bookcase, concealed between two other bookcases, with a few old books on its shelves.

"Of course," I murmured.

"You've got a new sofa?" asked Frederick, pointing to the couch Miss Whitfield had given us.

"Mhm," I grunted, still gazing at the bookcase. So there *was* another way into the west wing library.

Over the next few days I couldn't help feeling there was something about this whole business that didn't add up. Gina had thought Frederick was the faun, but he certainly hadn't given that impression when I'd met him in the underground tunnels. And there was a hidden entrance to the west wing library, and a set of footprints in the secret laboratory—but did the footprints belong to Gina? Was it true she wasn't the first girl to have gone missing in the woods? When was I going to meet the faun? And what did Frederick know that he wasn't telling me?

I spent most of the weekend flicking through the chronicle, trying to piece together some kind of explanation for this madness. I read through my own entries and the stories about the faun again and again, and I studied the ink drawings and wondered whether somebody I knew, somebody here in the castle, could really be an enchanted beast in human form.

Unfortunately, Charlotte and Hannah had no time that weekend to discuss my outlandish suspicions, because we had our math exam the following Monday. I probably should have spent a bit more time studying. But with the best will in the world, I couldn't keep my mind on integrals and functions. So, as the three of us sat in the west wing library bent over our math books, I left it to

Charlotte and Hannah to work out the answers to the study questions while I cast another eye over the lord of Stolzenburg's entries in the chronicle. I also reread Eleanor Morland's first forays into fiction; her early attempts at fairy tales were very interesting indeed.

On Sunday evening, as Charlotte and Hannah cheerfully packed away their calculators, I realized I still hadn't even glanced at my math. But at least I now had a slightly better understanding of how the chronicle worked. Not wanting to completely mess up my exam, I decided to make a virtue out of necessity and tinker with my test results a little.

It wasn't really such a big deal if I came up with a few questions for tomorrow's exam and worked out the answers ahead of time, was it? It wasn't as if I was going to use a crib sheet, so it wasn't really cheating. And next time, I promised myself, I'd work very hard and do plenty of studying. Then I pulled out my pen, turned to the next blank page in the chronicle, and wrote myself a lovely little exam paper.

When I'd finished that, I turned my attention back to my other problems. I was still waiting for the faun to materialize, but in the meantime I thought it might be a good idea to focus on something else. What if Darcy, in the course of his inquiries, were to stumble across a vital clue about what had happened to Gina? Once we knew what had happened to her we'd be able to figure out where she was, wouldn't we?

Yes—that sounded like an excellent plan.

I smiled to myself and started writing.

Today saw the founding of one of the first secret societies in the history of Stolzenburg. Its name is Westbooks, and its headquarters are located in the west wing library, which has been specially cleared out for the purpose. Regrettably, the first meeting of the club's founding members (who must, of course, remain anonymous) was disrupted by an unfortunate incident. It turns out that Darcy de Winter, who is currently staying at the castle, is a complete and utter moron. Although the club members offered in the most polite and accommodating way to turn down the volume on the literary film they were watching, so as not to disturb his sleep, he announced that his family owned the castle and proceeded to kick the whole club out. (I hope he chokes on the books in the library he stole from us.)

Other than that, of course, Stolzenburg remains the most brilliant school in the world. All the staff and students are back from their holidays, ready for the new school year, and everyone is looking forward to the next few months. Miss Berkenbeck and Dr. Meier in particular seem to be getting on very well lately. They practically kissed in the dining hall today. . . .

# 12

"HOW ABOUT A BIT OF CHOCOLATE?" I WAVED A CHOCOLATE bar under Charlotte's nose, but she merely shook her head and buried her face in her arms. Hannah looked pale, too, and so did the rest of our class. Since our exam had finished twenty minutes ago, we'd been sitting in the conservatory in a state of shock, trying to come to terms with what had just happened. Some people had started crying even before the end of the test; for others, like Charlotte, the panic had only set in after they'd handed in their papers. Some, like Sinan and me, hadn't even realized there was a problem until the others had told us.

But now we all knew that there had been something wrong with the exam questions—something very wrong indeed. When the chronicle had inserted my new questions into the test, it had somehow combined them with Mrs. Bröder-Strauchhaus's original questions; the result had been mathematical mash-ups so complicated that even a Nobel Prize–winning mathematician would have had trouble solving them.

I hadn't even realized there was anything amiss—I'd just sat there filling in the answers I'd prepared beforehand, without even looking at the questions. And to Sinan, who found any kind of math completely baffling, today's test had been just as impenetrable as any other. But for everyone else, the past two hours had been a form of torture. This was an important exam and Mrs. Bröder-Strauchhaus, who'd delivered the papers that morning and then promptly retired to bed with the flu, was not known for her leniency.

"We never learned any of that in class!" Hannah complained to Jana and Giovanni. The three of them were flicking feverishly through a book of formulas.

"There was something wrong with those questions. How on earth were you supposed to find the value of $x$ in question four?" demanded Giovanni, while Charlotte wept quietly beside me.

I huddled deeper into the sofa and gnawed at my bottom lip. Damn, damn, damn! This whole thing was my fault. I'd caused this chaos. And I felt terrible about it.

Perhaps that was why I'd slept so badly last night—because I'd had a premonition that something like this was about to happen? I'd dreamed that the paper dragonfly had appeared and warned me about the book, telling me to throw it in the river. (I hadn't taken the warning seriously, of course—and it would have been too late to change anything, anyway.) The dream had felt frighteningly real, though, and the dragonfly had seemed even creepier than usual. . . .

But never mind all that now: The question was, what was I

going to do about the exam? Apologize to the class? Go and see Mrs. Bröder-Strauchhaus and tell her the truth? "Erm, so, I have this magic book that can make things come true and I used it to change the exam questions—sorry"? It didn't seem like a great idea, unless I wanted people to think I was stark raving mad. Surely Mrs. Bröder-Strauchhaus would see for herself that something had gone wrong and give us a new test. Right? I desperately hoped so. But either way, I knew I had to apologize.

"Er, Charlotte," I whispered, tugging at her sleeve, "I think I might have messed up. Big time."

"What do you mean?" Charlotte sniffled. "Have you got a tissue, by the way?"

"Sure." I fished a pack of tissues out of my schoolbag, but before I could hand them to Charlotte I heard her blowing her nose. Someone had beaten me to it. Someone tall and blond, who was now settling himself on the sofa next to Charlotte.

"What happened?" asked Toby.

As Charlotte told him about the math exam from hell, I studied Toby closely. He looked almost as exhausted as Darcy. There were dark rings under his eyes and his hair was scruffy and unkempt. But something about Charlotte's presence seemed to have re-energized him. And now—now he was even putting an arm around her shoulder!

"Oh, man," he said. "Sounds like you're having a pretty terrible day."

Charlotte, surprised by the touch of his arm, turned toward him and gazed into his eyes for a long moment before nodding. "Pretty terrible," she agreed. Then she broke into a smile. Okay. . . .

I decided to give them some space. "I, um . . . have to go and sort something out," I said, and hurried out of the conservatory.

Five minutes later I reached the west wing, where I climbed the stairs and knocked on Darcy's door. It was a long time before I heard movement on the other side, but eventually a key turned in the lock, the door opened a crack, and Darcy poked his head out. "Emma," he said curtly. "What do you want?"

"You let Toby off the leash, then?"

Darcy made a face. "He's my friend, not a dog."

"Oh—I'm glad you finally figured that one out."

"I realized I had to let him make his own decisions," he said quietly. "And since you don't seem to think Charlotte is doing anything untoward . . ."

"Charlotte was just worried about me. She was trying to help."

"By poking around the west wing?"

"You don't get it."

"No, I don't, unfortunately."

I sighed. "Anyway, I'm glad you're not trying to come between them anymore."

He nodded, graciously and a touch too smugly. "Okay. I'm afraid I need to get on now." Darcy tried to close the door, but I shoved my foot in the way.

"Get on with what?" I asked.

He didn't answer.

"Listen," I began, "I know we get on each other's nerves and we're not exactly friends or anything. Especially not after what happened on the open day. In the woods, I mean, when you told me that you . . . but I didn't . . ."

"I'm not ashamed of my feelings," Darcy broke in. "Perhaps my words were a bit clumsy, but they were honest, just like your answer was. I don't hold it against you. It's water under the bridge."

"Er . . . good. Well then . . ."

"But I would be very grateful if you'd leave me to get on now, Emma. I don't see the point in continuing this conversation. And I really do have a lot to do. So. Good-bye." He edged my foot out of the doorway and closed the door with a bang.

"Wait!" I cried. After all, the main reason I'd come up here was to see whether my latest entry in the chronicle had had *any* kind of positive effect. "Have you found any more clues?" I called through the door. "I found a secret entrance to the west wing library on Friday night! I really think you should let me help you look for Gina!" Had I really just offered to help him find his sister?

The key turned in the lock again and Darcy's head reappeared. He looked at me, frowning.

"I'm sure you could do with some help, couldn't you?" Ever since Miss Whitfield had told me how much Gina's disappearance had changed Darcy, I'd found his arrogance less off-putting. And I needed answers, too, just like he did. Darcy looked thoughtfully at me for a moment, then cleared his throat. "Would you like to come in?" he said.

The room was unrecognizable. I'd only seen it once before, through the en suite bathroom that led onto the west wing library. But I definitely didn't remember it being this messy. The four-poster bed in the middle of the room had at least been usable before: Now every square foot of space was covered in stuff. There were piles of clothes and cuddly toys on the bed, and the floor was littered with books, Barbie horses, CDs, several laptops, girls' shoes in various sizes, board games, dolls, bottles of nail polish, a silk painting frame (accessories included), and various cardboard boxes overflowing with notebooks, photos, and letters.

"Erm . . . ," I said as Darcy closed the door behind us. I looked from him to a pair of pink sandals on the floor (which were definitely too small for him) and back again. "What is all this stuff?"

"It was Gina's."

I surveyed the piles of children's toys. "I thought she was sixteen when she went missing."

"She was." Darcy stepped gingerly across the room, trying not to tread on the bottles of nail polish, and sat down on the floor beside a battered cardboard box. He picked up one of the plastic horses (a unicorn with a pink mane and a glittery horn on its forehead) and turned it over gently in his big hands. "This is pretty much everything she ever owned. Everything I could find, anyway. I brought some of it with me from England, but a lot of it was still here in the castle. Packed away in one of the lofts."

"So now you're sorting through her things?" I spotted a stack of French vocabulary flash cards by his left knee.

"I thought it might help me understand."

"And? Is it helping?"

He tilted his head, and suddenly he didn't look sullen and sneering anymore, just exhausted. Only now did I notice his tousled hair. It was almost as if he'd tried to tear it out in handfuls. The rings under his eyes looked dark blue against his pale skin, and his cheeks were haggard; he probably wasn't eating enough, closeted away up here all the time. It was as if I was suddenly getting a glimpse of the real Darcy. As if he'd not only invited me into his room, but also allowed me to look past his mask of reserve and pride.

"I've been reading through her old exercise books and lesson schedules and I've found out a few things," he said, "but what I really need is a diary or something—I could have sworn she told me she kept a diary. But wherever it is, I can't find it. I've been through all of her stuff, and I've even searched the classrooms and her old bedroom—sorry about that, by the way—but I haven't found anyth—"

"Sorry about what?" I stepped over a pile of dolls and sat down on the floor beside him.

Darcy shrugged. "I thought she might have kept it in a secret hiding place under the bed, or under a loose floorboard or something. It's possible."

I let out a long breath. "Are you telling me it *was* you who trashed the library? You've been lying about it this whole time?"

"No, of course not!" Darcy shook his head vehemently. "I'm not talking about the library, I'm talking about Gina's old bedroom. Which is now occupied by other students. You and Hannah, to be precise.

"You searched *our* room? Without asking us?"

"Yes—as I said, I'm sorry. But I had to know, I couldn't wait. I hadn't been here very long and I didn't really know you. Otherwise I might have asked you if I could search your room, instead of climbing in through the window in the dead of night. Or at least I would have realized that no one patrols the school corridors at night anymore, so I could have just walked up the stairs instead of nearly breaking my neck scaling the castle walls."

"Oh—you *might* have asked me. How very considerate of you," I scoffed. Perhaps behind his mask Darcy was still a stuck-up, arrogant . . .

He sighed, and suddenly two pieces of the puzzle slotted together in my mind.

"That was the night of the First Lesson, wasn't it?" I remembered how I'd woken up shivering, and found the window ajar and the chronicle lying open on my bedside table.

Darcy nodded. "I didn't find any secret hiding places in the room, but one of your books did catch my eye—I just opened it quickly to see what it was, but then you suddenly woke up. I managed to hide behind the curtain just in time. Obviously, I never would have read *your* diary without permission."

I closed my eyes for a moment. So Darcy had still been in the room when I'd sneaked off to the kitchen to make myself a sandwich. That was why the window had been open again when I got back. He'd waited for me to leave and climbed out the window, empty-handed. Gina hadn't hidden her diary anywhere in her bedroom. Although perhaps she'd . . .

Oh.

My.

God.

I went cold. Goose bumps crept up the back of my neck, and for a moment I forgot to breathe.

How could I have been so stupid this whole time?

So blind!

So dense!

"Emma?" Darcy returned the plastic unicorn to its herd, then put out a hand and gently touched my shoulder. "What's wrong?" he asked, alarmed. "Why have you gone so pale? Don't you feel well?"

"I . . . ," I croaked. "W-wait here, okay?" I leaped to my feet. "I'll be right back. Stay where you are!"

I dashed out of the room and ran all the way to the east wing, taking the stairs to my bedroom two at a time. When I got there I lurched over to the dresser, yanked the sock drawer open, grabbed the chronicle, and set off back to the library at a run. I fumbled with the book as I went, trying to open it to the page I was looking for, and halfway to the library I almost collided with Hannah as she emerged from the conservatory. "Has something happened?" she called after me, but I was in too much of a hurry to answer. "Later!" I panted as I veered around the next corner.

When I got back, Darcy was pacing up and down the room (which was no mean feat, given the amount of clutter on the floor), but the moment he saw me in the doorway he stopped and came toward me. "Please tell me what's going on," he said.

"Here." I held out the book. On the way back I'd opened it to one of the pages written by my predecessor—the person who'd been using the chronicle four years ago.

Darcy's eyes widened as he took it from me. He ran his fingertips gently over the paper. "Gina!" he stammered. "This is her writing, this . . ." He tore his eyes away from the page and looked at me with fierce intensity. His dark caramel-brown eyes blazed. "*You*," he breathed. "You had her diary?"

"Yes," I said. "No."

He raised his eyebrows.

"It's not really a diary—it's actually a kind of chronicle,"

I explained. "About the school and the castle. Lots of people have written in it—I have, too. And . . . well, so has Gina, but I didn't realize that until just now. I think before she disappeared she must have been using it as a diary. But the thing is, it's . . . it's not a normal book. This book is special. It's . . ." I took a deep breath. "It's different from other books."

I'd been about to say *magic*, but the word had gotten lost on its way to my lips. I couldn't bring myself to say it out loud. And perhaps that was for the best. Did I really want Darcy to know the whole truth? I did feel I could trust him now, in spite of everything. But it probably wasn't a bad idea to be cautious.

Darcy hefted the chronicle in his hands. "It looks old," he remarked, turning the pages very gently. "And valuable." He didn't understand, of course. For him, the most important thing about the book was the fact that it was Gina's diary. It was no more and no less than the vital clue he'd been searching for all these weeks. The vital clue I'd written that he should find! At least I'd gotten something right.

Darcy hurriedly swept aside some of the books and boxes, making enough space on the window seat for us to sit comfortably side by side. "I think we should go through everything Gina wrote, line by line. This is going to help us find her, I'm sure of it." He grabbed my wrist and pulled me toward him. I'd never seen him like this before—so excited, so animated, with that hopeful tremor in his voice. Was this what he'd been like before Gina had gone missing? I found myself smiling.

"Okay," I said. "Let's do it."

We sat down on the window seat with the book between us and started reading.

I was already familiar with a few of Gina's entries. The one about the First Lesson four years ago, for example. And the one about the blueprints for the new sports hall. I'd also read some of the passionate poems she'd written (although as a rule I was *not* a fan of dramatic declarations of love). But there was much, much more to discover. Gina had been extremely prolific. I found several entries I'd never noticed before—as if there were hidden pages in the chronicle that gradually revealed themselves over time.

We spent the next few hours poring over Gina's entries. But they were so confusing—sometimes even unsettling—that our initial euphoria at having found a new clue soon turned to unease. Clearly, Gina had not been very happy. Many of her entries spoke of homesickness, self-doubt, and how upset she was that her brother had no time for her anymore. She wrote that keeping a diary wasn't helping, but was only causing more problems. Had Gina been one of the few chroniclers who'd realized how the book worked, and had gotten themselves helplessly embroiled in problems of their own making? It certainly looked like it. Because Gina, just as I'd suspected, had been looking for the faun.

We read about how she'd come across the old legends, how she'd started searching the castle, how she'd discovered and explored the secret tunnels. It all felt eerily familiar. Gina, too, had been impatient to meet the faun, and had spent hours lingering by the statue in the woods wondering where he could be hiding.

And then, one day, she'd found him.

Suddenly the tone of her entries changed. They sounded happier and more animated. Gina kept mentioning a new friend—a "creature." She wrote that she wanted to save him, that she would do whatever it took to help him. There was no doubt about it: Gina had found the faun. If her entries were to be believed, he might still be here in the castle even now!

I couldn't believe I'd never noticed these lines before; perhaps it was because I'd always found Gina's entries so dull that I'd tended to skip right past them. And Darcy seemed to be having trouble with these new revelations, too. "I don't get it," he said at last, after we'd read about twenty or thirty entries. "Gina wasn't some kind of fantasist. What made her suddenly start believing in fairy tales? Particularly some weird faun creature living here in the castle? It's ridiculous! Kids' stuff!"

"Well," I said, smoothing out the pages, "like I said, this book is different from other books. It . . . it sometimes makes you believe in things you'd never have thought possible under normal circumstances."

Darcy looked at me blankly.

I shrugged. "What would you say if I told you that . . . that for quite a while now I've been wondering the same thing myself?" I asked. "Whether the faun exists, I mean." My voice shook a little as I said it.

Darcy's nostrils flared. "I'd offer to take you to the doctor."

"I thought so. You and my dad have something in common there, you know . . . ," I tittered nervously.

"Er—Emma, are you okay?"

"Of course."

"You believe in the faun, too?"

I looked down at the chronicle without speaking.

"Come on, Emma, you can't be serious. I mean . . . *why?*"

Then my eyes fell on Gina's next entry, and I noticed that it was dated several months later than the previous one. "Well, you know what a naïve little kid I am," I muttered distractedly. Gina's tone had suddenly changed again; even her handwriting looked different somehow. Wilder. More rushed. Something must have happened between this entry and the last. Something important.

Darcy sighed. "I shouldn't have insulted you like that, and I'm s—"

"When exactly did Gina go missing? December 2013?" I broke in.

"Yes, December fourteenth." He took the book out of my hand. For a while he read in silence, and as he read, his breathing grew shallower. Then he passed the chronicle back to me.

Gina's entries for December made for horrifying reading. Something had clearly upset her very much. She kept saying she felt stupid and betrayed, and in some places the paper was rippled and the ink smudged with tears. Her poems became darker, bleaker. Gina seemed to have tried several times to speak to Darcy about something, but either she hadn't been able to find him or he'd given her the brush-off. And then she mentioned another name: Frederick.

Frederick?

*It's time*, she'd written in her last ever entry. *He's waiting for me by the river.*

Oh God.

I looked up. "She was going to meet Frederick by the Rhine," I whispered. "The night she disappeared."

Darcy had turned even paler. He pressed his lips together so tightly that all the color went out of them, and his shoulders shook with rage. "I knew it," he shouted. "I always knew it! That bastard!"

Without warning he drew back his arm and punched a pile of books and boxes, hard. Too hard. They swayed for a fraction of a second and then toppled over toward him. I flinched, but Darcy didn't even bat an eyelid—he managed to catch the boxes in midair and stand them upright again. My heart was in my mouth: I'd had a vision of Darcy lying on the floor buried under a pile of Gina's schoolbooks, not breathing. The thought made my blood run cold, and I blinked hard in an attempt to rid myself of the horrible image.

"Frederick . . . ," I said. "Why was she going to meet him? What does he have to do with all this? Do you think they'd been planning to run away together and something . . . went wrong?"

Darcy took a deep breath. "What she wrote about the river— it fits with something I found out recently," he said. "It turns out the rowing club lost one of their boats that December. It wasn't discovered until a few days after Gina went missing, so nobody ever knew whether it had been stolen that night or washed away in a storm three nights later."

"So they stole a boat to escape in together," I mused. "But only Gina disappeared. Frederick's still here. Why would that be?"

"Perhaps Gina didn't leave of her own accord," said Darcy flatly. "Perhaps Frederick *made her disappear.*" His skin had taken on a grayish tone, and his fists were clenched.

What Darcy was saying made terrifying sense. Perhaps that was why Frederick had been so keen to find out how much Darcy knew. "But why would Frederick . . . ? Gina hadn't done anything to him."

"No," said Darcy. "I don't know. And I should have listened to her." He'd picked up the chronicle and was leafing through Gina's final entries again. "She needed me, and I didn't even realize it. She wanted to tell me something. I . . . I probably could have stopped it." He looked at me, his eyes dark with the despair that had gripped him ever since his sister's disappearance. Now it threatened to eat even deeper into his soul.

"You don't know that. It might not have changed anything," I said in an attempt to console him. But he wasn't listening.

"If only I'd been there for her," he murmured, bowing his head so that his forehead rested against the window pane. Suddenly I thought I understood: Darcy was not particularly forgiving of other people's mistakes, but he judged his own just as harshly. Forgiving himself was something he found very difficult to do. And now that he knew Gina had been in desperate need of his help . . . I laid a hesitant hand on Darcy's shoulder. I half expected him to shake it off, but he didn't move, so I left it there. What kind of a game was Frederick playing with us? What had happened between him and Gina?

"Should we go to the police? Show them Gina's entries in the chronicle, tell them they should question Frederick again?" I asked at last.

Darcy shook his head. "Not till we have proof. Not till we've figured out exactly what happened and what those bloody fairy tales have got to do with it."

"And how are we going to do that?"

Darcy turned to face me. The determination in his face made me drop my hand from his shoulder.

"We'll think of something," he said. "Are you . . . Do you still want to help me?"

I nodded and picked up the chronicle. "It's my diary, too, so I'd like to take it with me if that's okay."

"Of course."

I turned to go, but then a thought occurred to me. "What—er—what was going on back then, that meant you didn't have time for Gina?" I asked. "What was keeping you so busy?"

"Nothing," he said. "Nothing important. I was a stupid kid—I was only sixt . . . er, sorry . . . I mean, I was an idiot back then. But fortunately I've got a bit more sense these days."

"How come?"

But Darcy clearly had no intention of going into details. "Didn't you say you'd found a secret entrance to the west wing library?" he asked, edging past a heap of dolls, an iPod, and some childhood photo albums till he reached the bathroom door, then he beckoned to me to follow.

A moment later, we entered the library. I led Darcy over to one of the bookcases at the far end of the room, the one that had only a few books left on its shelves. I pulled them out one by one until I found the fake book that operated a hidden mechanism when you tilted it, unlocking the door. "I came through from the other side last time," I explained as the bookcase swung open to reveal the spiral staircase beyond. "You can get to the lord of

Stolzenburg's laboratory from here. Do you remember the foot-prints we found in the dust? There's another secret door in the wall just there."

"I see." Darcy pushed past me into the darkness and for a brief moment, as he drew level with the bookcase, my heart started pounding again and I was overwhelmed by a sudden, irrational fear that something was about to happen to him. This time, though, I understood why. My subconscious must have been trying to tell me this for weeks, but it was only now that I remembered. I remembered what I'd written in my first ever entry in the chronicle.

I pressed the worn cloth binding to my chest. Back then, of course, I hadn't known about the book's powers; I hadn't realized that whatever I wrote would eventually come true. I'd only written what I'd written because I'd been furious with Darcy for throwing us out of our beautiful library. But that didn't change the fact that I'd put him in terrible danger. I'd written that I hoped he would choke on the books he'd stolen from us.

I knew by now that it sometimes took quite a while for the book's magic to take effect. But it always did, sooner or later. It was just impossible to predict when and how it would happen.

Had I foretold Darcy's . . . ?

I didn't even dare think it. But I felt my own words hanging over us, dark and heavy, ready to come crashing down on Darcy at any moment. Probably when I was least expecting it.

Shit. I bit my lip and tasted blood.

Then I followed Darcy into the secret tunnel.

I still can't believe it!

Why?

Why?

WHy?

How could he do something like this? Is that how he sees me? As a joke? As a stupid little girl?

Is that all I am? That's how I feel at the moment. Stupid. And alone.

Where the hell is Darcy?

# 13

WHEN HANNAH AND I CAME DOWN TO BREAKFAST THE next morning, it was immediately obvious that there was something going on. The dining hall was full of little groups of students whispering to one another, and the table where Helena usually sat was surrounded by a whole crowd of people, although Princess von Stein herself was nowhere to be seen. The teachers also seemed less relaxed than usual. To judge by the looks on their faces, something pretty serious had happened.

Hannah and I exchanged a glance. "Have we missed something?" she asked.

I shrugged. "Looks like it."

We made our way over to our usual spot by the window, where Charlotte and Toby were feeding each other Nutella on toast while gazing deep into each other's eyes. Ah, young love!

"Morning," I said loudly, while Hannah sat down next to Toby and reached unabashedly for his bowl of muesli.

"Cool, they've got a new cereal!" she exclaimed. "Can I try some of yours?"

"Sure," mumbled Toby, with his mouth full of toast.

I poured myself a coffee. "So," I began. "What's going on?"

Charlotte raised her eyebrows. "Well: It turns out there's been a bit of a misunderstanding, but it's all sorted out now and . . . Toby and I are together!" she explained. "But you knew that, didn't you? You were there when we—"

"I didn't mean what's going on with you two," I said with a sweeping gesture that took in the rest of the dining hall. "I meant this!"

Charlotte looked around the room. The whole of the school seemed to be clustered around Helena's table by now, whispering excitedly. Meanwhile, Mrs. Bröder-Strauchhaus and Dr. Meier were walking grimly toward the table where my dad was sitting. "Have you noticed anything unusual?" Charlotte asked Toby.

He shook his head and wiped a bit of Nutella from the corner of Charlotte's mouth with his thumb. "No, why?" he asked, gazing at his girlfriend as if she were the eighth wonder of the world. "Your hair looks like liquid gold in this light, you know."

"Really? Thanks. And your freckles . . ."

I sighed. "Hannah, we won't get any sense out of these two today. Let's go and get you some muesli and see if we can figure out what all this fuss is about."

"Just a second." Hannah quickly polished off the last few mouthfuls of Toby's muesli and drank the rest of the milk straight from the bowl. Thus fortified, she followed me to the serving hatch, where the Berkenbecks, as usual, had laid out a generous breakfast buffet.

Sinan was there, shoveling scrambled eggs onto his plate, and he helpfully filled us in on the morning's gossip: Apparently, Helena had had a man in her room last night. (I wondered how Charlotte could have failed to notice *that?*) Mrs. Bröder-Strauchhaus had caught Frederick climbing out of Helena's window in the early hours of the morning; it turned out they'd secretly been dating for months.

When she heard this, Hannah reached instinctively for my hand and squeezed it. "That—that arsehole!" she exclaimed.

But the fact that Frederick had been giving me and everybody else the runaround didn't bother me as much as my friends might have expected it to. For a while now I'd suspected Frederick of being capable of something far, far worse than this.

So it was Helena he'd been visiting, then, the night Miss Whitfield had seen him climbing out the window. Now that I came to think of it, I'd seen him with Helena several times recently . . . at the ball, for example. And hadn't he taken her side against Darcy and Toby in that argument about the desk, when we'd been setting up the dining hall for the open day? The two of them had clearly enjoyed their little deception; Frederick had even gone so far as to flirt with me, when secretly he'd been seeing Helena all along. But none of that really bothered me. I'd known for quite a while now that I no longer had feelings for Frederick. And I now suspected him of such a terrible crime that nothing he did could surprise me anymore.

No: What really puzzled me was the fact that Charlotte hadn't known anything about it, despite the fact that she and Helena shared a room.

When we got back to our table a few minutes later I asked her about it. "Last night . . . oh, I must have . . . I must have slept very deeply," muttered Charlotte, blushing to the roots of her hair (which she usually did only when somebody mentioned *the incident*).

Toby took a sudden interest in some toast crumbs lying on his plate.

"Okay," I said. "I get it. But this thing with Helena and Frederick must have been going on for quite a while. Did you really not know anything about it?"

Charlotte shook her head. "We're not exactly bosom buddies. We only really speak to each other when we have to. I did suspect she had a boyfriend—she'd started spending ages on her hair and makeup, and she used to sneak out sometimes—but I never realized it was Frederick she was seeing." She lowered her eyes. "And you know I've been reading a lot recently, spending half the night in the library . . ." She broke off.

A shadow fell across our table. Only now did I realize that the noisy chatter in the room had ceased abruptly and a great many faces were turned in our direction. I turned around to find Darcy standing right behind me.

"Hi." I looked up at him, and he glanced at each of us in turn. It was the first time in over two weeks that he'd shown his face in the dining hall. And once again he looked as though he'd barely slept a wink. Yesterday we'd wandered around the secret tunnels for what felt like hours in search of fresh footprints, but apart from mine and Frederick's, we hadn't found a single one. Had Darcy carried on searching—was that why he hadn't slept?

"Come and sit with us," Toby offered.

But Darcy made no move to accept the invitation. Instead, he bent down so that his mouth was close to my ear. "I've had an idea," he said quietly. "Would you have time again this evening?"

"Yes—er—of course," I stammered. "What's the plan?"

"I'll tell you later. I'll come and knock for you. Shall we say six o'clock?"

"Okay."

"Thanks." Darcy nodded, then crossed the dining hall with long strides and was gone almost as suddenly as he had arrived.

Hannah, Charlotte, and Toby stared at me.

"Do you have . . . a *date?*" said Hannah incredulously. "I thought you two hated each other."

"Hmm," said Toby under his breath.

"We do," I assured her. "I'm just helping him with some research, that's all."

"About his sister?" asked Charlotte.

"Yes. Among other things."

"Well, good luck with that," said Toby wearily. "I'm at my wits' end, personally."

I was about to ask him what he meant when I caught sight of my dad staring down at his toast and marmalade, on the verge of tears. Had something happened? This had to be about something more than Helena and Frederick's secret rendezvous. Was my mom okay? My throat felt tight.

"Excuse me." I got up and hurried over to the teachers' table. Usually my dad and I stayed out of each other's way during the school day; he liked to talk to his colleagues at mealtimes, and I always sat with the other students. But now Miss Whitfield was patting his shoulder sympathetically. *Something must be very wrong.*

To my relief, however, it turned out that my mom was fine. What had happened was that the school office had received a call with some very disappointing news: My dad's prize had fallen through.

The lady from Brussels couldn't apologize enough: There had clearly been some kind of mix-up and my dad's name had accidentally ended up on the wrong list. She had no idea how it had happened, but the whole thing had been a mistake and although she was sure Dad was doing fantastic work at Stolzenburg, the prize obviously had to be awarded to its rightful recipient.

Oh, no! Had the book's effect worn off too soon?

I gave my dad a hug. "Don't be upset. You're still the best head of school I know."

"We'd already told everyone! The press, the parents, the alumni! It's so embarrassing!" wailed my dad, blowing his nose into a tissue.

"No, Dad!" I said. "It's the jury who should be embarrassed. They're the ones who made the mistake." Or rather: I was. I was the one who'd messed this whole thing up. It certainly wasn't my dad's fault. Oh lord, what had I done? "Shall I come over this afternoon and help you sort out your medicine cabinet?" I asked in an attempt to cheer him up. (My dad loved going through his medicine cabinet looking for out-of-date drugs that needed throwing away, or low stocks that needed replenishing.)

"That's bound to take your mind off things," Miss Whitfield chipped in, still patting my dad on the shoulder. "And after that you can both come over and have dinner with me. I'm making roast beef with roast potatoes and Yorkshire pudding."

My dad nodded and blew his nose again.

"Oh—er—I'm busy this evening, actually," I stammered. "I promised Darcy de Winter . . ."

"Young Darcy can come, too. That's a wonderful idea," said Miss Whitfield. "I promised his mother last week that I'd keep an eye on him. She was ever so surprised when I mentioned to her on the telephone that he was here."

"I don't know if we'll be able to make it—we've got . . . ," I began, but Miss Whitfield was having none of it.

"You must come. It's an old family recipe I don't often cook anymore," she insisted so emphatically that to refuse the invitation would have gone against all the rules of etiquette we'd learned in her classes. My dad seemed to have reached the same conclusion. "Thank you, we'd love to come," he said, although the look on his face said he would much rather have spent the evening tucked up in bed with a hot water bottle and a copy of *The Modern Child*.

Miss Whitfield hurried off, perhaps to tell Darcy the good news. Weird.

My dad's medicine cabinet was (as expected) in tip-top condition. But we still managed to spend over two hours sifting through bottles of pills and arranging them in order of color and size. As we did so, Dad's mood lifted considerably: He always felt happier after reminding himself of all the ailments, injuries, and illnesses he was equipped to cure. I was feeling so guilty that I even agreed to count all his tablets for him one by one, so it was pretty late—nearly six o'clock—by the time I headed back to the castle.

I didn't have time to change when I got back to my room, but that didn't matter—after all, Darcy and I were *not* going on a date, as I had to explain to Hannah (who was sprawled on her bed reading a magazine) for the second time that day. I had just enough time to hang up my wet swimming things and tie back my hair, which I'd allowed to dry naturally, in a bun that closely resembled a small bird's nest. I still had my school blouse on, and a well-worn pair of favorite jeans, and the whole ensemble looked a little bit rough and ready. But who knew: Perhaps I would set a new trend among the lower school?

Then there was a knock on the door.

Darcy leaned against the doorframe while I put my jacket on. He glanced at my hair for a moment, then back at my face. "We'll need to be quick," he said. "I have an invitation to dinner at Miss Whitfield's. Thanks to my overprotective mother."

"So do I—thanks to my father." I zipped up my jacket. "So, what's the plan?"

"We're going to do a little breaking and entering," Darcy whispered, quietly enough so that Hannah couldn't hear.

I gasped. "Where?"

"Come on."

Darcy had to duck his head as he lowered himself into the driver's seat of the dark green Mini, now parked in a proper parking space. I clambered into the passenger seat and scanned the dashboard in front of me—it was littered with used ferry tickets (Dover to Calais), three empty bottles of Gatorade, a bag of peppermint drops, and a map of Cologne that Toby must have used during his trip there.

The in-car computer flashed into life as Darcy started the engine, but he didn't turn on the radio or enter a destination into the GPS. Instead he drove straight out of the parking lot and down the hill. Wherever we were going, it seemed Darcy already knew the way.

Being a sensible person, I would never have gotten into a car with a stranger. And Darcy wasn't a stranger—I'd known him for almost a month, after all. But I still felt slightly uneasy as we sped through the woods. I had no idea where Darcy de Winter was taking me: Darcy, who spent his nights rooting through his sister's old toys and barely slept a wink, who was arrogant and rude, who'd told me he liked me and been rebuffed. . . . I couldn't help but recall that the last time I'd left the castle with a guy, it had not ended well.

"Er—where are we going?" I asked, and at the same moment Darcy steered the car into a space between two trees and stopped.

"Here," he said. "We could have walked, but given that we're a bit pushed for time I thought it would be better to drive. Logistically speaking."

We got out of the car. A few yards ahead of us was a sign saying STOLZENDORF, and Darcy strode past it in the direction of the village. As I followed him, I vowed to myself that I would not set foot in the Golden Lion again under any circumstances. But Darcy wasn't taking us to the pub. He turned down a side street and stopped in front of a crooked little half-timbered house. There was a carpentry workshop on the ground floor, and on the window ledges of the floor above were window boxes full of faded geraniums. LARBACH BROS—CARPENTERS AND JOINERS was painted in peeling letters above the door.

"So you really are planning a break-in," I observed.

Darcy shrugged. "We'll just have a quick look around his room and see if we can find any clues."

"And what if he catches us? Or his parents do?"

"They go bowling in Rindsdorf on Tuesdays, and Frederick's working at the castle till eight o'clock. So there shouldn't be anyone at home. But we probably shouldn't hang around here in the street for too long—it looks suspicious."

I looked discreetly up and down the street, but there was no sign of any neighbors or other witnesses. "Okay—let's go."

I half expected Darcy to have a master key for this house, too, but he didn't, and nor did he need one. The Larbachs had left their back door unlocked (as everybody did in Stolzendorf) and we were able to walk straight through their back garden into a storage room at the rear of the house and up the stairs to their flat.

Frederick's bedroom was at one end of a narrow hallway, and it was tiny. The wall was plastered with various posters of cars and one of Jessica Alba on a beach; the bed was unmade and the desk was cluttered with piles of books about plants and folders of lecture notes. On the windowsill was an empty yogurt container, which was starting to go moldy, and the air had a stale, musty smell. I would have liked to open a window, but I didn't dare touch anything.

Darcy did not share my scruples. He marched across the room and threw open the window. Then he opened the drawers in

Frederick's desk. "You could have a look under the bed," he told me, "if you want to make yourself useful."

I crouched down and peered into the shadows under the bed. But all I could see were a few socks and a spider with hairy legs. Ew!

"What exactly are we looking for, anyway?" I asked, without taking my eyes off the spider.

"Evidence," Darcy replied. "Anything that might lead us to Gina. Something that once belonged to her. A photo. Some clue as to what happened between them. I don't know."

"Hmm." I stood up again and had a poke around in the drawer of Frederick's bedside table, but all I found were a few magazines, a flashlight, and a packet of condoms. There was nothing interesting in the wardrobe, either—just a load of clothes, an old hockey stick, a couple of tennis balls, and a scuffed skateboard with no wheels.

"Somehow I don't think Frederick's the type to keep a diary," I said.

Darcy, who had just finished searching the desk and the bookshelf beside it, nodded in agreement. "It's not looking good." He sat down on the floor by the bed and leaned back against the mattress.

I did the same, but because I was so fixated on the spider (I was determined to keep as much distance as possible between it and me) I ended up sitting too close to Darcy, and for a moment our thighs touched. I felt his muscles tense, and then he shuffled away from me. Of course. Of course he didn't want *that* kind of closeness anymore. Not after I'd rejected him and hurt his pride. What was it he'd said? *It's water under the bridge.* Well, good.

Although . . . I was starting to think my first impression of Darcy hadn't been entirely accurate. He'd had his reasons for keeping Toby away from Charlotte, after all. And the way he'd rescued me after my embarrassing dip in the fountain, the way he was doing everything he possibly could to find his sister . . . He clearly wasn't as bad as I'd first thought. I almost felt sorry for the things I'd said to him by the ruins that day. I could at least have been a bit more polite.

"Sorry," I muttered.

Darcy acted as if nothing had happened. "This is a dead end," he said. "If there was any evidence here he must have destroyed it long ago."

"Or hidden it in a safe place."

"But where?"

"I don't know." I cleared my throat. "I . . . I was rereading some of Gina's entries last night," I began.

Darcy looked at me. "I'm listening."

I took a deep breath. What I'd read the night before had been weighing on my mind ever since. "I looked at her poems again. In the later entries, there are quite a few of them where she wishes she was . . ." I hesitated a moment, not wanting to say the word out loud; but then I did say it, quickly and sharply, like ripping off a Band-Aid. "Dead," I said. "She wishes she was dead, or that the world would end."

"I know. They're pretty melodramatic. But don't lots of teen-agers write stuff like that: about death and everlasting love and God knows what else?"

"I don't mean—it's just that . . ." I didn't know how to explain without sounding completely ridiculous. But perhaps that was precisely the point. Perhaps it was time I stopped caring what Darcy de Winter thought of me, stopped caring whether he saw me as a mature young woman or a naïve little kid. Perhaps it was time for me to genuinely help him: To tell him the truth. I gulped. "I think she might have gotten her wish. To be dead, I mean," I told him. "Because she wrote it down."

Darcy raised his eyebrows.

"The chronicle is not just an ordinary book, and I think Gina knew that. From the things she wrote in the weeks before she went missing, it sounds as if she knew what the chronicle was capable of, and she was acting on that knowledge. The book . . . the book has special powers, you see," I stammered. "It can make things happen. But it's dangerous, too—I realize that now. I was naïve to think otherwise." Then I told him everything, right from the beginning, about the lion, the math exam, my dad's prize, my fears about the faun. Darcy listened to me in silence. When I'd finished, he said: "I can't say I believe it, Emma. Magic! Magic doesn't exist."

I nodded. "Of course you don't believe it. Even *I* still think it's completely ludicrous." I sighed. "I thought I was so grown up. And here I am telling you, hand on heart, that I believe in magic. And a faun. And possibly a fairy queen. Sorry, but I . . ."

Darcy shot me a warning glance and put a finger to his lips. I fell silent immediately. Now I heard it, too: voices, from downstairs.

Shit.

There was a clattering sound. Footsteps on the stairs. A man and woman talking.

With one quick movement Darcy was at the door, listening through the gap.

The woman laughed at something the man had said.

I tiptoed over to where Darcy was standing. What were we going to do now? What were Frederick's parents doing back already? I looked at my watch. It was only twenty to seven.

Frederick's dad hummed to himself as he crossed the hallway, a door creaked on its hinges, and a moment later we heard him turn on the shower. From the other end of the flat came the clink of saucepans and cutlery. Okay, so they weren't coming into Frederick's room. They were both occupied, for the moment. I nodded to Darcy, who pushed down on the door handle very, very gently. Then he grabbed my hand and pulled me with him into the hallway.

We crept silently across the threadbare carpet. The shower was running and the radio was on in the kitchen. But still I held my breath as we tiptoed toward the front door. Then, out of the corner of my eye, I saw something moving—a shadow. I jumped. Darcy ducked behind a narrow cabinet and pulled me with him onto the floor. I pressed my back into the wall behind me and felt tiny beads of sweat forming on my forehead.

Frederick's mom came hurrying past us and opened the door to a little pantry. She was tall and bony, and made me think of a crow in a flowery apron. She stood for what felt like an eternity in front of a shelf of preserves before finally selecting a jar. My heart was pounding. This was only postponing the inevitable. When she turned around she was going to look right at us, and then . . .

We shrank even farther into the shadow of the cabinet. My heart was beating so loudly that it seemed a miracle she hadn't heard it yet. But she was too close for us to risk leaving our hiding place. Damn it! What we were doing might not exactly be a robbery, but it certainly counted as trespassing. My dad would not be happy. In fact, I wasn't sure his nerves could stand it if the Larbachs decided to call the police and Darcy and I were brought back to the castle in a police car.

The shower stopped running.

Frederick's mom picked up a jar of cherries in brandy, closed the pantry door, and turned around, still reading the label. She walked past us without looking up, and went back into the kitchen.

I was about to let out my breath when the bathroom door opened, directly opposite our hiding place. It opened slowly, because Frederick's dad was still drying himself as he stepped out into the hallway, and a cloud of hot, steamy air drifted toward us. He hadn't seen us yet. He finished drying his neck and stepped back into the bathroom to hang up the towel.

It was now or never!

At the same moment, Darcy and I leaped to our feet. This was our chance. We burst through the door into the stairwell and ran headlong down the stairs. We made a lot more noise than we would have liked, but by this point we didn't care: All we wanted was to get out of there. We rushed through the storage room, across the back garden, and out onto the street. From there we ran all the way back through the village to where the car was parked. Only then did we come to a halt.

Only then did Darcy let go of my hand.

We collapsed into the Mini, gasping for breath.

"That was close," I said at last. My heart was still hammering so hard, it felt as if it might burst. We'd snuck into someone else's house and nearly been caught. We'd committed a crime! The adrenaline coursed through my veins. But we'd escaped! We'd pulled it off! I suddenly felt wonderfully light.

Darcy looked at me. "Yes." He grinned. The twinkle in his eye made him look much younger than usual. "We did a pretty good job. Maybe we should turn professional."

"Professional housebreakers?" I asked, and now I found myself grinning, too. "Sounds cool."

"I reckon we've got what it takes. How about we try a bank robbery next?"

"Or a roast dinner?"

Darcy glanced at the clock on the dashboard. "Oh, crap!" he exclaimed.

Then he started the engine.

September 1794

"I have found the one who loves me for who I really am," the faun told the little fairy. "You must help me take off this cloak, so that I can show my beloved my true face."

The fairy fluttered up into the air and buzzed around the faun's head for a moment.

Then she started to laugh.

# 14

Darcy and I arrived at Miss Whitfield's cottage about five minutes late.

"Well, you both look very chipper, I must say," she said as she let us in. "And it's a good thing, too—your dad could do with a bit of cheering up, Emma."

My dad was already in the living room, where Miss Whitfield had set up a small table; he had his head in his hands and was staring gloomily at the wall. The cheering effect of our afternoon sorting out the medicine cabinet seemed to have worn off, I thought as I sat down next to him. Miss Whitfield seated herself at the head of the table and removed the silver covers from an array of plates and bowls, all full of piping hot food.

"Do help yourselves," she urged.

I unfolded my white linen napkin and arranged it on my lap. What was the etiquette for an informal dinner again? Did you have to do things in a certain order? Did you have to offer a dish to the other guests before serving yourself?

"Come along now, don't be shy," said Miss Whitfield as I was pondering these questions. "We don't want it to go cold!"

Fair enough. I helped myself to vegetables and gravy. Yorkshire pudding wasn't really my thing, but the rest of the food was delicious. I hadn't realized until now how starving I was after a day of swimming, clearing out my dad's medicine cabinet and, of course, breaking into the Larbachs' house. Crime certainly did give you an appetite.

"So you two met up before dinner, did you?" Miss Whitfield inquired as I shoveled a second helping of beef onto my plate. "What did you get up to?"

"We just went for a little walk down to the village," said Darcy. "And by the way, Miss Whitfield, I'd be grateful if you didn't mention anything else about my stay here to my mother. I'm sure my parents aren't particularly happy that I've come here without telling them."

"I'm sorry I gave the game away," said Miss Whitfield. "And I do understand that you want to find out what happened to your sister. I respect that."

"Thank you," said Darcy.

"Could you pass me the green beans, Emma?" said my dad, and I handed him the bowl.

"Have you been able to find anything out? Any new information? Something the police overlooked, perhaps?" Miss Whitfield asked.

Darcy and I exchanged a glance. We silently agreed not to mention our suspicions about Frederick for the time being.

"Not really," Darcy replied. "I'm still going through Gina's old school stuff. But Emma recently found an old diary of Gina's." He shrugged. "We're hoping that might tell us something."

Miss Whitfield smiled. "Yes, it might—young girls confide all sorts of things in their diaries. They did in my day, anyway. I hope it will prove useful." She turned to my dad. "Can I interest you in a little more roast beef, Rasmus?"

"No, thank you," said my dad. "I have to watch my cholesterol. And I must say, I don't feel very well all of a sudden. I feel as though my throat's swelling up. And my tongue feels so heavy."

I sighed. "Have a drink of water then," I said. My dad, when he spent too long poring over the instruction leaflets for his various medicines, had a tendency to start suffering from imaginary side effects: This evening was clearly no exception. He'd probably convinced himself he was having some sort of allergic reaction. "Take a deep breath, and . . ."

But I got no further, because at that moment Dad passed out.

His eyes rolled back in his head and he slumped forward. I only just managed to grab him by the shoulders before he fell face-first into his plate of food.

"Oh my goodness!" cried Miss Whitfield.

Darcy already had his phone out. "I'll call an ambulance."

"Yes, quick!" I bit my lip. Dad hung limply in my arms. Why did it have to be the school nurse's day off today, of all days?

Together we maneuvered my dad onto a little sofa by the window. I put a cushion under his head and two more under his feet. Was it his blood pressure? How small he looked, lying there motionless with his eyes closed, his skin pale, and his hair straggly. Dad felt ill most of the time, of course, but his ailments were usually imaginary, and it was a shock to see him like this. For the first time in all these years there was genuinely something wrong with him.

This situation was new to me, and I was completely at a loss as to how to deal with it. What was Dad suffering from? An allergic reaction? Epilepsy? A heart attack? How did you put someone into the recovery position again? Shit, I had no idea! Might it even have been one of my entries in the chronicle that had caused this? Had *I* done this to Dad?

My mouth went dry, and the blood pounded in my ears.

Darcy paced up and down the room while we waited; he kept going to the window to look for the ambulance. Miss Whitfield held Dad's hand, and I stroked his cheek and checked every few seconds that he was still breathing.

"Wake up," I whispered. I vowed to myself that I would never be careless with the chronicle again. "Please wake up."

And then, after a few minutes, Dad's eyelids twitched. They fluttered open; he blinked and peered at me as if he was returning from somewhere very far away. "What happened?" he mumbled.

"You collapsed," I whispered, choking on a sob. "It was so sudden. It was awful!" A tear slipped out of the corner of my eye and rolled down my cheek. "How do you feel now? Can you breathe?"

He seemed to ponder this for a moment, then nodded.

"You gave us quite a shock!" said Miss Whitfield.

When the paramedics arrived a few minutes later, they couldn't find any indication of Dad having suffered an allergic reaction, an epileptic fit, or a heart attack. They said he must have become dehydrated and had a dizzy spell. In all the commotion about his prize, he simply hadn't had enough to drink (which meant that his collapse was mainly my fault; man, I felt so guilty). So the paramedics put him on a drip, and as the fluid flowed into his veins the color gradually returned to his face. Soon he was able to sit up again.

I put my arms around his neck and buried my face in his shoulder. If anything had happened to him I would never have forgiven myself. "I'm sorry, Dad," I whispered into his shirt, as he stroked my hair with a trembling hand. "My poor little Emma," he whispered. "My poor little Emma. I'm so sorry—I didn't mean to frighten you."

"How about a nice strong cup of Earl Grey?" Miss Whitfield suggested.

After we had drunk our tea my dad got up to leave, saying he was tired and wanted to go to bed. At first I wanted to go with him and keep watch by his bedside overnight, just in case, but Darcy and Miss Whitfield persuaded me not to. After all, the paramedics had assured us that there was nothing to worry about, and that Dad just needed to make sure he kept drinking lots of water.

Later that evening, as I headed back to my bedroom, I was still feeling guilty about Dad's fainting fit. I certainly wasn't in the mood for a conversation with Frederick Larbach. But Frederick Larbach was the very person I happened to run into—sneaking around on the girls' corridor again! He just couldn't help himself.

"Hey, Emma!" Frederick smiled his crooked smile. He looked perfectly normal. His ponytail looked normal, his gardening overalls looked normal. But this was the guy whose house I'd just broken into, whose bedroom I'd searched; this was the guy I suspected of having been the last person to see Gina de Winter alive, of having stolen a boat, rowed her out into the middle of the Rhine, and then . . .

"H-hey," I stammered. *Do murderers look normal? Come on, Emma, keep it together.* "I thought Mrs. Bröder-Strauchhaus had banned you from the castle. Because of last night," I said, in what I hoped was a chatty tone.

He nodded. "Yes," he said. "The news has gotten out, then."

"What did you think would happen?"

He rubbed the back of his neck. "Now you're pissed off with me."

"You think I'm *pissed off*?" This seemed so absurd, what with everything else that was happening, that I almost had to laugh. I wasn't "pissed off" with Frederick. I had way more important things to worry about.

He lowered his eyes. "Well, I did flirt with you a bit, and I thought you'd noticed and you—"

"Don't worry about it. I wasn't interested."

He sniffed. "Okay."

"Or rather, I stopped being interested quite a while ago," I corrected myself. Why did I feel the need to justify myself to somebody who'd led me on like that, who'd made me think he liked me when in fact he already had a girlfriend? Somebody who, I was fairly sure, had committed an unspeakable crime four years ago? I pushed past him.

"Good night," I said with as much dignity as I could muster. But Frederick hurried after me and grabbed me by the shoulders. "What were you and Darcy doing this evening? What did you find out? You have to tell me, Emma, do you understand me?" All trace of the crooked smile had vanished.

I bit my lower lip. "Nothing," I said, looking at the floor.

Frederick scoffed. "I'll find out, anyway," he said, "with or without your help. So do us both a favor and tell me what Darcy de Winter is up to. Tell me!" He shook me so hard that my head jerked back and forth. Fear shot through me. Had he been this rough with Gina?

"You're hurting me," I hissed, and I had a sudden urge to run, to get away from him. It wasn't far to my room. But Frederick held me in a viselike grip.

"If you don't let go of me right now, I'm going to scream. I'm going to scream at the top of my voice," I threatened. If he was caught here again it would cost him his job, at the very least.

Frederick loosened his grip. Furiously, I wrenched myself free and strode off without a word.

"If you start spreading rumors about me, you'll regret it," he murmured from behind me. "You have no proof of any of this bullshit. Darcy has nothing on me. Nothing at all."

I didn't wait to hear any more but ran off down the corridor, threw open my bedroom door, and slammed it shut behind me. Then

I leaned back against it and took several deep breaths, waiting for the pounding of my heart to subside.

"Just five more minutes," muttered Hannah. She was sitting at her desk, where she'd dozed off over her homework (English poetry). Now she stretched and yawned widely. "I should probably go to bed," she murmured. Only then did she catch sight of my face. "Has something happened? You look as if you've seen a ghost."

"Something like that," I said. "My dad fainted, and then I had a bit of a run-in with Frederick." To say nothing of my and Darcy's narrow escape from the Larbachs' house. I sighed. All in all it had been a pretty rough day.

But the rough day gave way to an even rougher night. For a long time I couldn't get to sleep, and I tossed and turned fretfully. There was too much going on in my head, too many questions gnawing at me. The chronicle, the stories about the faun, my dad's collapse, the secret tunnels, Gina's poems, Darcy's search for clues, Frederick's strange behavior . . . They all seemed to be related somehow, but I just couldn't see how. I couldn't help feeling I'd overlooked something important. Something that was right under my nose.

No—enough now. I had to stop letting my imagination run away with me, otherwise I really would end up going mad. Just like the lord of Stolzenburg. So I forced myself to stop going over and over everything in my mind; I even resisted the urge to pick up the chronicle and start looking back at the things I'd written to see how they'd turned out. Instead I focused on counting sheep, with my headphones plugged into my phone and the music turned up so loud that it drowned out the voices in my head.

It must have worked, because some time later I woke up with a jolt.

There was somebody standing over my bed, looking down at me.

It was somebody I never would have expected to see here. Well—obviously I wouldn't have expected to see *anyone* here, in my bedroom, at this time of night, except perhaps the paper dragonfly from the dream I'd just been having. I blinked, and suddenly I was wide awake.

It was dark—it must have been the middle of the night. The sound of quiet snoring issued from Hannah's bed.

But I hadn't been imagining things—there really was a figure standing by my bed.

"Emma," Miss Whitfield whispered. "Where's the book?"

I sat up. "Wh-what?" I stammered. "What are you doing here?"

She put her hands on her hips. "Give it to me. Now."

"What?" I said again. "What's going on? Is it my dad? Is he okay?" I swung my legs out of bed and started searching frantically for my slippers, but then I realized that if Dad had fainted again— if his life was in danger—it hardly mattered whether I had warm feet or not. I lurched toward the door, barefoot.

But Miss Whitfield barred my way. "This has nothing to do with your father. I want the chronicle, Emma. *The chronicle!*" Her voice shook, but her tone was adamant.

So it wasn't about my dad, thank goodness. Relief flooded through me, immediately followed by confusion. What *was* Miss

Whitfield doing here then? How did she know about the chronicle? I decided to play dumb for the time being. "What chronicle?" I asked innocently.

But Miss Whitfield wasn't fooled. "Don't lie to me, Emma," she snapped. "I know you have it. You told me so this evening. Gina's diary. That's when I realized."

I narrowed my eyes. I'd never seen Miss Whitfield like this before—shoulders quivering, lips pursed, and a look in her eyes that was enough to chill the blood. I'd never known her to be so rude, either. What had happened to the friendly old lady who just a few hours ago had been serving us tea in flowery china cups?

I gulped. "The chronicle," I said. "What do you know about it?"

"Enough," Miss Whitfield replied. "More than enough, I'm afraid to say. But I never realized it was . . . When Dr. Meier had that funny turn in the dining hall, and then the very next day a lion appeared in the woods—that was when I first suspected somebody might have gotten hold of it. But I had no idea it was you. After all, the creature almost attacked you and Charlotte and your young friend." She sighed. "Be that as it may. I have been searching for this book for a very long time. It is dangerous, and I need you to give it to me before something dreadful happens." She held out her hand.

But I didn't move.

"So you know about it? About its *powers*?" I whispered, a thousand questions flashing through my mind. "How? What is it? Why is it so . . . special? What was it doing lying around in the west wing library?"

"*That's* where you found it? Well, well, well."

"Er—"

"That's interesting. Very interesting."

"Really? How come?"

Miss Whitfield looked me in the eye. "Legend has it that the book is cursed, Emma," she said. "There was a paper mill on the banks of the Rhine . . ."

"Yes, I know the story. An evil fairy queen put a curse on the monks and their paper, and the seven books that were made from that paper had supernatural powers, which brought misfortune to their owners."

"Exactly."

"So you believe in the legend? You think it's true?"

Miss Whitfield nodded.

The fact that she was barring my way to the door, and the angry glitter in her eyes, should have shocked and scared me. But instead I felt an overwhelming sense of relief that there was somebody else out there as crazy as me. Somebody who believed in the existence of a fairy queen. What was more, that that *somebody* was a grown woman—a teacher. And she'd always seemed so sensible and matter-of-fact.

"Okay," I said. "What about the faun in the fairy tale? What do you think about that? Does he really exist? Could Frederick . . ."

Miss Whitfield sighed impatiently. She batted away my questions with a quick wave of her hand. "Give. Me. The. Book," she ordered, taking a step toward me. "Then I'll explain everything, I promise. Where have you hidden it? Is it here in your room?" She came even closer, close enough for me to see that she was trembling with suppressed agitation.

I took a faltering step backward. "W-well," I stammered, but my eyes instinctively darted toward the bed and gave me away.

"Under your pillow?" Miss Whitfield exclaimed. "Emma! Everybody knows that's the first place a thief would look!"

She marched past me before I could do anything to stop her, plucked the pillow off my bed, and dropped it carelessly on the floor. "Good," she said. "I would have been surprised if you'd hidden it there. I knew you were clever enough to find a more creative hiding place." She knelt down to look under the mattress, then opened the drawer of my bedside table and rummaged around inside it.

I made no move to stop her.

I was too busy looking at the empty space where my pillow had been.

Oh, crap.

Where was the book? I'd put it under my pillow that morning and I hadn't touched it since. It couldn't have fallen down the side of the bed or Miss Whitfield would have found it by now.

Damn, damn, damn!

I snapped out of my reverie and threw myself to the floor. Panicked, I groped around under the mattress, grabbing the lamp from my bedside table and shining it into every nook and cranny.

"Emma!" barked Miss Whitfield at last, having given up on her own futile efforts to locate the chronicle. She stared at me for a moment. "Please tell me this doesn't mean what I think it means. Where is the chronicle? Give it to me! GIVE IT TO ME! NOW!"

"What's going on?" piped up Hannah sleepily from across the room. It was a wonder she hadn't woken up before now, really, given that we'd just turned half the room upside down a few yards from her bed.

But Miss Whitfield took no notice of my roommate. She was still staring at me, unblinking. "Think, Emma. Where could it be? Who might have taken it?" she demanded.

"I—I don't know," I admitted. "I honestly don't."

"Miss Whitfield?" Hannah was up and out of bed in a flash. "What are you doing here? In the middle of the night?"

But Miss Whitfield clearly had no desire to explain herself again. She rounded on Hannah. "Did you take it?"

"N-no. Take what?"

"The book," I said.

Hannah pressed her lips tightly together. "I don't know what you're talking about."

Miss Whitfield heaved a deep sigh. "Think, Emma! Think hard," she insisted. "And as soon as you think of anything, come to me. We have to find that book." Then she stood up. Her long skirt swished as she hurried to the door, and in the doorway she turned back for a moment. "It's important. The chronicle has done terrible damage in the past. Anybody who comes into contact with it is putting themselves in grave danger."

"Why, though?" I asked. But Miss Whitfield had already disappeared.

Hannah and I exchanged glances. "What was up with her?" said Hannah. "And what does she know about the book?"

I shrugged. "A lot, by the sounds of it. But that's not even our biggest problem. The book's gone."

"WHAT?!" Hannah cried. "I thought you were just bluffing so she wouldn't be able to take it away from us."

I shook my head. "Somebody must have come into our room and stolen it."

"Somebody other than a nutty old deportment teacher, you mean?" said Hannah. "But why? Anyway, I've been here all evening. If somebody did come in it must have been during the day—during lessons or at lunchtime . . ."

"Yes," I said distractedly. I'd suddenly realized what it was I'd been missing all this time. The thing that had been right in front of my nose but that I'd never quite been able to grasp. Perhaps that was because I'd never really given very much thought to Miss Whitfield. She'd never seemed even remotely suspicious, and before now it wouldn't have crossed my mind to associate her with the faun or the chronicle or any of the other weird things that had been going on at Stolzenburg.

But now, looking back, I remembered something: The night Hannah and I had gone to Miss Whitfield's cottage to collect the furniture for the library, I'd caught a glimpse of one of her old family photo albums. Suddenly the black-and-white photographs came back to me in vivid detail.

In the background of one of the pictures, I'd spotted the entrance to the secret tunnel at the foot of the faun statue. I'd been so transfixed by the underground staircase that I'd hardly paid any attention to the woman in the foreground of the picture: a woman in a lace dress and gloves, holding a parasol, who had posed for the photographer by the ruins over a hundred years ago.

But if I had, I surely would have realized at the time that the woman in the photograph looked exactly like Miss Whitfield.

September 2017

This is obviously ridiculous. There's no way this thing actually works. A magic book! Seriously?!

But hey, I'm gonna give it a try—just for a laugh. Obviously it won't work because it's completely impossible. But in the unlikeliest of unlikely events that this is not a complete joke and everything I've ever believed about the world we live in is false, I'll give it a try. Just in case this isn't a joke. Just in case it's the explanation I've been looking for all this time.

I think someone should . . . go sleepwalking. Yeah, that would be funny. Emma Morgenroth is going to get out of bed tonight and roam the corridors of Stolzenburg in her sleep, having a weird dream she can't wake up from. And she won't be the only one. Let's think, who could I get to keep her company?

# 15

I N MY DREAM THE FAUN AND I WALKED IN THE SHADE OF THE woods. Side by side we wandered through the trees and the undergrowth, our steps cushioned by a carpet of pine needles. The air was mild and smelled of flowers and the faun played a tune for me on his flute, silvery notes that shimmered in the leaves and branches.

It was a sad tune, and the melody felt familiar—so familiar that I instinctively began to sing along: "And I wait between the lines, in the darkness of the night, I hear . . ."

I was still wondering where I'd heard or read the words to the song before, when I heard a steady pattering sound in the treetops, a sound that felt out of place on that summery morning. The soft forest floor turned cold under our feet, and wet, and slippery.

The flute fell silent.

Suddenly an icy wind began to blow, driving raindrops into my face. The faun, and my dream, slowly melted away.

And then I opened my eyes and gasped. All of a sudden I was wide awake.

Just inches from my toes was a sheer drop. I was balanced on a narrow wall, seven stories high, swaying dangerously in the wind. What the hell was going on? How had I ended up here?

I'd been safely tucked in bed, I knew that much. After Miss Whitfield had left our room (and I'd realized that, for reasons I couldn't explain, she appeared in a photograph that was over a hundred years old) I'd tossed and turned for quite a while. But I had eventually managed to get to sleep—only to wake up teetering on the roof of the west wing tower. I wasn't alone, either: Out of the corner of my eye I saw something moving. A tall, dark-haired young man was walking along the battlements, perilously close to the edge, with his eyes tight shut. As I watched, Darcy de Winter placed one foot in front of the other, wobbled in the wind, and leaned out over the gaping void beneath us.

Shit!

Without thinking I launched myself at him, grabbed him by the shoulders, and hauled him back from the edge in the nick of time.

We fell backward off the slippery battlements and onto the roof of the tower. We landed so hard that the back of my head was dashed against the stone and I almost slipped back into unconsciousness, back into the dream I'd been having a moment ago. A fragment of song drifted through my mind: *I hear wings, gossamer-fine* . . .

But then I remembered where I was; I saw the misty early

morning sky above me and felt the ice-cold raindrops on my cheeks. I heard Darcy groaning beside me.

"Aargh," he moaned, rubbing his head. "Emma? Where are we? What happened?"

I shook my head. "No idea. I was asleep—I only just woke up." I gulped, and added in a whisper: "Right on the edge of the roof."

Darcy looked blankly at me for a moment. "So we've been *sleepwalking*?" he said at last. "Both of us? And we both just happened to end up in the same place?"

"I'm pretty sure it wasn't a coincidence," I said darkly.

We sat up. Only now did I notice what Darcy was wearing—I was sure I'd seen that flowery fabric before, the night I'd run into Miss Whitfield in the woods. "That's not yours, is it?" I said.

Darcy looked down at himself. The thin cotton was even thinner than I remembered, and it wasn't concealing much. I could see Darcy's boxer shorts through the nightdress. The fabric was stretched tight across his chest and shoulders, and the overall look was not much improved by the frilly hem.

"Of course not," he snorted, plucking gingerly at the nightie. "I'm not really into dresses, believe it or not. On me, I mean." He looked up. "Is this yours? Why am I—"

I felt myself blushing. "No," I broke in hurriedly. "I think it's Miss Whitfield's."

Darcy stopped plucking at the nightie. "Is this some kind of sick joke? Did I go back to her house or something while I was sleepwalking? Surely not!" He frowned.

"I think my subconscious mind must have wanted me to check on my dad," I said, pointing to my dad's corduroy shirt, which I was currently wearing like a dress. "Simultaneous sleepwalking," I added slowly. "We're lucky we didn't both fall to our deaths." A shiver ran down my spine.

Darcy blinked. "I can't think how we . . ." But then he broke off: suddenly, mixed in with the drizzle, lots of small, hard, pink objects had started raining down onto our heads and shoulders. They bounced off us and went skittering across the roof of the tower. Darcy brushed one off his arm. "Are they . . . *mice?*"

They were. Pink sugar mice, the sweets I'd loved so much as a child that one Christmas, when I'd been given a bagful of them, I built them their own house out of shoe boxes. (It had been an architectural masterpiece of cardboard, pipe cleaners, and real Gouda, and I had christened it "The Palace of a Thousand Cheeses." My dad had had to throw it away after a week because it had gone moldy and started stinking to high heaven.)

I gathered up a few of the mice and bit off one of their tails. Sugar, no doubt about it. As I chewed, I tipped my head back and peered up at the sky, trying to locate the source of this weird meteorological phenomenon. But I saw no sign of any plane, helicopter, or even hot-air balloon that might have been dispensing the mice. They seemed to be raining down on us from the clouds themselves.

I must have well and truly lost it this time.

"Er . . . ," said Darcy. He'd gone as white as a sheet, and was staring dazedly down at his flowery nightdress and the pile of mice accumulating around him. They were still tumbling from the sky thick and fast.

I closed my eyes for a moment and took a few deep breaths. There must have been a logical explanation for what was going on;

in fact, I'd had an inkling of what it might be ever since I'd woken up on the edge of the turret roof. "Darcy," I said quietly, folding one of the sugar mice into his hands, "the chronicle has been stolen. Yesterday when I got back to my room, it was gone. And I think whoever took it is messing with us."

"You mean . . ."

I nodded. "I know you don't believe in magic. But just look at what's happening. It's not normal. It's impossible. That's why I'm sure that whoever has the book is playing games with us."

Darcy stood up, a little unsteadily, and leaned out over the battlements. I did the same, and together we looked down into the courtyard, where the gravel was now blanketed in a layer of pink sugar. The downpour of mice was growing heavier now, and had even spread to the parkland beyond the castle gates.

Again I described the book's powers to Darcy. I also told him about Miss Whitfield coming into my room. While I was speaking, he gripped the stone parapet so hard that his knuckles went white and his fingernails turned slightly blue. But when I'd finished, he nodded, very slowly, without taking his eyes off the mice that were still raining down into the courtyard below. "It's completely insane. It's nuts. I don't believe in magic," he said quietly. "But I do believe you about that book. I don't really have a choice. This is too much, it's too . . . I keep thinking I'm still dreaming, or I've got a fever and I'm hallucinating or something. . . ."

"I know. But unfortunately, we are very much awake."

"And not exactly dressed for it." He glanced at my bare legs. Although my dad was a lot taller than me, his shirt wasn't quite long enough to pass for a dress.

"True," I said, tugging down on the hem.

Darcy dragged his eyes back to my face. Now he, too, bit into a mouse, and then he cleared his throat. "So whoever it was that stole the book—they created this sugar rain, put us in these stupid clothes, and sent us up here onto the roof?" he mused.

I nodded.

"That's terrible," he said quietly. "We could so easily have fallen. We could have died. It's terrifying that a stranger has the power to manipulate us like that." The muscles in his jaw stood out as he clenched his teeth.

"I know," I said. "I know." We were still being pummeled by the deluge of sugar mice. I was trembling with cold, and with anger at the thief who had almost killed us. "Let's go inside and figure out what we're going to do. We have to get the chronicle back, and fast."

Darcy nodded grimly. "Whatever it takes," he said.

An hour later, Hannah, Charlotte, Toby, Darcy, and I assembled in the west wing library for an emergency meeting, fully dressed now and ready for anything. Technically Hannah, Charlotte, and I had lessons to go to. But although we knew we'd get into trouble for skipping class, this just couldn't wait. We had to do something, and there was no time to lose.

We'd let Toby in on the secret of the book and its magical powers, but he didn't seem to be as worried about it as the rest of us. He was more amused than shocked by the sugary downpour, and by the idea that we were actually dealing with real magic. Perhaps that was because the lower school students were currently having a riotous sugar-mouse fight in the courtyard, while the police, summoned by my dad to investigate the mysterious pink mass, confirmed that they were not treating the mice as terror-related.

"Perhaps it was Miss Whitfield who took the chronicle," said Charlotte, sitting on the new sofa next to Toby.

"I don't think so. Why would she have come to our room if she already had it?" said Hannah. She, like me, was perched on one of the armchairs, while Darcy paced up and down the room (a little too close to the bookshelves for my liking).

"There is something a bit fishy about her, though, if you ask me. . . . She knew the old legends about the chronicle, *and* she knew you were the one who'd been using it," Charlotte mused.

"But not until it was too late; I'm sure the chronicle was already gone by the time she came to our room."

"But she must be wrapped up in all this somehow," Darcy muttered. "From what you've told us, it doesn't sound like she doubted the chronicle's powers for a second."

"No." I put my chin in my hands. "She even warned us about them. And then there's that old photo . . ."

"Perhaps all the women in her family just look really, really similar?" Hannah suggested.

"No. I think it was *her* in the picture." I had no idea how I knew this, but a prickling sensation in my stomach told me I was right.

"It's a bit creepy, but kind of cool," said Toby. Darcy, on the other hand, sniffed skeptically. "What are you saying, Emma? That Miss Whitfield is this mysterious faun you're always telling us about?"

I shrugged. That thought hadn't occurred to me before. Was it possible? Might the faun be a woman?

"I think we need to tackle this one thing at a time," said Charlotte, "and the most important thing is to get the book back before whoever took it does something even worse. So: What do we know so far?"

"Well, it went missing yesterday, at some point during the day. In the morning, before I went to class, it was still there. And by late last night it was gone," I summed up.

"And after dinner I was in our room all evening, doing my homework," Hannah added. "So it must have been gone before I got there."

I shook my head. "You were asleep when I came in, remember?"

"Yes. But I would have noticed if—"

"Either way, that doesn't narrow it down very much," Toby broke in. "Not enough to give us an idea of who the thief might have been, anyway. But it must have been somebody who already knew how the book worked. Otherwise they wouldn't have had you wandering around naked in a shower of sugar mice a few hours later."

"We were not *naked*," Darcy said haughtily.

"Well, anyway, *I* wouldn't have started writing in the book straightaway if I'd happened to find it," said Toby, "and I'm sure it took you a little while to figure out how it worked, too, Emma?"

He was right, of course. "But apart from us—and Miss Whitfield, evidently—nobody even knows the book exists. I haven't told anyone, anyway."

"Me neither," said Charlotte, planting a soft kiss on Toby's cheek. "Not even you."

Hannah cleared her throat.

At that moment, several books slid to the floor with a crash right by Darcy's feet. "Sorry," he muttered and bent down to pick them up. My heart skipped a beat. Damn it! I couldn't go on like this. Although I'd vowed never to write in the chronicle again, I was going to have to do something about Darcy and the books I'd said he should choke on. Hannah, meanwhile, had gone bright red.

"Um—Hannah?" I said. "Are you okay?"

She looked at the floor. "I might—I might have accidentally told someone how the chronicle works," she said flatly. "I don't know what I was thinking—it was quite a while ago, and I thought he must have forgotten by now, but . . . now that I think about it, maybe—"

"Who?" we cried in chorus.

Hannah blushed even deeper. "Frederick," she whispered. "Do you remember how he asked me to dance at the ball? He was so funny and nice and—well, we got to talking about all the old myths and legends that have sprung up around Stolzenburg. I didn't mean to give anything away, but he asked me where I thought those stories came from." Hannah's face was so red it looked as if it was about to explode. "And I said somebody makes them up and writes them down and then they come true. But I didn't mention the book and I definitely didn't say you had it, Emma, I swear. I honestly don't know how he figured it out."

"Frederick!" Darcy and Toby exchanged a glance.

"I do," I murmured, and sighed. The penny had just dropped. Toward the end of my date with Frederick, in my drunken state, I must have let something slip while I was blathering away to myself. I couldn't remember exactly what I'd said, but it must have been enough for Frederick to go off and wheedle a bit more information out of Hannah—and that had given him everything he needed. Now he'd realized Darcy and I were onto him, he'd decided to use what he knew. Damn it! "It was me," I said. "It was my fault."

Then I told the others about my encounter with Frederick in the girls' corridor; I'd assumed he was on his way to see Helena, but now I realized he'd been coming from the direction of my bedroom. And all the while Hannah had been fast asleep, having nodded off over her homework. Damn it!

Darcy clenched his fists. "Come on then! Let's go and get the bastard! Anyone know where he might be this morning?"

But no one had any idea where Frederick might be, so we decided to split up. Charlotte and Toby would search the grounds and talk to Miss Whitfield again, Darcy would drive down to the village and pay Frederick's parents another visit, and Hannah and I would search the castle. If any of us found Frederick, we'd text the others to tell them. Our plan was soon complete, and a few minutes later we set off.

Hannah and I started with the common rooms, then worked our way through the dining hall, the kitchens, the conservatory, and every single corridor of the main building. We moved on to the west wing, passing through the de Winter portrait gallery into the ornate ballroom, where dust sheets had already been draped over the furniture to keep it clean until next year. We searched the secret tunnels last—and then we went back to the beginning and started all over again.

We carried on searching all day, but none of us found any sign of Frederick or the chronicle or even the slightest clue as to where either of them might be. Even Helena von Stein seemed to have vanished without a trace. And Miss Whitfield stubbornly refused to open the door of her cottage, no matter how many times we rang her doorbell or knocked on her living room window. We could see her through the glass, sitting in a rocking chair, reading a novel by Eleanor Morland. She was utterly engrossed, as if nothing and nobody else in the world existed. It was very frustrating.

Despite these setbacks, we kept up the search until late into the evening. Then we reassembled in the west wing library, exhausted and dispirited, and sat around the fire staring into the flames. Charlotte and Toby had raided the larder and returned with some bread, fruit, and a bowl of custard, which we devoured with relish (we'd all missed dinner) while sitting in front of the TV. There was an item on the news about Stolzenburg.

Until a few hours ago, the school had been crawling with journalists and camera crews eager to report on our "meteorological phenomenon." One of the TV news reporters was now putting forward an unlikely explanation involving a cargo plane with a broken hatch. The sequence of events that had allegedly caused the shower of sugar mice was improbable to say the least, and was being hotly debated on the Internet. But we knew what was really behind it. Unfortunately, that didn't help us at all right now.

Hannah was the first to succumb to fatigue; at half past nine she nodded off on the rug in front of the fire. When a crackling log woke her up again a few minutes later, she bid us good night and headed to bed. A little while later Charlotte yawned and did the same, and Toby offered to walk her back to her room.

I was exhausted, too, of course, after hours of wandering round and round the castle without getting any closer to our goal. But at the same time I felt I couldn't—or shouldn't—let myself fall asleep right now. I was genuinely afraid to close my eyes. Last time I had, I'd woken up to find myself inches away from the edge of a turret roof. Who knew what Frederick had in store for us next? No—I didn't dare go to bed.

The same thought seemed to have occurred to Darcy, because he made no move to leave the library, either. We watched in silence as the fire burned down, and we pushed Miss Whitfield's sofa closer to the embers to warm our feet.

"Do you really think Miss Whitfield could be a hundred-year-old mythical creature?" said Darcy quietly. My eyes were burning now from the effort of keeping them open.

"I have no idea," I said, leaning back against the sofa cushions. It was almost midnight, and apart from the usual rustles and creaks of the ancient building, the library was completely silent. "I don't know what to think."

"Me neither." He stretched out his long legs and linked his hands behind his head. "I'm shattered. Perhaps we should go and make ourselves a strong coffee. . . . The thing is, though, we can't stay awake forever. Sooner or later we're going to *have* to sleep."

"Later, hopefully—once I've come up with a plan." I sighed. "None of this makes any sense. This whole time I've been thinking that if the faun did exist, it must be Frederick. And if not him, I'd have been more inclined to think that *you*—" I stopped myself. "But Miss Whitfield? I'd never *ever* have suspected her. You'd have thought new information would help us make sense of things, but the more I find out the more confused I get. Or am I missing something?"

Darcy turned to face me. "So it wouldn't surprise you if *I* suddenly turned into an enchanted beast with hooves and horns?" His lips twitched in amusement.

"Yes," I said. "Of course it would. Now stop making fun of me."

At once he was serious again. "I'm not making fun of you, Emma, I promise," he said. "But the fact that we're sitting here, seriously contemplating the possibility that somebody in this castle might not actually be human . . . If I was going to make fun of anyone, it would be myself. Because I'm so scared of a magic book that I can't even go to sleep. Like a kid who's scared of monsters under the bed."

"Except that monsters under the bed are imaginary. Whereas you and I waking up on top of the west wing tower this morning was very real."

"Life-threateningly so."

"I wish I'd never found that stupid book!"

"No, don't say that! It's still the best clue we have about what happened to Gina."

"I don't know. . . . It's not as if her poems have brought us any closer to finding her. She wished she was dead—she wished for the end of the world. That could mean anything. The consequences of what gets written in the book are completely unpredictable."

Darcy stared into the embers for a while. Their reddish-orange glow made his face look softer than usual. He, too, looked exhausted—the shadows under his eyes were even darker than before. But then, all at once, his face lit up. "Dead, or the end of the world," he muttered, then leaped to his feet. "That's it!" he cried. "That's it!"

"What?" I stood up, too. Darcy looked as though he was heading toward the bookshelves again, so I stepped hurriedly into his path and blocked his way. "What do you mean?"

"It's so obvious! If the book has the power to make it rain pink mice over Stolzenburg, then surely it must have had the power to send my sister to the end of the world!" He beamed at me.

"Um—there is no end of the world? The world is round . . ." Were we seriously having this conversation?

"But there's a pub in Edinburgh, for example, called the World's End."

"You think Gina could be in Scotland? But then why has she never made contact?"

"Who knows? But it doesn't matter. There must be loads of places called the World's End. We just need to do a bit of Googling."

"Okay," I said. There was something to be said for the idea. It was a glimmer of hope. A possibility, even if just one among many. Another possibility was that Gina was nowhere: not at the end of the world or anywhere else. And Darcy knew that, too—I could see he was trying to curb his euphoria. He breathed deeply, evenly, and moved toward the window.

"Tomorrow," he said, with his back to me. "We'll look into it tomorrow. I still have to be prepared for the worst."

But his shoulders were shaking with excitement. Without thinking, I went over to him, took his hand, and squeezed it. "We'll find her," I said.

Darcy turned to me. He stared down at our joined hands for a moment. "Thank you," he said. "You've helped me so much the past few days. Without you I'd still be sitting there sorting through Gina's toys." He looked into my eyes. "I know you can't stand me, Emma. I know you're not doing this for me. But I still feel like we could be friends, or something like friends, when all this is over. Thank you."

I looked at his eyebrows, which I'd always thought had such a snooty, superior arch to them, and the long, straight nose he'd wrinkled in disdain when we'd first met. But now, as I looked into that proud face, I no longer felt any resentment toward Darcy de Winter. I knew him well enough now to know that behind his mask there was more than just an arrogant rich kid. There was a brother who was desperate to find his beloved twin sister. A good friend who was eager to protect those he cared about, and who'd helped me out of a jam more than once.

True, Darcy had his flaws: He'd kicked us out of the library, he'd come between Toby and Charlotte, he'd made me fall in the fountain and told me I was a naïve little kid. He could be grumpy and antisocial at times. But I'd been proud and rude to him, too, and I'd formed a judgment about him without even getting to know him. Not to mention the chaos I'd caused with my experiments in the chronicle . . .

I took a deep breath. "It's not that I can't stand you," I said. "Actually, I guess I . . . quite like you. Sort of." Why was this so difficult? Why was it so hard for me to admit I'd been wrong about him? "I mean, not just sort of. I'm sorry for the way I treated you. And all the things I said to you at the ruins that day."

Darcy shook his head. "I deserved it. I insulted you and then tried to kiss you. I deserved all those things you said."

"I don't know about that." I suddenly became aware that our faces were very close together and that we were still holding hands. Now Darcy took hold of my other hand.

"When I said it was all water under the bridge, I . . . I lied," he murmured. "The last thing I want to do is to offend you again, so I won't try to do what I did that day in the woods. But . . ." He cleared his throat. "My feelings haven't changed."

"Really?" I whispered. "Because mine have." Until that moment I hadn't realized it. I hadn't been able to admit it to myself. But now I knew. My feelings for Frederick had been nothing more than an infatuation: Darcy was the one I liked being around, the one who was important to me, the one I'd fallen in love with. I stood on tiptoe so that our noses were almost touching. My heart started to beat faster.

Darcy smiled. "Oh, I see," he murmured, and his lips moved closer to mine.

I was about to close my eyes and let it happen . . . but before I could find out whether his lips really were as soft as they looked, I spotted something moving out of the corner of my eye. The moment burst like a bubble. I turned, pressed my face to the window, and saw a figure running toward the castle.

It was Princess von Stein. "That's—that's Helena!" I said falteringly. "She must have been out in the woods."

I heard Darcy let out his breath. Now he, too, was peering out into the darkness. "You're right," he said, tugging at my arm. "And I bet she knows where Frederick is. Come on."

"Leave me alone!" Helena hissed when we caught up with her on the main staircase. Her hair was a mess, her clothes disheveled. "What do you want? I've just been in the conservatory, reading."

She tried to push past us, but I blocked her way. Darcy grabbed her by the wrist.

"We saw you coming out of the woods," I said. "Where have you really been?"

"Nowhere." She tried to wriggle out of Darcy's grasp, but he held firm.

"Where . . . is . . . Frederick?" said Darcy through gritted teeth, emphasizing every word.

"Let go of me right now or I will scream this whole—"

"And where's the book?" I broke in. "What have you and Frederick done with it?"

Helena blinked. "You know about that weird diary thing?"

"Of course," I retorted. "Who do you think Frederick stole it from?"

Suddenly, Helena stopped trying to wriggle free and hung her head, something I'd never seen her do before. Suddenly, she didn't seem to care if we saw her that way. The fear and exhaustion of this surreal day must finally have caught up with her. "I'm worried about Frederick," she whispered. "I think he's losing it. He turned up at our secret meeting place last night with that book, and he hasn't let it out of his sight since. He keeps reading bits of it, scribbling in it, muttering weird things to himself."

She sighed. "And then this morning he suddenly announced that it was too dangerous in the castle and we had to go and hide. But he wouldn't tell me why or where. I went to the cave with him— you know, Darcy, the cave on the riverbank where you and Vera used to go. That seemed to calm him down for a while, but then he started going on and on about the book again, and I just couldn't take it anymore, so I left."

"So he's still there?" Darcy breathed. "He's there right now?"

Helena shook her head.

"What cave?" I chimed in. "I know the grounds like the back of my hand and I've never heard anything about a cave . . ."

"My sister, Vera, found it. You can only see it from the water. Vera and Darcy spent a lot of time there four years ago, didn't you, Darcy?" said Helena, trying to wrench her arm free again. "Jesus, Darcy! Would you please let go of me! I won't run off, I promise. And you're hurting me."

Reluctantly, Darcy loosened his grip. Helena rubbed her sore wrist.

"Vera?" I asked.

"She was in Year Twelve at the time and—well, she was my girlfriend," said Darcy quietly. "We soon realized we weren't compatible and we didn't stay together very long. But I was pretty besotted with her at first, and I . . ." He cleared his throat. "I spent too much time with Vera and not enough with my sister."

"I see," I said, and felt jealousy start to gnaw at me. This was just great—we hadn't even had our first kiss yet, and here we were talking about Darcy's ex! But in the grand scheme of things, it didn't really matter. I had bigger problems right now. And at least this explained why Darcy had been so distracted four years ago, and why Gina had found it so hard to talk to him. "It would have been a good idea to search that cave this morning," I remarked.

"Yes, I should have thought of that," Darcy murmured, as I turned back to Helena.

"So where's Frederick now?" I asked.

Helena shrugged. "He followed me through the woods—still going on about the book—and then just as we got near the old monastery I suddenly realized he wasn't behind me anymore. The last thing I heard him say was *it's about time they found a body*, or something like that. But when I turned around he was gone." She shuddered. "And then I freaked out and ran all the way back here."

Darcy and I stared at each other, and I knew the same thought was in both of our minds.

"Do you think . . . ?" I blurted out.

Darcy gave a brusque nod.

Then we ran.

December 2013

Again I sit here alone and write
As I await the final act,
I drown in secret scribbled words
That may be fiction or may be fact.

In this book of a thousand places
There is no place for this lonely girl,
And nothing left to do but hope
Either for death, or the end of the world.

# 16

W E RAN THROUGH THE DARK WOOD. BRANCHES SNAPPED under our feet, and twigs clawed at my face in the darkness. But we couldn't waste time looking for a path. There wasn't even time to think. We just had to run, faster than we'd ever run in our lives.

It was a matter of life or death.

Literally.

Darcy crashed through the undergrowth ahead of me and reached the ruins first. I saw him disappear down what had once been the church nave.

I followed.

There were two possibilities: Either Gina was dead, or she was at the end of the world, wherever that might be. She'd mentioned both options in the chronicle, so they were both equally possible and equally likely. Gina's life hung in the balance.

But if Frederick had decided he wanted Gina's body to be discovered, the balance would tip conclusively in that direction the moment he committed the words to paper. There was no knowing exactly how it would happen, but one thing was for certain: If Frederick wrote in the chronicle that Gina was already dead and that someone was going to find her body, it would be her death sentence. There would be no going back.

Darcy and I sprinted along the aisle toward the statue of the faun. The secret staircase had been opened, but Frederick was sitting cross-legged on one of the weathered tombstones beside it. The book was in his lap, lit by a flashlight, and he was scribbling something in it. Even when we stopped just a few yards away from him, he didn't look up. Was he so engrossed in what he was doing that he hadn't even noticed us?

"There you are!" he murmured, just as I'd decided to make the most of the element of surprise and snatch the book out of his hands.

Frederick greeted us with his usual wry smile. "I was wondering when you two were going to show up," he said. "Luckily, I've already figured out how this thing works. Just in time."

He lowered his pen to the paper again.

"Stop!" cried Darcy. "Don't do this! Wait!"

Frederick frowned. "What?" he said. At the same moment, Darcy and I launched ourselves at him. Somehow, whatever it took, we were going to get that book away from him.

But Frederick had turned his gaze back to the chronicle, where he'd already written several words on the next blank page. "I could write any name I want here in the time it takes you to get to me," he said calmly, almost casually.

Darcy froze, rooted to the spot, and held me back, too. I squinted at the book in Frederick's lap, trying to read the words upside down. It wasn't easy to decipher his handwriting, but eventually I managed to make out what he'd written: *At last, the mortal remains of . . .*

I gasped. He was about to write Gina's name; the pen nib was almost touching the paper.

"Are you crazy?" I screamed. "You'll kill her!"

"Oh, really?" said Frederick.

"I thought you understood how the book worked? That everything you write in it comes true? For God's sake!"

Frederick grinned. "Of course I understand. At first I did have trouble believing all those fairy stories you told me on our way back from the pub, Emma. But then I asked Hannah about it, and her reaction was so intriguing that I thought I might as well give it a try—I had nothing to lose, after all." His grin grew even wider. "Interesting weather we've been having today, isn't it?" The flashlight in his lap illuminated his face from below, bathing it in a ghostly light. Had Frederick gone mad? What was he planning?

"Please," I pleaded. "Don't do anything stupid! That book is more dangerous than you think!"

Frederick tilted his head and looked at me. "You don't know *what* I think, Emma. You don't know *what* happened that night four years ago. You didn't even know Gina. So do us a favor and stay out of it!"

I gave him a piercing stare. "I *found* the book. I'm the one who's been studying it, I'm the one who knows best out of all of us how to use it. I'm the one who realized Gina had been writing in it," I hissed.

"And it's my sister's life we're talking about here," said Darcy quietly.

Then Frederick tipped back his head and started to laugh, loudly and without warning. His voice echoed around the monastery walls and seemed to linger in the trees. Was I imagining it, or had the night just turned a shade blacker? Was the darkness closing in around us? A sudden gust of wind brushed my skin like the icy breath of a stranger.

Instinctively, I moved closer to Darcy. I felt the warmth of his body against mine, and I felt him trembling with rage. "Enough of this bullshit," he growled, and at that Frederick fell silent and stared into our faces as he lowered his pen to the paper and started writing a capital *G*.

Then he spoke. "You have no idea what it's like to be someone like me," he said abruptly. "I've always had to fight for everything. My family isn't rich, my dad isn't a famous academic and headmaster. If something goes wrong for me, I'm screwed. I don't have money or a family name to fall back on. People like me aren't allowed to make mistakes. We can't afford to. We can't afford to even be suspected of doing something wrong, do you see? And your darling sister, Darcy—she used me. She risked everything I'd worked so hard for!" He practically spat the last few words. "Yes, I pretended to be that faun she was always going on about. For a laugh. I didn't know she was going to take the whole thing so seriously. I thought it was just going to be a private joke between us, a bit of fun."

He formed the curve of the *G*.

"But it wasn't my fault she had a screw loose! That she was dumb enough to actually believe all that rubbish! It wasn't my fault she went and fell in love with me, and thought she had to save me from some tragic fate."

"She must have been devastated when she found out you'd been lying to her the whole time," I said.

Frederick raised his eyebrows. "Just because *you* felt that way, doesn't mean—"

"Oh, shut up! I don't give a flip about you!"

"That's pretty much what Gina said. And then she used her little book to make me row her out onto the river. I didn't want to, but it was like I was on autopilot or something. Now I see why. The chronicle was controlling me. It forced me to take Gina out in that boat and watch her jump overboard. She wanted me to get the blame for her death," he said bitterly. "For four years I've lived in fear that someday, someone will uncover some evidence against me. That I'll be accused of a crime I didn't commit, and my whole life will be ruined. But not anymore. I'm going to make sure her body is found in the underground tunnels, and I'm going to make it look like an accident. You should be grateful I'm fishing her bones out of the river for you, Darcy. At least now you can finally bury her."

Frederick extended the curve of the *G* a little, but he got no further because Darcy let out a roar like a wounded animal and charged straight at him. "Murderer!" he bellowed, throwing caution to the wind. "MURDERER!"

"Darcy!" I cried. "She might still be alive! If the chronicle can make pink mice fall from the sky, then who knows—anything could have happened! Maybe Gina jumped out of the boat but didn't drown—maybe she got swallowed up by a giant fish and carried off to the other side of the world or something. Like in 'Jonah and the Whale.' Darcy!"

But Darcy wasn't listening—he and Frederick were now just a tangle of kicking, punching limbs. I remembered, not all that long ago, wondering which of them would win in a fight. But nothing could have been further from my mind now. All I could think of was Gina and the very, very slim chance that she had survived. That she was out there somewhere, alive, waiting for her brother to find her.

Darcy and Frederick were rolling around on the ground now, dangerously close to the underground staircase. Frederick had fastened his hands around Darcy's neck and was trying to strangle him. Darcy landed a punch on Frederick's nose. Frederick groaned and rammed his knee into Darcy's stomach. But Darcy hardly seemed to notice—he didn't even flinch. He was delirious with rage. A vein pulsed at his temple, and he didn't take his eyes off Frederick for a second. Then I heard a metallic *crack* as something smashed against the stone pedestal of the statue. There was a sound of splintering glass, and the flashlight went out. Frederick and Darcy became a dark, shapeless, grappling mass.

And where was the chronicle?

I groped frantically along the ground. Damn it! If only I'd thought to do this before, when I could still see! The chronicle must have been around here somewhere: Frederick must surely have dropped it in the tussle. I crawled closer and closer to him and Darcy, feeling moss and stone under my palms. And then my fingertips found the cloth binding! I snatched the chronicle up from the ground where it lay.

And then I ran.

I knew I couldn't stay there any longer watching them fight. Although I'd flinched at every blow Darcy had received, at the end of the day it didn't matter who won this brawl. All that mattered right now was saving Gina.

And so, forcing myself not to look back at Darcy and Frederick, I entered the underground staircase. I didn't so much run as tumble down the steps, before charging blindly along the passageway that led to the castle. I hoped that was where it led, anyway: It was pitch black down here, as if I'd fallen headfirst into an inkwell, and I couldn't see a thing. There could have been anything at all in the thick darkness on either side of me—a sheer drop, or a fairy kingdom—and I wouldn't have been any the wiser. I groped my way along the rough stone wall with one hand, and clutched the book to my chest with the other. My heart hammered against the book's worn binding through the thin fabric of my shirt, and little by little my fingers turned numb with the cold. I stumbled on, barely noticing when I grazed my shoulder on the rocky walls or stubbed my toe on the ground. I had to get the book somewhere safe, and fast. I racked my brains feverishly, trying to think of the best place to hide it.

Under my pillow wouldn't do, obviously. Nor would anywhere else in my and Hannah's room. That was bound to be the first place Frederick would look. What about the west wing library? Wouldn't the best thing be to put the chronicle back in its secret compartment and pretend I'd never seen it? But even that probably wouldn't be secure enough: After all, it wasn't long ago that somebody had come in and searched the library from top to bottom, pulling every piece of furniture in the room apart. . . .

As I went on, my breath and my footsteps started to echo in the air. Suddenly I could no longer feel the wall beneath my fingertips. I must have reached the lord of Stolzenburg's laboratory. This gave me an idea: Perhaps I could find somewhere to hide the book in here!

I slowed down, came to an unsteady stop, and felt in my jacket pocket for my phone. It filled the underground room with a bluish glow as I switched it on . . . and almost dropped it again in my shock.

I was standing, as I'd thought, in the secret laboratory. To my left were the workbenches, piled high with dusty apparatus, and a few yards farther on I could see the copper basin filled with little leaves. Beyond that was the entrance to the other secret passage, the one that led to the west wing of the castle. No surprises there.

But what I hadn't been expecting to see was a new tunnel.

Directly behind the copper basin, yet another passageway had opened up in the wall. It was slightly narrower than the others. Narrower and darker. As I moved closer to it, the light from my phone revealed more of the little silver leaves—hundreds of thousands of them.

Where did this new tunnel lead? "New" to me, at least: The tunnel itself was clearly anything but new. It looked even older than the alchemist's laboratory I was standing in. Its stone walls were darker in color than the other walls and somehow smoother, worn down by the breath of the centuries. There were cast-iron torch brackets set into the walls at regular intervals, and some of them still contained lumps of charred wood covered in soot.

I wondered whether there was a secret lever that I'd accidentally pressed while I was stumbling through the darkness. How else could the tunnel have been opened? Or perhaps there was a lever somewhere above ground, and Darcy and Frederick had fallen against it while they were fighting? Either way, I was glad to see this new tunnel.

Very glad, in fact.

I didn't have the faintest idea what I would find at the end of it, but I was sure it would make the perfect hiding place for my precious cargo. Yes—this was exactly what I'd been looking for. I stepped resolutely into the tunnel, and followed the trail of leaves into the unfamiliar darkness.

The light from my phone bobbed along the ground ahead of me. My heart was still pounding in my chest. From somewhere far behind me I heard Darcy and Frederick shouting, and the sound of running footsteps. Were they chasing each other through the tunnels?

Now the rocky walls began to narrow; the silvery leaves rustled under my feet and the smell of damp earth grew stronger and stronger the farther on I went. After a while I realized that the color of the light in the tunnel was changing: the bluish glow from my phone was being eclipsed by a warmer light, one that flickered and danced. Eventually, the tunnel turned a corner, and as I rounded the bend I saw that there were flaming torches mounted on the walls every few yards or so, lighting the way. Only now did I see the footsteps in the dust. They were identical to the ones Darcy and I had seen the day we'd discovered the secret laboratory.

Perhaps Gina was somewhere nearby after all? I sped up, almost breaking into a run, and didn't stop until the tunnel suddenly opened onto another room—or rather, a chamber—or was it a cave? It wasn't man-made, at any rate.

I tipped my head back and gazed up at the roof, which, now that I was out of the tunnel, arched high above my head. Glittering conical rock formations hung down from the cave ceiling, long and jagged, and similar formations stretched up from the ground toward them. They sparkled like prisms, and I wandered amongst them openmouthed. This was magical. I'd never been in a stalactite cave before, but I'd seen them on TV and I knew that this cave must be one of the most beautiful of its kind in the world.

The silvery leaves shimmered even brighter now; there were so many of them that they'd formed a soft, thick carpet on the ground. The footsteps I'd been following had vanished beneath them. The leaves seemed to multiply as I got closer to the center of the cave, and at last I came to a kind of pit in the ground that was overflowing with them, like a rustling silver sea. Standing at the edge of the pit, I found the source of the mysterious footprints.

"Emma," she greeted me serenely, and smiled.

Instinctively I pressed the book closer to my chest. *"Who are you?"* I whispered.

"That's a good question," Miss Whitfield replied. "It is the right question, the first question you should ask. I will answer your question, and then you will give me the chronicle." She spoke as matter-of-factly as if she'd been explaining a piece of homework. As always, she was wearing a long dark dress, high-necked and hopelessly old-fashioned. As if it came from a different era. She was holding something I couldn't quite identify, something small and white and fragile-looking. . . .

"You!" I cried, starting angrily toward Miss Whitfield. "You're the faun, aren't you? You've been deceiving us all this time. You're not really a teacher. You want the book for yourself. To break your curse, and set you free. I recognized you in that old photo."

Miss Whitfield shook her head. She opened her mouth to reply, but at that moment Frederick and Darcy came bursting out of the secret tunnel into the cave. They both looked exhausted. Their clothes were streaked with dirt, Frederick's nose was bleeding, and Darcy had a bruise around his left eye, which was already starting to swell.

"Emma," he panted, "I was worried."

Frederick, meanwhile, was turning slowly on the spot as he gazed around the cave. "Wow! What is this place?"

I decided to ignore them for the moment, and turned back to Miss Whitfield. "What is that thing you're holding?" I pointed to her cupped hands, and she opened them slowly to reveal an object made of folded paper. A piece of origami.

A dragonfly.

I moved closer, bent down, and examined the miniature work of art sitting in the palm of Miss Whitfield's hand. Its wings were delicate and translucent, its body was covered in little letters, and its eyes were made from gleaming mother-of-pearl. It was very similar to the dragonfly I'd dreamed about so many times over the past few weeks. But unlike the creature in my dreams, this dragonfly was not alive. Its legs were stiff and rigid, and I could see the individual folds in the paper it was made from (which seemed to be a page out of a book). This dragonfly was mute and motionless.

"Did you make it?" I asked.

Miss Whitfield nodded. "I make one every time there's a new moon. I've been making them for . . . well, for a very long time.

And then I bring them here and set them free. This one was made from a page of an old botany book I found in the west wing library. I'm sorry I had to be so . . . so ruthless in my search for the chronicle. But after the incident with Dr. Meier and Miss Berkenbeck in the dining hall, I had an idea that somebody . . . Well." She broke off, drew back her arm, and hurled the paper dragonfly into the air. The origami insect spiraled upward toward the roof of the cave, and it wouldn't have surprised me if it had suddenly come to life in mid-air, flapped its wings, and flown away, never to be seen again.

But instead the dragonfly simply sailed through the air like a paper airplane, veered in a wide curve around our heads, and finally landed in the sea of silver leaves in the middle of the cave. Only then did I notice all the other dragonflies that must have been brought here by Miss Whitfield over the years. There were lots of them. Too many to count. Hundreds, maybe. Some of them were yellowed and torn; some were falling apart, half-buried under piles of leaves. Some looked a lot newer—bright white specimens that perched on the surface, gazing at us with their lifeless eyes.

I shivered and looked from the dragonflies to Miss Whitfield and back again. What did all this mean? Questions raced through my mind. What had Miss Whitfield done—and why? How old was she really? Why did she make the paper dragonflies? What *was* this place? And where on earth was Gina de Winter? Rather than attempt to unravel the tangle of evidence, clues, and theories inside my head, I blurted out the first question that sprang to mind. "*You* destroyed our library. Was that because you were looking for the chronicle?"

Miss Whitfield pressed her lips together. "Yes. I had no choice.

That book is dangerous—it cannot be allowed to fall into the wrong hands. For a long time I hoped that it had been lost or destroyed, like the other six, but . . ." She cleared her throat. "I had suspected for some time that that might not be the case, and eventually I realized I had to do something. As I said, I am truly sorry about the library."

I sniffed. "At least it made a change from your weird hobby." I cocked my chin toward the paper dragonflies. Then I couldn't hold back any longer, and all my questions came tumbling out at once. "Why?" I shouted. "Why do you make these things?" My voice cracked. "What were you doing in that old photo? What do you know about the chronicle? And *how* do you know about it?"

Miss Whitfield sighed. "Listen carefully, Emma, and I'll explain." She turned to look at the sea of silver leaves. "There's a fairy tale. In the chronicle. The tale of the faun and the fairy," she began.

I moved to stand beside her. "I know. By Eleanor Morland."

"Yes," said Miss Whitfield quietly. "But the fairy tale doesn't have an ending. It breaks off where the faun reminds the fairy of their pact. Where he tells her he has found his true love, and that she must turn him into a real man."

I'd never noticed that there was no ending to the fairy tale anywhere in the chronicle. Again I became very aware of the book's cloth binding beneath my fingertips. "And how *did* it end?" I whispered, almost forgetting to breathe.

"Not happily," said Miss Whitfield. "Not happily at all. The faun . . ." But she got no further.

Darcy and Frederick had finally gotten their breath back.

For a while they, too, had seemed mesmerized by this strange place, and by Miss Whitfield's dragonflies, and they'd stood rooted to the spot. But now Frederick must have sensed an opportunity to finish what he'd started, and he lunged toward me with a shout. Before I could react, he'd grabbed hold of my wrist and snatched the book out of my hand. Darcy was by my side in an instant, wrapping his arms around Frederick's neck and trying to drag him backward. But even as he gasped for breath and his face turned scarlet, Frederick managed to open the book and pull out his pen.

"No!" I cried, grabbing hold of the book's back cover. Miss Whitfield came to my aid. We tugged at the chronicle with all our strength, while Darcy tightened his grip around Frederick's neck.

"Let go of it," Darcy snarled, through clenched teeth.

"You don't know what you're doing!" cried Miss Whitfield.

Frederick said nothing. He didn't make a sound; he couldn't even breathe. But his pen was sliding over the paper, finishing off the *G* he'd started, forming the beginning of an *i*.

"Stop!" I screamed.

Darcy was yelling, too, and for a fraction of a second he let go of Frederick. Then he flung his whole body weight against him, so hard that all four of us lost our balance. Miss Whitfield and I toppled over backward, plummeting through the air just like the paper dragonfly. I saw the glittering rock formations above me as I fell, and I glimpsed the fluttering pages of a book, and a hand that might have been Darcy's or might not have been. The world blurred before my eyes.

Then came the leaves.

I fell backward into the rustling sea, which was not nearly as deep as I'd thought. Silvery letters swam before my eyes as I landed on the stony ground at the bottom of the pit, hitting the back of my head on the rock. The shock of the impact left me momentarily stunned. I gasped for breath, inhaling little scraps of paper through my nose and mouth. Then I wiped my face with my hands, accidentally crushing something that felt like an origami dragonfly. At last I managed to sit up.

I look around, dazed.

To my left sat Darcy, coughing up a leaf. To my right, Miss Whitfield was leaning over Frederick, who was lying motionless beside her. "I think he's unconscious," she murmured, but I hardly heard her because I'd just caught sight of something—

No, not something. *Someone.*

As we'd fallen into the pit, we'd caused most of the little leaves and paper dragonflies to scatter, so that the stony ground lay exposed. We could see, now, what had previously been hidden: a bright white skeleton, the bones jutting sharply into the air. My mouth went dry. A chill ran up the back of my neck all the way to the crown of my head.

This wasn't just a pit.

It was a grave.

I saw a rib cage. A gleaming jawbone. A collarbone. A shoulder joint. A pelvic bone. The bones looked peaceful; beautiful, even.

"Gina?" I whispered. I felt sick. So Frederick had done it. That bastard had killed her. He'd murdered her.

Beside me, Darcy choked on a sob and sank to the ground.

Trembling, I crept closer to the skeleton, staring at the smooth thigh bones, the individual vertebrae of the spine, the teeth. And the skull, with its two protuberances on the forehead that curled upward and outward. Only then did I realize that I was wrong: This wasn't Gina de Winter.

This was my meeting with the faun.

September 1794

"Why are you laughing?" the faun asked the fairy. "You promised to help me. Now you must keep your promise."

But the fairy merely glared at him. "You fool!" she cried. "You fool!"

# 17

So the faun did exist. Or he had existed.

He was dead. But he had lived!

I stared into his empty eye sockets. I noticed the fine lines that snaked along the bones in dainty flourishes, coming together to form letters and words. The same handwriting appeared on the silver leaves that spilled out of the gaps between the bones and the cracks in the skull. The huge horns on the faun's head were just as imposing as the ones in the lord of Stolzenburg's sketches. And the lower leg bones ended in cloven hooves instead of human feet.

The faun!

I still found it almost impossible to believe. The chronicle had created a living creature! And that living creature had died, long ago. Was that where all the silvery leaves had come from? If the faun had been made of words—if words were what had given him life— then perhaps he was returning to words as his body decayed, as dust returns to dust. Perhaps the silvery sheen of the leaves, and the words that were written on them, bore testament to the life they had once created. The rustling of the leaves around me suddenly seemed deafening, and it grew louder and louder the more I thought about the faun.

But above the rustling I could just make out the sound of suppressed sobs. Darcy was crouched on the ground a few yards away from me, his face buried in his hands.

"It's not Gina," I said softly. And then I almost shouted it: "It's not Gina!"

Darcy looked up, held his breath for a moment and then moved toward the skeleton. The look of despair vanished from his face, to be replaced by relief, then confusion, then disbelief. "Th-that's . . ." he stammered, "that's . . ."

"He was my friend," said Miss Whitfield, who had come to stand beside us. She brushed a few stray leaves off her long skirt as she spoke. "I'll tell you the story," she said. "The whole story. But not here. It's cold." She beckoned to us to follow her.

Darcy and I got to our feet, a little unsteadily. Instinctively we held hands, and Darcy slipped his fingers through mine. I squeezed his hand; the warmth of his skin was comforting. As Miss Whitfield climbed out of the pit, I caught sight of Frederick. He was still lying on his back with his eyes closed. But his chest was rising and falling steadily and he seemed to be more or less unharmed.

"He'll come round eventually and make his own way out of here," said Darcy.

Miss Whitfield nodded. "And we need to put as much distance

as possible between him and the chronicle before that happens. He seems a little . . . unhinged."

"Okay," I said as I clambered over Frederick. As I did so, I checked to make sure he hadn't cracked his head open or anything: *I* didn't want to be responsible for somebody's death. Luckily, however, he didn't seem to be in need of first aid.

Miss Whitfield reached the mouth of the tunnel and Darcy followed, dragging me along behind him. "Gina still has a chance," he whispered. "Everything might still turn out okay. We escaped the book's curse."

He smiled at me, but I didn't reply. I wasn't so sure about that. After all, Gina might well have died years ago. And as for the book's curse . . .

Miss Whitfield, Darcy, and I hurried through the tunnels back to the castle, and a few minutes later we pushed open the secret door in the west wing library, the one that was disguised as a bookcase. It creaked softly as it swung shut behind us.

"Okay," I said to Miss Whitfield. "Fire away."

She surveyed the room, glancing unhappily at the marks where the bookshelves had been ripped off the walls. "Here?" she asked. "Wouldn't you rather come to my cottage and I'll make us a nice cup of Earl—"

I shook my head. "We need answers. Now."

Miss Whitfield sighed and lowered herself into one of the armchairs. The embers in the fireplace were almost extinguished, but Darcy was already laying more logs on top of them and rekindling the flames. I realized I was pacing up and down in front of Miss Whitfield as I waited for her to start speaking. Only when Darcy touched me gently on the arm did I force myself to take a few deep breaths and sit down on the sofa.

Miss Whitfield seemed tense all of a sudden. The corner of her mouth twitched and her eyes glittered. Or was that just the firelight flickering across her face? For a moment, the only sound was the crackling of the fresh wood on the fire. Then Miss Whitfield cleared her throat, sat up very straight in her armchair, and said resolutely, "Whitfield is not my real name. My real name is Eleanor Morland."

*Eleanor Morland?* echoed a little voice in my head.

"Like the author?" asked Darcy, puzzled, as a chill ran down my spine.

"Not *like* the author," I whispered, looking wonderingly at our teacher. "She *is* the author."

Darcy scoffed. "That would make her over two hundred years old."

"Two hundred and forty-one, to be precise," said Miss Whitfield. "I was born on the sixteenth of December 1775. And I am still going strong."

I heard Darcy give a sharp intake of breath beside me, but Miss Whitfield went on, unfazed. "It was the chronicle. It was an accident." She flicked through the book, and showed us an entry from 1794. "I wrote it here myself, in my last ever entry. *I will take my leave of this book and return without it to England, where I will live as an ordinary writer forever and always, without recourse to magic,*" she read aloud. "*Forever and always*—do you see?"

"Yes," I murmured, "and no. Where does the faun come into all this?"

"You made yourself *immortal?*" said Darcy.

"As I said, it was an accident. If I could take it back I would, believe me," said Miss Whitfield, leaning back in her chair. "But anyway—I promised to tell you the whole story, and here it is. For the first eighteen years of my life I was just an ordinary English girl. I spent my childhood in England; I learned needlework and French and German and how to play the piano. Occasionally, I wrote stories and plays that I gave to my family to read. In the summer of 1794 my parents sent me to Germany, to stay with friends of the family at Stolzenburg. I was to spend several weeks here practicing my German.

"I had a wonderful time—the de Winters made me feel very at home, and I loved the castle and its grounds. I spent most of my time roaming around the old building looking for secret passageways. And I badgered the servants to tell me all the stories and legends they knew about Stolzenburg: I had already developed a keen interest in fairy tales, and I knew that every castle worth its salt has its own ghost story. At first they didn't want to tell me much— nobody wanted to frighten young Miss Morland. But eventually I managed to get one of the kitchen maids to share what she knew. She told me about the legend of the seven enchanted books, and about the lord of Stolzenburg (who had died just a few decades earlier) and his obsession with creating a supernatural being. From then on there was no stopping me. I immediately started searching for clues.

"I combed the whole of the castle, every corner, every room, every staircase, no matter how obscure. And I found them both. The book and the faun."

Miss Whitfield's eyes took on a dreamy look, and a sad smile flitted across her face as she continued. "He was wonderful. The first time I saw him—the faun, the word-eater—was one balmy full-moon night as I was sitting by the window in my bedroom. The sweet, heavy scent of the roses drifted up to me on the night wind. It was dark—the woods were casting a shadow across the parkland—but I knew he was there, at the edge of the courtyard. I saw him moving out of the corner of my eye, and I heard the crunch of the gravel. Perhaps he thought everyone in the castle was already in bed, or perhaps he wanted me to see him, I don't know. All I remember is that he suddenly stepped out into the moonlight, closed his eyes, and tipped back his head, turning his face up to the heavens.

"I'll never forget that sight: His face and his naked upper body were those of a man, but his legs were covered in hair like a goat's and he had hooves instead of feet. The two curled horns growing out of his temples reached right around his head to the back of his neck, and his skin shone silver in the darkness; it was covered with little letters, like a web of tiny tattoos. I leaned farther out of the window to get a better look at this wondrous creature, but I accidentally knocked the window frame with my elbow and the faun heard me. He looked up at me for a moment with his golden eyes, then he disappeared back into the darkness with one great bound."

I sighed. "Did you ever see him again?"

Miss Whitfield smiled. "Many times. The next few nights I waited for him, down in the courtyard, and when at last he plucked up the courage to return, I stepped out of the shadows and spoke to him. He almost ran away, but when he realized I was not afraid of him, he stayed. I think I was the first human being he had ever seen close up, because he seemed just as fascinated by me as I was by him." Miss Whitfield brushed a lock of hair out of her face, the way she must have done as a young girl.

"Neither of us could understand what the other was saying, for the language the faun spoke was neither German nor English—it was a sound like the rustling of paper. Nonetheless, we became friends. We met in secret in the underground tunnels he showed me, and we walked together in the woods and around the castle. I showed him my human world, and he played to me on his flute."

"Well, um—that must have been lovely for you," said Darcy, his chin propped on his hands. "But what does all this have to do with us? The faun may have existed once upon a time—but he's long dead now."

Miss Whitfield nodded. "I know. That's what's so tragic. The faun wasn't human; he was a magical creature. He was immortal. It should have been him, not me, sitting here with you. But I was too young, too inexperienced, too rash in everything I did. I thought I was an adult, I thought I knew what I was doing, but unfortunately the opposite was true.

"When I came across the book in a dusty corner of what used to be the lord of Stolzenburg's bedroom, and realized how it worked, I wrote things in it that I regret to this day. And the thing I regret most of all is the story of the faun and the fairy." Miss Whitfield's voice had grown brittle. She stood up from her chair in silence and walked over to the fire, where she gripped the mantelpiece with both hands, rested her head on the marble, and stared into the flames for a moment.

"Miss Whitfield?" I asked quietly. "What happened?"

"I wanted to help him," she whispered. "I knew how lonely he'd been before we met, and I knew we had only a few weeks left together until I had to return to England. So I decided to write something that would set him free, something that would grant his dearest wish and help him to become human. I thought I would combine the old legends about the fairy queen on the banks of the Rhine with my own ideas, so that later on they could all become part of the same legend. I thought it was a simple yet brilliant plan."

She sighed. "But it went terribly wrong. I worked on the fairy tale for several days, but as I was writing it . . . events overtook me. The story ran its course before I had finished telling it. And so it ended in a way I had never meant it to." Miss Whitfield was still standing by the fire with her back to us. "The fairy queen from the old legend was a bad fairy. She gave the faun a test—and when he failed it, she took his life in return," she said flatly.

"B-but . . . ," I stammered. The very idea of "bad fairies" made my head spin. Did they exist, too? Because they'd been written about in the chronicle, just like the faun? But according to the old legend it was a fairy who had first cursed the books. . . . Did fairies exist because the book did, or did the book exist because fairies did? My mind was racing. And I felt so sad for the faun.

"But . . . couldn't you have written a different ending, and changed how things turned out?" I asked. "Couldn't you have saved the faun?"

When Miss Whitfield turned back to face us, her eyes were shining with tears. "I tried," she said. "I tried, but it was too late."

"Oh," I said.

Miss Whitfield nodded. "When the faun died—that was when

I finally realized how dangerous the book was. That was when I decided never to write in it again. I hid it in the secret tunnels, at the foot of the copper basin, and covered it with the little silvery leaves that were all that was left of my friend. And I returned to England, where I started writing books—but never fairy tales. My novels were always set in the real world. I had vowed never to write another word about fairies, fauns, or magic of any kind, and I kept that vow.

"The faun had suffered a terrible fate, of course, but after his death I thought it was all over—that the chronicle couldn't affect me anymore. It wasn't until years later that I realized I wasn't aging in the same way as other people. At some point in my forties I simply stopped getting any older. It was quite some time before I remembered my last entry in the chronicle, and realized what I'd done to myself." Miss Whitfield rubbed her eyes with her thumb and index finger. "But there was nothing I could do about it, and in the end I was forced to fake my own death and leave home so as not to attract attention. Over the past two hundred years I have traveled the world, making my home in South American rain forests and Siberian villages, on a Chinese tea plantation and in various European cities, mainly in France, Germany, and England. I turned up at Stolzenburg from time to time to visit the de Winters, claiming to be the distant cousin of a great aunt, so that I could keep an eye on what was happening at the castle. For many years life here went on as normal, although after a while I discovered that the chronicle was no longer in the hiding place where I'd left it, and I thought it must have ended up in one of the libraries.

"But then, four years ago, I heard a rumor that made me think the chronicle must have resurfaced. I was on an expedition in the Arctic when I heard about Gina de Winter's disappearance, and I immediately returned to Stolzenburg. I was afraid the chronicle must have had something to do with Gina going missing—that someone had not only found it, but realized how it worked—so I took a job as a teacher at the school and resolved to stay here until I had found the chronicle and destroyed it once and for all. But Gina must have created a new hiding place for it, because for four years my search remained fruitless. I'd started to think the book must have vanished into thin air along with Gina, but then there was another spate of mysterious incidents: first Dr. Meier's strange behavior in the dining hall, and then the lion. . . . So once again I started to search the castle—more thoroughly this time. And to cover my tracks, I left little piles of the faun's silver leaves around the castle and the grounds. I wanted to make it look as though there was some sort of ghost haunting Stolzenburg, so that whoever had the chronicle would be put off the scent."

"I see." I remembered Miss Whitfield picking up one of the little silver leaves at the ball, and realized that it must have fallen out of her pocket. "But you had no idea it was me writing in the chronicle."

"No; I thought it was Frederick. And later, when your father won that award, I did briefly wonder whether it might have been him. I invited him to dinner and slipped a mild sedative into his food, hoping to loosen his tongue. But then you and Darcy told me about the book yourselves, and—"

"So that's why my dad passed out? Because you *drugged* him?"

Miss Whitfield lowered her gaze. "I am truly, truly sorry about that, too. But you must believe me, Emma—your father was never in any real danger."

I sniffed.

Darcy had stood up, too, now, and was pacing up and down the room. "So you think Gina used the book to write herself into oblivion? You think something went wrong?" he asked.

"Yes," said Miss Whitfield. "That's exactly what I think."

"So how do we find her?"

Miss Whitfield opened her mouth to reply, but before she could say a word Darcy had spun around and was staring at the secret door. "What's that noise?" he said in alarm.

And it was true—over the crackling of the fire I could hear a strange noise that hadn't been there a moment ago. It was coming from the other side of the secret door. Muffled, yet somehow ominous. Was it footsteps? Or the rustling of paper? Was it the sound of hundreds of dragonfly wings whirring through the air?

Miss Whitfield snatched up the book and held it close. "P-perhaps Frederick has woken up?" she said falteringly.

Darcy and I exchanged a glance. It didn't sound like Frederick, at least not Frederick alone . . . and it was getting louder.

The best thing to do would have been to take the chronicle and run. But Darcy seemed to have lost control of his limbs (and possibly his mind, too). He walked toward the secret door as if on autopilot, reached out a hand toward the imitation book that acted as a lever, and watched as the bookcase swung open before him. All at once the rustling swelled into a deafening roar, rushing out of the darkness toward us.

Darcy moved forward like a robot programmed to keep putting one foot in front of the other.

"NO!" I shouted. "Stop it! What are you doing? Get away from there!"

But Darcy had already taken another step forward, and he was standing right in the middle of the doorway when suddenly the frame started to creak and splinter. The heavy bookcase that formed the secret door began to tremble. With a sudden jolt (it was impossible to say what had caused it), the bookcase swung backward toward Darcy. I saw him spin around, his eyes wide. But it was too late.

The bookcase slammed into his chest, trapping him in the doorway.

I screamed.

I lurched toward him. He was gasping for breath, and all the color had gone out of his face. "Darcy!" I cried, tugging at the edge of the bookcase. "Are you hurt?"

"Don't know," he said. His breath rattled. His upper body was crushed between the bookcase and the door frame. "I can't . . . I can't . . . breathe."

Shit!

My blood ran cold. This was the book's curse. This was the moment I'd been dreading, the moment my first ever entry in the chronicle would come back to haunt me. I'd written that Darcy de Winter should choke on the books he'd stolen from us . . . I gritted my teeth as I tugged at the heavy wooden bookcase.

I wasn't going to let a few stupid words on a bit of paper take away someone I cared about. I wasn't going to lose Darcy the way Miss Whitfield had lost the faun!

"Help me, quick!" I shouted, but then I saw that Miss Whitfield was already beside me, clinging to the bookcase and leaning her entire body weight backward to try to shift it. Together we heaved and strained. But the mechanism that opened the door seemed to be jammed. The bookcase wouldn't budge. It was hopeless.

Darcy stared at me, his eyelids fluttering.

I let go of the bookcase. "Okay, okay," I muttered, turning to Miss Whitfield. "Give me the book. It's our only hope. Quick!"

I held one hand out toward Miss Whitfield and with the other I rummaged in my trouser pocket for a pen—I knew I had one somewhere. But Miss Whitfield didn't move. What was wrong with her? Hadn't she heard me?

"GIVE ME THE BOOK!" I repeated, my voice cracking.

Miss Whitfield took a step backward. "Emma," she said quietly. "You can't write anything else in the book. It's too dangerous."

I could hardly believe my ears. Didn't she get it? "This is Darcy's *life* we're talking about. He's CHOKING! We can't just let him die!" I yelled, wondering whether I should make a lunge for her and take the book by force. But suddenly she held it out to me of her own accord.

"I know what it's like to live with a terrible burden of guilt," she said, "so I'm going to leave it up to you to decide. But I'm begging you not to do it, Emma."

I snatched the chronicle out of her hands and opened it. I lowered my pen to the paper and . . . hesitated.

Darcy's skin had taken on a bluish tinge. He must have been on the verge of losing consciousness. Miss Whitfield was tugging at the heavy oak bookcase again. Was it my imagination or had the roaring sound gotten louder? Was there something drumming against the door from the other side?

I didn't care. If I wanted to save Darcy I had to be quick.

I'd already composed the sentence in my head. *September 2017: Today the hinges of the bookcase-door in the west wing library were so rusty that they completely gave way.* All I had to do was write it down.

But what if something went wrong again?

What if the hinges didn't break until tomorrow? What if half the castle came tumbling down along with the door?

I weighed the book in my hands. My eyes darted from Darcy's bluish-gray face to the flames in the fireplace. "And . . . what if we threw it in the fire?"

Miss Whitfield was panting with the effort of tugging at the door. "Yes . . . that might be the best thing to do. If you destroy it we'll be rid of it once and for all, and its magic will be undone. I just don't know what will happen to Gina, if we destroy it before we find her."

I bit my lip, tasted blood again. Miss Whitfield was right. I probably should destroy the chronicle. If I threw it on the fire and the words inside it ceased to exist, then they would no longer have the power to suffocate Darcy, would they? But what would he say if he survived this ordeal only to find his sister gone for good? What if, when the flames obliterated the book's magic, they also obliterated the only thing that was keeping Gina de Winter alive? Was that how it worked?

I didn't know. To be honest, I didn't have the faintest idea what would happen if I threw the book on the fire, whether it would save

Darcy and kill Gina or the other way round or neither. Everything about the chronicle was unpredictable. Everything.

I couldn't do it.

I couldn't do anything.

Could I?

Later on, I sometimes managed to persuade myself that I'd dropped the book because my fingers were so sweaty. Or because I'd somehow sensed we'd be able to free Darcy without using magic.

But in reality, it was the sheer terror of having to make a decision I might regret forever that paralyzed me in those horrible, endless seconds as I watched Darcy choking to death before my eyes.

It was that terror that left me frozen, helpless, unable to think straight. And it was that terror that eventually made me drop the book to the floor and grab hold of the bookcase again in the hope of busting the hinges with plain old muscle power. Darcy was unconscious now; there was no time to try anything else.

But the bookcase still wouldn't budge. Darcy was deathly pale. And the noises on the other side of the door were so loud by now that whatever was making them must have been right behind the wooden paneling. I could still hear the swishing and rustling of paper, but now there were footsteps, too. Something was hammering on the other side of the wood, making it shudder—something that sounded like a pair of fists. And then a hand appeared in the gap above Darcy's head, and a flurry of little whitish scraps of paper came spilling out from behind it. The owner of the hand shouted for help. It was Frederick.

"The door's stuck!" I called to him above the noise. "Something must have gotten jammed!"

The hand was withdrawn and the hammering grew louder, more desperate. Then it stopped abruptly, for a second or maybe two. And then the bookcase was rocked by a powerful blow, and then another. Frederick must have been hurling himself against the other side of the door.

I looked at Miss Whitfield, and she nodded at me. The next time Frederick buffeted the door with his shoulder we were ready, and we pulled with all our strength. I dug my fingernails into the wood and heaved.

Then there was a loud *crack* and, at last, the heavy oak bookcase began to move. The hidden mechanism creaked and grated. As the bookcase swung toward us, Miss Whitfield and I both lost our balance and fell over backward onto the rug.

At the same moment, something shot past above our heads: a silvery white cloud of rustling paper. The fluttering of countless wings filled the air. I couldn't be certain, but I thought I could make out a few shimmering dragonfly bodies in amongst the cloud, which now darted toward the fireplace and hung in the air for a moment, dangerously close to the flames, before whisking up the chimney and out into the night. In the blink of an eye the cloud was gone, vanishing as swiftly as it had appeared. I found myself wondering whether it had really been there at all, or whether I'd just imagined it.

I sat up.

Darcy had fallen to the floor, too. Was he still breathing?

Miss Whitfield was crawling over to where the chronicle lay.

Frederick was staggering around the room, disoriented. His cheeks were covered in red scratches that looked like paper cuts. And he was rubbing the back of his head.

"I . . . think . . . I just had a really weird dream," he stammered, lurching toward Darcy's bathroom. I didn't see whether he went in or not, and I didn't care. All I could see was Darcy, lying pale and still at the foot of the bookcase. Was he . . . ?

As I got closer I could see his chest rising and falling. He was breathing. He was alive! For the first time ever, I was glad the chronicle was so unpredictable—this time, instead of following my instructions to the letter, it had spared us the worst. Tears of relief welled up in my eyes.

"Darcy!" I whispered. "Darcy!" I bent over him, studying his dark eyebrows; his long, straight nose; his chiseled cheekbones; the little veins on his eyelids; and the bruise where Frederick's fist had caught him. This face had become so familiar to me over the past few days and weeks. It was angular and serious, sometimes proud, sometimes arrogant. But I didn't care, because it was Darcy's face, and now I knew the real Darcy.

Gently, very gently, I placed my lips on his blue lips. They felt completely different from how I'd imagined they'd be. Softer and firmer at the same time, cool and warm. And at my touch they gradually came back to life.

September 2017

At last, the mortal remains of G

# 18

THE DARK GREEN MINI WAS PARKED IN THE COURTYARD AGAIN, in front of the steps leading up to the main door. The trunk was open and Darcy was lifting his wheeled suitcase into it. This was proving a greater challenge than you might have thought. Firstly, Darcy still had pain in his chest where the bookcase had pressed into it over a week ago. (He had some impressive bruises on his ribs, and it was a miracle none of them were broken.) And secondly, there was hardly any room left in the trunk because my backpack and Miss Whitfield's luggage (three suitcases and a hatbox) were taking up almost all the available space.

But Toby, as always, was there to assist his friend in his hour of need. He helped Darcy reorganize the bags, cases, and backpacks so that everything just about fit into the trunk. My dad, meanwhile, discreetly tucked a packet of chewing gum into my pocket to guard against travel sickness, and Charlotte and Hannah danced about excitedly on the bottom step.

"You have to let us know as soon as you've found her," said Hannah for what must have been the hundredth time that afternoon.

"And please be careful with the . . . you know what," added Charlotte, with a sideways glance at my dad. We'd decided not to inflict the knowledge of a magic book and a dead faun on him just yet.

"We will," I assured her, patting the handbag in which I was carrying the chronicle. There'd been no doubt in my mind that it would have to go in my hand luggage—partly to make sure I didn't lose it if our suitcases went missing, and partly because I'd started feeling slightly paranoid about the book in general. Whenever it wasn't right next to me, I found it almost impossible to concentrate. And even when I carried it around with me like I was doing now, I felt anxious. It was as if I was holding a ticking time bomb that could go off at any moment.

Now that we were setting off, I felt even more apprehensive. Not for the first time, I wondered whether the long journey Darcy, Miss Whitfield, and I were about to undertake was really justified. How could we be sure we weren't chasing a red herring?

It was now three days since I'd found the article, on the website of a local newspaper: It was a couple years old, a few lines long, and had probably been read by only a handful of local residents. It talked about a girl who, in December 2013, had suddenly turned up in the middle of nowhere suffering from memory loss. She was now said to be working in a local gas station. The description of the girl closely matched that of Gina de Winter, and the location sounded promising, too: The amnesiac girl had been found one morning by a group of hikers near the entrance to a big national park, close to a gas station that went by the distinctive name of the World's End. It was located on an island called Newfoundland, off the east coast of Canada.

My dad was less than enthusiastic about our trip. We hadn't even left the castle courtyard yet, and already he was sick with worry. He looked on warily as the boys loaded up the car, his right hand resting on my shoulder as if to hold me back, to stop me from getting into that car and driving off to the airport and flying away.

"Has that thing even passed its inspection?" he whispered.

"Of course," I said. I didn't actually know whether it had or not—I had no idea what a British inspection sticker looked like— but it didn't really matter. "I'm going to be fine. Darcy and Miss Whitfield will be with me," I reassured him, hugging him close.

My dad had had quite a lot to cope with over the past few days. First I'd told him I had a new boyfriend, and that the new boyfriend was Darcy de Winter; then I'd told him that this new boyfriend and I were proposing to travel to the other side of the world, for three whole weeks, in the middle of term. Even a more laid-back father than mine might have had a little trouble getting his head around all this. Which made it all the more remarkable that my dad had finally agreed to let me go. The fact that Miss Whitfield was coming with us had helped, of course. As had my fully up-to-date vaccination card—and the fact that we had information that might just lead us to Gina de Winter.

But he still found it difficult to let go of me when, at last, all the luggage was safely stowed in the car, and Darcy came over and took my hand. As I walked toward the Mini, I saw a telltale glitter in my dad's eyes. "Make sure you always fasten your seat belt. And only drink boiled water. And stay on the marked paths. And watch out for wild animals," he said hoarsely, as I settled myself on the back seat beside Miss Whitfield's hatbox and Darcy slid in behind the steering wheel.

Miss Whitfield lowered herself onto the passenger seat and was about to close the car door when somebody came hurtling down the steps and pushed past Toby, Charlotte, Hannah, and my dad, all of whom had just been getting ready to start waving or crying or a mixture of the two.

For a fraction of a second I was afraid it was Frederick, making a last-ditch attempt to get the book back, and instinctively I clutched my handbag to my chest. But then I realized it couldn't possibly be Frederick; after that surreal night in the tunnels he'd gone tearing back to Cologne like a bat out of hell. And now I recognized the slender figure of Miss Berkenbeck, holding an enormous picnic basket out in front of her.

"For the journey," she said, depositing the basket on Miss Whitfield's lap. "It's just a few sandwiches. And a cake. Some pickles. A bit of fruit. Some hard-boiled eggs. A bowl of chocolate pudding. Lemonade. Potato salad. A few pints of milk. And a meatloaf—I found the recipe in *OK!* magazine the other week, and . . ."

"Thank you," said Miss Whitfield, visibly taken aback by the volume of unexpected provisions that had just landed in her lap. "This ought to keep us going all the way to Canada. Perhaps we'll even be able to offer some to Gina, if we find her."

"What do you mean, *if*?" exclaimed Miss Berkenbeck. "Of

course you'll find her. We made that chocolate pudding especially for her, you know."

Darcy and I exchanged glances in the rearview mirror. I saw a flicker of amusement in his eyes. Like me, he'd been feeling increasingly nervous over the past few days—but hopeful, too, that we might find his sister. And what could make for a more perfect reunion than being able to present Gina with a bowl of three-day-old chocolate pudding that had traveled halfway around the world? I grinned to myself, while Miss Berkenbeck produced a flowery handkerchief and waved it vigorously in farewell as Darcy started up the car. Soon we were pulling out of the castle gates, away from Stolzenburg and all its legends.

Two days later—after more than twenty hours in the air, and layovers in Brussels and Toronto—we landed at the airport in Saint John, the oldest city in North America. The air was crisp and clean, and the moment we stepped off the plane we were greeted by adverts for whale-watching trips, drifting icebergs, vast forests, rocky plateaus, and prehistoric ravines. But we hardly noticed them: We weren't here for the breathtaking scenery or the geological marvels. The only things we were interested in were a shabby old gas station called the World's End and the young woman who worked there (or who *had* worked there a few years ago, at least, if the article in the local paper was to be believed).

Darcy was all for driving our rented car inland straightaway, but after the long plane journey all three of us were exhausted; I was longing for a hot shower, and neither Darcy nor Miss Whitfield was really in a fit state to drive. So we bought ourselves some sandwiches (the picnic basket, unfortunately, hadn't made it past Belgian Customs) and checked into a motel. In the morning we would set off for Gros Morne National Park and the log cabin we'd booked before leaving Germany.

The World's End gas station was aptly named, as we realized the next day, after driving for several hours through ravines, forests, and swamps to get to it. By the time we arrived we hadn't seen another car on the road for at least two hours. The gas pumps were so rusty you could hardly tell what color they must once have been, and the panes of glass in the windows of the little kiosk looked dull and grimy, as did the windows of the houses in the tiny hamlet behind it. Beyond the village, the road turned into a dirt track that disappeared into the foothills of a mountain range.

This was it, then.

The world's end.

We didn't know what Gina was calling herself now, but we had several photos of her: The most recent one had been taken at the Autumn Ball four years ago. If we went from house to house showing the photos to the villagers, then sooner or later one of them was bound to recognize her. Assuming our theory was correct. Assuming Gina de Winter had ever been here at all.

We left the car by one of the gas pumps and walked slowly toward the kiosk, clutching the photographs. A movement behind the grubby glass showed that there was somebody there, and as we got closer we could see that it was a young woman with dark hair. All of a sudden, it was as if the mountains around us were holding their breath.

Then everything seemed to happen in slow motion. I watched as Darcy dropped the photos—we had no need of them now—and ran inside the kiosk. I was about to follow him, but Miss Whitfield held me back.

"Let them have this moment," she murmured, and I nodded. She was right, of course.

We stood there watching through the dusty window as Darcy entered the kiosk and barged past the shelves of sweets and magazines, oblivious to everything but the woman behind the counter. She stared at him, wide-eyed with terror, probably thinking this was a robbery. He was standing in front of her now, his shoulders trembling. I couldn't see his face, because he had his back to us. But I saw the dark-haired young woman give a start, and then I saw the fear vanish from her face to be replaced by a look of confusion. A moment later, I saw recognition course through her like a lightning bolt. Tears ran down her face as Darcy put his arms around her.

"Shall we take a little stroll?" asked Miss Whitfield, and we linked arms and walked away.

Gina de Winter was twenty years old, and for the past four years she had been going by the name of Lindsay. She was as tall as her brother, with the same proud arch to her eyebrows, the same straight nose and fierce look in her eyes. But she seemed less arrogant. Less lonely. And that evening, as we sat around the fire outside our log cabin wrapped in blankets, she told us her story.

She told us about her time at Stolzenburg and how homesick she'd been. About the ill-fated trick Frederick had played on her, about the chronicle and her search for the faun and how she'd been so brokenhearted that she'd grown reckless. Those poems she'd written in the book had set off a chain of events she couldn't control, and that was why she'd climbed out of her bedroom window one December night four years ago and gone down to the river. She'd known it was wrong, but the magic of her own words had been too powerful. She hadn't been able to resist it—and neither had Frederick, who'd rowed her out onto the river against his will. The boat had gotten caught in a strong current and capsized.

At this point Gina's memories became hazy. She couldn't remember how she'd managed to get out of the river and climb into a freight container. And she had no idea how she'd ended up on the back of a lorry, parked at a gas station in the middle of nowhere. All she knew was that she'd crept out of the container into the wilderness where, a few hours later, she'd run into a group of hikers—and hadn't even been able to tell them her name.

People had assumed she'd run away from home, and she'd been grateful when Meg, the elderly lady who owned the gas station, had taken her in and given her a job. She'd sensed that she was missing somebody but it wasn't until today, when she'd seen her twin brother standing there in front of her, that everything had come flooding back and she'd remembered who she was, where she came from, and what had happened to her.

Now, as I showed Gina the chronicle in the flickering firelight, she let out a sharp cry and recoiled from it as if from a poisonous snake.

"Well then," said Miss Whitfield. "I think it's time." Very

gently, she lifted the book out of my hands and stroked the worn cloth binding. "We should do it now."

"Do what?" I asked, but in the same moment I realized what she meant. I leaped to my feet and stepped in between her and the fire. "No. Wait. It's too dangerous. We don't know what'll happen if we destroy the book. We might break its curse. But what about all the magic it's already done? What if all of that was lost?"

Miss Whitfield shook her head. "Do you really want to go on living in fear, Emma? You've seen what happened to Gina. What if the book falls into the wrong hands? And are you sure you want to spend the rest of your life wondering whether Darcy is about to be crushed by a bookcase?"

I thought about how panicky I'd felt, the past few days, whenever I'd been more than a few feet away from the chronicle—during my swimming lesson, for example, when I'd had to leave it in my locker. Miss Whitfield was right: I couldn't spend the rest of my life carrying the book around with me, worrying about its curse. "Th-then we'll hide it in a safe place. In a Swiss bank vault. Or somewhere out here in the wilderness, in a hollow tree or something," I stammered.

"No." Miss Whitfield pushed me aside. "That's what I did two hundred years ago and, as you can see, it didn't work. Let's put an end to this once and for all."

"But—" I began. But Gina and Darcy had both stood up now, too.

"I want to do it," said Gina firmly, and Darcy put his arm around me.

"It's for the best, Emma," he said quietly. "We've found Gina. We don't need magic anymore now."

I let out a deep breath, looking from Darcy to the book to Miss Whitfield and Gina, and finally the flaming logs.

At last, I nodded.

Gina took hold of the chronicle and traced the embossed outline of the faun with her finger. Then she turned, quickly, and threw the book onto the fire. The red and orange flames licked at the paper and the cloth, turning it black, eating away at all the words, all the thoughts, all the events that had been preserved in those pages for centuries.

Gina, meanwhile, had dropped to her knees and was bending dangerously low over the fire, as if she wanted to be sure that every last scrap of paper was destroyed. That there really was nothing left of the book that had done her and Darcy and the faun and everyone else so much harm.

Yes, it had been the right thing to do. It was the only way to break the curse. But it still hurt to see all those centuries' worth of words going up in smoke. In spite of everything that had happened, it felt like I'd just lost a dear old friend.

"Don't cry," Darcy whispered, brushing a tear out of the corner of my eye with his thumb. I hadn't realized I was crying. Darcy pulled me toward him and I hid my face for a moment in the warmth of his shoulder.

"We're free now," he whispered into my hair, and then he kissed the skin beside my ear, then my cheek, the side of my nose, and finally my mouth. We'd been together for over a week now, but this kiss was different from all the others. It was soft and passionate and it tasted of the wood smoke from the fire and of the forest all around us. And there was a promise in it: a promise that now, at last, everything was okay. Everything was going to be okay.

As we moved apart, we saw Gina standing a few yards away from us. She, too, was crying—crying and laughing at the same time. "Let's go home!" she cried. "Let's go now! I have to call Mom and Dad! Come on, let's go!"

"Our flight back isn't for another three weeks, though. I wonder if we can change our tickets?" I asked, turning to where Miss Whitfield had been standing. But there was no reply.

Miss Whitfield was no longer standing by the fire. I spun around. Even the tree stump she'd been sitting on was gone. And something told me she hadn't just gone inside the cabin.

"She . . . ," I whispered.

Gina shrugged. Darcy was silent. I felt a lump in my throat.

Miss Whitfield was gone. Of course she was. I should have seen it coming. She'd vanished along with the book, whose magic had kept her alive for over two hundred years.

"She knew," I said. "She must have known, mustn't she?"

"Yes," said Darcy. "I think this was what she wanted."

I reached for Darcy's and Gina's hands and squeezed them. "Good-bye, Eleanor Morland Whitfield," I whispered, and suddenly I knew that when we got back to Stolzenburg there would be no more sheep and no more secret tunnels, no more paper dragonflies and no more faun bones. Stolzenburg would be a perfectly ordinary, wonderful school with perfectly ordinary, wonderful people in it. Now and then they would tell old legends and fairy tales about the castle, the way people always do about old castles. But they would be just that: fairy tales.

Nothing more, and nothing less.

## The Faun's Song

And I wait between the lines,
In the darkness of the night,
I hear wings, gossamer-fine,
Approaching with the thunder's might,
The strangest sound I ever heard,
I almost dare not look,
Oh, how I long for different words,
New paper, a new book!
Seek me in between the lines,
Where once my father sought,
For I no longer wish to be
This creature that he wrought.

Thank you for reading this
FEIWEL AND FRIENDS book.
The Friends who made

possible are:

JEAN FEIWEL, PUBLISHER
LIZ SZABLA, ASSOCIATE PUBLISHER
RICH DEAS, SENIOR CREATIVE DIRECTOR
HOLLY WEST, EDITOR
ANNA ROBERTO, EDITOR
CHRISTINE BARCELLONA, EDITOR
KAT BRZOZOWSKI, EDITOR
ALEXEI ESIKOFF, SENIOR MANAGING EDITOR
KIM WAYMER, SENIOR PRODUCTION MANAGER
ANNA POON, ASSISTANT EDITOR
EMILY SETTLE, ADMINISTRATIVE ASSISTANT
REBECCA SYRACUSE, JUNIOR DESIGNER
MANDY VELOSO, PRODUCTION EDITOR

Follow us on Facebook or visit us online at mackids.com.
Our books are friends for life